AN UNUSUAL GRIEF

AN UNUSUAL GRIEF

Yewande Omotoso

Abuja – London

First published in 2022 by Cassava Republic Press

Abuja – London

Copyright © Yewande Omotoso 2022

A CIP catalogue record for this book is available from the National Library of Nigeria and the British Library.

ISBN: 978-1-913175-13-9
eISBN: 978-1-913175-14-6

Cover design: Leah Jacobs-Gordon
Book design: Deepak Sharma (Prepress Plus)

Printed and bound in Great Britain by Clays
Distributed in Nigeria by Yellow Danfo
Worldwide distribution by Ingram Publisher Services International

Stay up to date with the latest books, special offers
and exclusive content with our monthly newsletter.
Sign up on our website:
www.cassavarepublic.biz

Twitter: @cassavarepublic
Instagram: @cassavarepublicpress
Facebook: facebook.com/CassavaRepublic
Hashtag: #AnUnusualGrief #ReadCassava

For my father.

Because dying, too, is one of our assignments in life. There as well: "to do what needs doing." – Marcus Aurelius

1

The Drawings

It feels good to have come away, a relief. Titus won't stop calling but she doesn't answer. He is in a panic, he is upset, but she has left. She has come further than her legs can carry her: she has flown.

'Mrs Owolabi,' a woman says, through a cracked open door.

Mojisola assumes it is the same woman she spoke to at the gate via intercom, two guards looking on. She has only the sharp, cautious voice to go by.

'Thank you,' Mojisola says, although she hasn't felt true gratitude for many years now. 'For letting me in.'

'Well... I....' The woman will struggle to find the words, everyone does. 'I'm not sure what to say, Mrs Owolabi.'

'Please don't worry,' she says. And then, 'Call me Mojisola.'

'Zelda. Zelda Petersen. I didn't expect you. I didn't know you were coming.'

'It was sudden.' Mojisola hopes the landlady will not invite her in, just give her the keys so she can be on her way. She doesn't wish to make small-talk or pretend to be polite. And, really, it becomes apparent that there is no risk of hospitality: even with not much light and through only a crack Mojisola can see (or perhaps it is in the tone of the voice) that Zelda Petersen is, by necessity, a hardened woman. Zelda speaks with the suspicion of someone whose whole life has been about receiving visits from strange people looking for stranger things.

'Well.' She opens the door a little wider. 'You're straight from the airport?'

'Yes.'

'I suppose you want to see the place, collect her things. I'll get the key. Everything is as it was, more or less. I haven't advertised, although I will soon.' Zelda leaves the door open, still just that small crack, and retreats into the darkness. 'Wait,' she says, across her shoulder.

There it is, Mojisola thinks, *the caution*. And from the way Zelda said, 'Wait', Mojisola understands that the woman is used to giving this instruction and not being defied. Mojisola stands to attention in the corridor, staring through the gap, seeing nothing. A cat with a striking white pelt, possessing what can only be referred to as cat-pride, goes past the small suitcase she'd packed in a hurry. The cat looks like royalty visiting the proletariat, inspecting the lands: 'How is the crop this season? Are you ready for harvest?' The animal winds about her stockinged legs and enters through the dark gap. She hears the tinkle of keys.

'There you are.' Zelda Petersen is addressing her cat. 'Who told you to run off, hmm? Who told you to leave and scare me like that?' From the way she talks to the cat, Mojisola understands that they are friends and that much of the friendship relies on the fact that the cat does not talk back.

'Will you return it when you're done?' she asks, as she hands her the keys. Then she dips her head and seems, as if for the first time, to take in the suitcase. 'Oh,' Zelda says, as realisation dawns. 'You'll be staying?'

'I'll pay. If, as you say, the apartment is still available, then I'll pay.'

'Oh.' Zelda's lips are small and manage to fit into a rough circle just above a pale brown fleshy chin. The woman swallows, as if this action is now necessary in their short acquaintance. 'And how long do you intend to stay, Mrs Owolabi? Ah, perhaps, if we're talking money, you should come inside.'

Zelda Petersen holds open the door and Mojisola crosses in. It is daytime outside but in Zelda's apartment, night prevails.

Even so, Mojisola sees a tail disappear through an open door at the end of the hallway.

'In here,' Zelda says, and they enter a room with only one chair. 'Please sit.' She puts on the glasses that have, until now, hung by a red thread on her bosom. 'I'll get my ledger.'

Mojisola sits. Zelda Petersen is a woman with only two gears: caution and business.

'It's 3000 for the month. I can do pro rata.' She has a calculator.

Mojisola doesn't know why, suddenly, they are doing sums. In fact, she has no money but she will not tell Zelda this. 'I can make a deposit, perhaps?'

At the mention of a transaction that requires some modicum of trust, Zelda Petersen's face tightens; her lips wrinkle, lines form. She seems unhappy but Mojisola hopes she, too, has an intimidating face. Zelda and she are about the same age. Mojisola decides to shame the woman.

'Do you have children, Zelda?'

At the question, the muscles in Zelda's face relax. It is not that she now looks kind or contrite, it is simply that she is a natural woman of war. At the mention of children, she understands that, at least for this battle, Mojisola has won.

'I'll give you the banking details,' says Zelda. 'I have them written down.'

At the door again, Zelda watches Mojisola pick up her suitcase.

'It's number 81. Just along here and to the left. You didn't respond to my enquiry about her things.'

'Oh, didn't I?'

'Well, if you did, I didn't get it. Anyway, I started packing, I hope you don't mind. I had no choice. Space and time are money.'

Mojisola nods.

'Just as well you're here,' Zelda continues. 'I couldn't have risked sending the stuff down, couldn't have risked footing the bill with no guarantee of reimbursement. I'm sure you can appreciate that.'

Mojisola makes a smile. She has the bunch of keys squeezed into the centre of her fist. 'Thank you,' she says.

'Please, Mrs Owolabi, don't forget the payment.'

*

When Mojisola had alighted at the airport someone had addressed her in Zulu and she'd shaken her head, said, 'I don't understand' — had to repeat, 'I don't understand,' a few times until she realised there was no need. The person had understood her perfectly the first time. She had to cross through a crowd of people and get outside to find transport. Her attention was momentarily arrested by a little boy and his mother, she holding his hand while dragging a large suitcase.

'You okay? How are you feeling?' the mother asks the boy, who cannot be older than four.

'I'm okay,' he says.

'You're not sad,' the mother says. Her voice is needling and Mojisola, walking just a few paces behind them, cannot stop herself from eavesdropping. Something, perhaps in the mother's tone, is familiar and embarrassing to her. 'Are you happy?' When the boy nods she says, 'Promise?'

Mojisola slows her pace and ducks to find a bathroom. She feels conquered even without leaving the airport building, without venturing further than the lavatories.

Finally outside, a taxi driver approaches. Mojisola is angry with the casual manner in which the man swings her towards his Corolla. He is too comfortable with himself; she is newly suspicious of the comfortable, the content.

'Hey, Mama,' he says, by way of greeting (too casual), and she nods because she is worried that if she opens her mouth, she'll scold him.

'Nice flight, Mama?' He attempts small-talk for the first ten kilometres, then turns on a music station that she finds unsuitable. A person is talking staccato and Mojisola can pick out a swear word every few seconds. Unable to bear it, she asks him to switch it off.

Her phone rings. It's Titus. She ignores it.

The taxi driver is unhappy with the silence. Mojisola can tell because his jaw is tightened. From the back seat she can see the added definition caused by him grinding his teeth. Perhaps he feels chastened. Maybe, later, he will complain to someone, his wife, about how difficult the job is, how unfriendly people are.

Although he addressed her as 'Mama', she wonders about his age. It is something she has been doing lately. She wonders whether or not she could have given birth to him. One cannot tell just by looking, but Mojisola will be 60 soon. She decides he is in the vicinity of 30, which means she could well be his mother. Outside, Johannesburg is vast and unending. She closes her eyes but doesn't sleep, a familiar pain keeping her alert; no doctor will cure it. When she opens her eyes again, she sees that the driver is staring at her in his rear-view mirror; his eyes dart back to the road. She notices some dirt on the seat beside her and wonders whether to point this out. Maybe she should make conversation after all, but she cannot muster a sense of duty to appease the driver, to make his drab job of ferrying passengers any more bearable by being agreeable. Not only, as she's just discerned, is she old enough to be his mother, but she is tired. And, of course, she is grieving and so, at least for a time, owes nothing to anyone.

They arrive at the complex and, even while bending at the intercom to ask for a Ms Petersen, Mojisola is unable to ignore the fact that Cove Crescent is neither cove nor crescent. She feels an anger disproportionate to the offence.

*

Zelda explains the bunch of keys.

A blue rectangle the size of a matchbox: 'For ingress and egress,' says Zelda. 'This is the button for egress.'

Two keys for two locks. 'This one is for the security gate. We've had a few instances...'

Mojisola wonders whether Yinka was ever robbed. The question is plainly on her face.

'Not in number 81,' Zelda says. 'But, yes, just last month that evil man on the ground floor thought he'd take a leak. I always say, at the Body Corporate meetings, I always say it: "Don't leave the open door unattended." He likes to leave his front door open — he says the apartment gets no light otherwise. The man is evil but for reasons I don't have to mention. Point is, he said he just popped in for a quick call of nature. But I'd warned for that specific thing. I'd said, "Even a quick visit to the bathroom, lock the door." Well, he's either deaf or stubborn 'cause look what happened. He went for a leak and in that time, they managed to steal his TV.'

Mojisola is assailed by the long story, surprised to be given so much more information than necessary. 'And? Did they hurt him? Is he okay?'

'No. He died last week, actually.'

Mojisola's face drops.

'Prostate cancer,' says Zelda. 'Look, Mrs Owolabi, the point is, lock up.'

'So the block is unsafe, then?' Mojisola feels her second thoughts arriving. She's had none since she'd made her decision in her kitchen in Cape Town.

'Well, I won't say "unsafe". The point is, lock your doors. That's the point. This is Gauteng.'

Two trinkets attached to a silver keyring. 'Those are hers. I suppose, when you eventually return the keys, you can keep them.' Zelda Petersen gives you what belongs to you and extracts your gratitude all the same.

Two keys stand between Mojisola and the apartment. One short and multi-grooved for the metal gate Zelda informed her about, doom of Armageddon in her voice. The other key is more regular in its features, for a wooden door that gives way with a scrape when Mojisola puts her weight on it. She has lost weight but, even so, she will always remain a soft, round woman.

As a girl growing up, as a teenager, she was good. She wasn't popular but she was liked well enough. Liked for being quiet and kind, too intelligent (top of the class) to ignore but insufficiently forward or noisy to be popular. She was contained. Held together in the checkered green uniform of her school, her sash always bowed and her shoes always polished. With her grades and neat appearance she would have been an easy pick for school prefect if not for her impossibly soft voice. Mojisola had said so little in school that some of her classmates believed the rumour of a stutter. But Mojisola does not stutter and never has. Instead she simply learnt, very early, how to bite her tongue.

Her mother was known in the community as a respectable woman, with the church, the women's council, the lay preachers and prison visits, the visiting of the sick. Her mother took her little girl along on her duties. All through childhood Mojisola sat quietly beside a praying mother, a hymn-singing mother. She had to sit still; fidgeting in front of the dying did not bode well.

Her recent weight loss is due to mourning. As a neighbour, coming round with a plate of condolence, put it, 'You have dropped.' Growing up, flesh and heft had always been the measure of feminine beauty. Mojisola remembers waking up a teenager and the fellowship circle warning her mother to be careful, to train her daughter accordingly. For this reason Mojisola can barely remember a time she was not protecting the world (and herself) from her body. This body of hers is shorter than average, which she accepts with grace. Perhaps from the influence of a childhood steeped in Bible study, and a simple appreciation for how things are, she understands that her height, her weight, her nose, everything about her, is all right and fine.

Mojisola's eyes are small and precise, her cheeks not high-boned but pronounced and soft. Her skin is okay, not great because of an outbreak of acne in her 16th year that left her even more shy and uncertain of her beauty. Still, Mojisola has shiny hair, an enviable bust, a melodic voice and a melancholic look that, when courting was finally appropriate, attracted poets and accountants alike. Titus, her husband, is neither. In her adult years, her university years, away from the judgement of her mother, Mojisola was complimented — mostly by her female classmates — on the loveliness of her calves, their length and generous shape, the bones in her ankles. In fact, the entire stretch of leg (the pair of them) was admired.

It is with these legs (they have not changed) that she walks slowly into her daughter's apartment, shuts the door behind her, takes two steps, hangs her head, closes her eyes. She must stand here. Eventually she must move too. Because she knows she won't die, not yet. She'll live long. That's her charge. She opens her eyes and looks about. Someone has left her a note but in a language she does not speak. It is not sufficient to translate: the note must be read in its original language. If she had lived a different life, she, Mojisola, would be fluent by now and in no need of translation. But she has lived the life she has, and it has brought her here, now. The task ahead is daunting but clear: she must learn the language in which the note is written and ultimately read the message.

This is what it is like for Mojisola to be standing in No. 81, standing in the home of her dead child, a space she has never been in, was never invited to. She is still for a moment. There is a coolness — perhaps a window is open somewhere. But then this reasoning is surpassed by a louder assessment. Mojisola feels, on entering the apartment and closing the door behind her, that she has entered a space of perverse quality. It feels subterranean, which is not logical since she is two floors up. She takes a few steps further in. Subterranean or interstellar, in defiance of ground rules. The place is a crypt or a rocket shuttle. This is something to arm herself with.

Mojisola cradles the notion and bends to take off her shoes. She does so not because it is her habit but because there is a line of shoes at the entrance door. It is a clue to the laws of this home and Mojisola is obligated to comply. She places her black court shoes beside a pair of leather sandals, straps darkened from sweat. There is, too, a pair of red heels (squeaky vinyl) and an evidently much-loved pair of bedroom slippers. Also, disconcertingly, there is a single rubber slipper.

She walks, her feet touching the terracotta tiles, absorbing the cool of them, their take from a cold night. There is a breeze. A window must be open and Mojisola decides to find it. Somehow, the coolness of the house offends.

In the first part of the home, everything is conjoined: a compact open-plan kitchen separated from the dining area by a counter laden with bank letters and a bunch of flyers — Fruit 'n' Veg, We Do Boards, Cameraland. There is a small dining table with four mismatched chairs; a little beyond is a sea-grey couch, a large cardboard box and a wingback covered with a once-white bedsheet. The spare furnishings, the absence of photographs or little flourishes, the pale curtains, drawn: Mojisola notes all this, accepting that she'd held a curiosity for something as mundane as what kind of bedsheets her daughter had bought, or if she used placemats. She'd imagined that her personality, otherwise indecipherable, could be revealed through such choices.

Her mind returns to the draught. She checks the kitchen: the windows above the sink are closed. Mojisola stands for a while in the hallway, a contracted space that separates this first part of the home from the second. There are two bedrooms; a bathroom sits between them. She is standing because she doesn't know which room is her daughter's. She doesn't want to make a mistake and enter: she is not ready. She has to guess, somehow, which room is the guest room. Into here she should carry her suitcase and perhaps lie down for a few minutes, think a bit.

She is presented with two doors, neither forthcoming as to what lies beyond. In a second she hazards a guess, pushes against the handle and it gives, slides as if it needed no persuasion.

It hurts her eyes to stand in this room. Yinka hasn't slept in it for weeks but it still smells of her; it looks like her. The whole thing is her face, bright with curtains. Mojisola is surprised by her sense of calm. She moves past the bed, using the side of her leg to press into it, wanting to touch solid things; the door had not fought her but instead just given way. There's the window, wide open to the weather. She pulls it in, glancing outside where the morning is passing. Yinka's bedroom window looks out onto a garden. There are roses, white and pink, their heads bobbing as if in conversation.

The phone rings — she'd left her bag on the kitchen counter. At the door to Yinka's room she plays with the light switch. On. Off. On. Off. On. Off.

'Hello?' She'd told him not to call, to give her time, not to ask for any explanations. If he pushes, she'll remind him about the broken vows, will throw that in his face.

'Moji?'

'Titus.'

After each other's names, nothing else is said for a while, as if that in itself is the sum of a real phone call; a roll-call.

'Listen.'

'Yes?' He is so anxious he is naked, in a way that their years of marriage have never revealed. 'Yes, Moji?'

Or maybe he has always been so, and it is she who has never seen.

'You there?'

Now that she has his attention, she isn't sure what else to say. She makes her breath audible — lets that fill the silence.

'How are you? How's your stress?' Titus asks, when she still says nothing.

She shakes her head, thinks, *I asked him not to call me. Not for a while, a long while.*

'Moji?'

The silence continues, the silence that is their marriage, both comfort and curse.

'How's Mouse?' She can ask about the family cat, a stray Yinka rescued. Mojisola has no special affinity for cats but she can ask. In turn, she hopes he will simply ring off. He responds and she moves from the kitchen, with the phone to her ear, down the hall again. The door to the room is open. Had she left it so?

'You there?' he asks.

'Ehn? Yes…yes, yes.'

He is silent. So is she.

*

When she peeks inside, Mojisola sees that the cardboard box is full of Yinka's things. She sits down on the wingback, grabbing the box by the ear and dragging it to settle between her thighs. This position reminds her of the years she spent plaiting Yinka's hair into cornrows for Staff School, when they were still in Ife. The memory comes like a window, sweet and polished, unbidden. Mojisola smiles, cracking the skin on her face. One week Sade Adu, the next ṣùkú with the plaits all starting from the forehead, sides and nape, and climbing upwards to the crown. There was a clever way to collect the braided hair on the top of the head that Mojisola was unable to master. She blamed this inability on being born left-handed, then converted into a right-hander.

She'd endured what to her young self had felt like years, but must have been several months at the most, of sitting at the table to do homework, the Bible weighed down upon her left hand, her mother walking past occasionally to check that her right-handed letters were straight. On and off she got rashes on the offending left hand. The doctor prescribed creams, and the rash would disappear for a while, then return, disappear, return and so on. Her handwriting was barely legible. She entered varsity and read geography. At the start of each lesson her head would hurt. She believed these recurring headaches to be some sort of miswiring; it was the brain arguing with itself about how to think, as a left-handed person or as a right. She excelled in her studies, though, and the headaches subsided. Her letters were never quite straight and her corn-rows often messy.

Her own mother had insisted on short hair (never allowed to grow beyond half an inch) until the end of secondary school. In university, finally free, Mojisola cultivated an Afro and then, when her hair grew even longer, used her scholarship money to get her tresses twisted and greased. She spent her spare time sitting in salons with the styles of the day plastered about the walls; unfashionable in every other sense, she never lost her passion for hair and keeping to trends. Years later when mothers popped in and said, perplexed, 'Sade Adu?' Mojisola knew the style, could draw it for them. Sunday evenings were often a frenzy of mothers phoning around to find out what the prescribed hairstyle for the week was, especially those mothers who were not Nigerian and didn't understand the school rule for all the girls' heads to look the same. Mojisola was often consulted and was happy to answer questions with confidence: she knew the styles even if she didn't know how to execute them perfectly. Anyhow, much later, after the Owolabis left Ife for Cape Town, a teenaged Yinka asked to straighten her thick hair; she asked for a hairband to hold the limp strands. Mojisola's braiding abilities — poor or otherwise — were no longer required. But sitting like this, just now, with the cardboard box between her thighs, all the hairstyles line up in her memory. Pàtẹ̀wọ́, where the cornrows come from the sides and clap together down a line that runs from crown to nape.

Mojisola opens the flaps. Since Yinka had left them, moved out, Mojisola had asked many times to come and visit but always the child's strong response: No. Once she'd said, 'Not yet,' but only once. Right at the top, upfront, like a signpost, is a picture of Yinka. She doesn't touch it. So hard to look, but she must. After all, she is here to see: what a waste it would be to come all this distance only to turn away. Or, more accurately, stay blinkered. Mojisola bats her eyelids several times, then focuses on the photograph. Immediately she notices that in the many months she has not seen Yinka (seen, spoken to, written to — what other forms of absence exist?) her daughter had put on some weight. A very tiny bit. Yinka had always been ferociously slender (that was her term). In high school, their second year in South Africa, the guidance counsellor had grouped her with a few girls who could not (would not) keep their food down. A note was written to the parents and Yinka was marched to the family doctor, who proclaimed her healthy. 'I'm just ferociously slender,' she began to say.

Mojisola picks up the photograph. It is a Polaroid and the edges are sharp. Her suspicions that it was taken recently are confirmed by the fact that Yinka is wearing a dress she does not recognise, a fire-truck red, dangerously short at both ends. Her cheeks are full and perhaps her bottom somewhat more generous. Mojisola doesn't know how to feel about this. That in the many months of their (in the end, final) separation, her daughter had started to fill out. She stares as if looking at a person for the first time; the first chance to study them without the fear of being noticed, being looked at in return — the grace of replicas. Really she is and can only be looking for one thing, she is trying to make a decision as to whether Yinka looks happy or sad. Was the extra eating due to nerves or had her daughter been thriving, eating up life in a way? If she considers the extra eating as a product of nerves or melancholy, she is affirming the notion that something was wrong, that Yinka was unhappy, that she, Mojisola, had failed her own child. The failure is plain and unavoidable because, just two weeks ago, her baby, Yinka Owolabi, had died, 24 years old and alone.

When the policeman had started talking, Mojisola had wanted to interrupt and say, 'But I'm on my way,' as if she wasn't the mother of a dead child, rather a mother fractionally late, delayed but on her way. Just that morning she'd decided she would phone Yinka and tell her that she was coming, not ask permission. She would say, 'Send me the address, I'm your mother.' As if that was a magic word to set the world right-ways again. 'Ma'am, are you there?' the policeman had asked. 'Did you hear me?' Yes, she'd heard. The person she'd made was no more. For many days afterwards she'd wanted a gun. Never having considered herself a killer, suddenly she'd lusted for blood. She collected all her anger — at herself, at Yinka, at Titus, at the world that won't wait — and held it at the base of her throat. It hurt to talk. And she was brimstone. If she'd owned a gun, people would be dead by now, but common sense prevailed: the world is better off without a gun-toting Mojisola Owolabi. No, violence was not the answer. Instead here she is, come to see, to check. She cannot really afford to come away but nonetheless she has done so. It's her savings she will use and whatever Titus supposes he ought to deposit into her account. For now he is confused and beseeching, but if he becomes resentful, she may get nothing. She is momentarily bitter about a lifetime as a housewife, but her grief overtakes her regret. It is, after all, the more pressing of the two.

*

Yinka's laptop. Mojisola slides the machine out of its leather sleeve and clicks it open. After an image of a red hibiscus flashes on the screen she is presented with 'Password' and a slot for her to fill in, the cursor blinking. She knows it will be wrong but, somehow reflexively, she types in her own name. 'Incorrect,' says the screen. 'Try again.' She is returned to a fresh empty slot.

She is sitting, attempting to imagine what Yinka would have used as a password when there is a knock on the door. Mojisola struggles to pull herself away from the task at hand, and when she does, she is sorry — there in the doorway is the tight-mouthed landlady.

'Have you made the deposit, Mrs Owolabi?'

'You can call me Mojisola.'

'Perhaps after your payment has cleared, I will.'

She checks to see if the woman is joking. She isn't. Zelda's question remains unanswered between them. Mojisola enjoys the knowledge that possession is nine tenths of some law somewhere in the world and, for now, she is in possession of the flat: it is on her to invite Zelda in, close the door in her face, keep her standing at the gate. It is all on her.

'By the way, I noticed you didn't lock the door,' Zelda says.

Mojisola waits. Zelda's topics are money and warnings. Apparently they've exhausted money, now come the warnings.

'You shouldn't leave the door unlocked, Mrs Owolabi. I understand Capetonians might be naïve but, really, here you must be careful.'

'There is crime everywhere,' Mojisola says, almost bored.

'In fact, no. There is theft everywhere. Petty attempts to grab at what isn't yours. What I am speaking of, Mrs Owolabi, here in Gauteng is proper *crime*. Organised crime.'

Mojisola looks amused; there is pride in Zelda's voice.

'I mean stealth,' says Zelda. 'And precision.'

Mojisola is not in the mood to compare the criminalities of the two cities. She has been a guest at dinner parties, some colleague of Titus's, Professor Such and Such, and she has witnessed this rally play itself out. A visiting Jo'burger attempting to impress by telling hijacking tales, someone from East London sufficiently horrified, a Capetonian with an anecdote about getting caught up in a robbery at the Pick 'n' Pay on Main Road, Rondebosch. Someone knows someone whose neighbour had their house cleaned out by the very woman they'd hired to clean it — this told for laughs, for wordplay, so much sacrificed at the altar of entertainment. Someone knows someone whose daughter was transported in the back of a Toyota for eight hours, the assailants occasionally stopping the car to come round, open the boot and taunt the young woman with rape. They seemed to get off on the taunting, as if that was a kind of rape in itself. This told to buy silence, to prohibit laughter, herald grim departures from the party and solemn speechless agreement as to the dire state of the nation.

Mojisola recalls a day she went on foot to the grocery store. She just needed a carton of milk. Normally she'd have driven but she reasoned it was just a five-minute walk through a neighbourhood she'd lived in for years. What could possibly befall her? And yet the thought having surfaced — that there was a danger — she entered the sunny road and walked slowly down the way, turning. Just before she arrived at the shop there was a patch of open grass she had to walk past and, in a split second, her heart jumped as a looming figure approached. And then she stopped and laughed and laughed and laughed — she'd jumped at the sight of her own shadow.

'Who are we more afraid of? The criminals or ourselves?'

Zelda looks a little stunned by the question, her eyes startled as if by a sudden flash. Mojisola remembers the dark apartment.

She is about to follow up the question with something soothing and apologetic when Zelda finds her way to a response.

'It is not a joke, Mrs Owolabi.'

Mojisola wants to say she isn't joking but Zelda, fully recovered from the cryptic question, has the air of someone who has settled an argument and is now generously looking to change the topic.

'So,' Zelda says, and she cranes her neck to look into the apartment.

Mojisola feels tired and hopes that, without her having to say another word, Zelda Petersen will exhaust her repertoire of conversation and leave.

'Are you packing her things?'

'Well, I—'

'I'm assuming you don't mean to stay too long.'

'I...I—' The phone rings in the back. Bloody Titus.

'I hope you found everything as expected. I didn't snoop, but when you didn't respond to my letter, well, then I had to... you know.'

Zelda looks expectant and it takes only half a second for Mojisola to understand that she is fishing, that even the stuffy nose-in-the-air landlady is not above some titbit of information she can later use as batter for gossip. She is looking at her, the failed mother, the spectacle of the mother who lost a child.

'Everything is fine,' says Mojisola. 'Is there something you are specifically worried about?' She can feel a sulphuric bubble in her chest.

Zelda is like all the others, their humanity disfigured by curiosity. The neighbour with the condolence plate of koeksisters had already asked the same thing. They don't ask it outright, but it is tucked into the corners of their speech, and all the while they're looking at her, the mother, asking with their eyes, 'How did you let this happen?'

'Mrs Owolabi, I was asking an innocent question. I only—'

Before any more can be said there starts up, in the background in an apartment somewhere among the many, the cries of a woman in sexual ecstasy. Mojisola sees her own combination of horror and longing mirrored on Zelda's face as they absorb the noise. As desired, Zelda speaks no further. She simply backs away down the hall until Mojisola can no longer see her.

*

She goes to bed in her flannels. Feels muggy in the head. Mugged. All the talk of crime, she gets up from bed and checks the locks twice before cursing Zelda and trying to fall asleep. After all her trepidation (promising herself she would rather sleep on the floor), she has collapsed onto Yinka's long and wide bed. It seems a small thing but when she came to lie down there was a curl of hair on the pillow. She'd collected it and placed it in the pocket of her pyjamas.

Every home has its sounds. Mojisola is accustomed to the night sounds of her home in Cape Town. There is a tap that defies correction and has dripped for as long as they've lived in the house. During the bustle of the day the sound is imperceptible but at night, in bed, the tap in their bathroom can resemble a footfall. Titus had never minded. Over time Mojisola, too, grew accustomed to it, but every now and again she'd hear it and startle. 'It's just the tap,' Titus would say.

Yinka's home has night sounds Mojisola cannot interpret. There is a rhythmic scratching noise that must be a neighbour, she decides, someone living above, but what are they doing and at such regular intervals? There is a noise that sounds like someone trying a door handle — it is this noise that has her check the front door before swearing off such paranoia and deciding, henceforth, to ignore all noises.

Her mind goes then to her earlier stupidity, that desperate conceit that had made her type in her own name when seeking a password for Yinka's laptop. After Zelda left, Mojisola hadn't returned to the task of working out the password. Instead she'd closed the laptop, realising caution was required. She doesn't know for sure, but she assumes she will not be given endless opportunities to guess. Maybe she has all of three chances and already one has been squandered on silliness. Or maybe she has five. There was also a cellphone in the box, which Mojisola set up to charge. In the morning, possibly, it will demand a password too, but she will worry about that then. First, she has to fall asleep.

When she'd first decided and then booked her flight to Johannesburg, Mojisola'd had no way of knowing what lay ahead, only that she must leave Cape Town, leave Titus and come here. She had the address of Yinka's flat because the landlady had written and mentioned the personal effects that needed to be sent. By that stage, Mojisola had become used to the sting of being contacted by strangers telling her things she didn't know about her own child. The humiliation of it.

Dear Prof. and Mrs Owolabi,

My name is Zelda Petersen. I was your daughter's landlady here at Cove Crescent, Midrand, Gauteng. I am sorry for your loss. I had expected someone to come by the flat but as I have not heard from you, I thought it appropriate to write. I have this physical address because it is the alternative address Yinka provided when we performed the security check. I hate to bring up anything unpleasant but some of Yinka's things remain and I, as life dictates, am required to let the flat. Which brings me to another delicate matter. As per law the lease does not terminate on the passing of the tenant (Yinka). In fact her executor (I assume that is you, her parents) is required to terminate the lease. Can you please do so, in writing, post haste. Monies owing (for instance if you require that I courier her belongings) will be sent to this address in the form of an invoice, and I would appreciate prompt response. I apologise for interrupting your grief with these seemingly trivial matters. Thank you for taking the time to attend to my requests.

Kind regards,

Zelda A. Petersen

In person Zelda Petersen is much less courteous than her letter suggested. Having now met her, Mojisola is left with the impression that the woman is only rude because she has not the time to compose the polite version of herself. Is that all courtesy is then, a few seconds, bought or stolen, to tame one's beast? But, regardless, the letter had come as a final piece to a plan that had been forming in Mojisola's mind ever since she'd received the phone call. That call no parent wishes to answer, that no one really, in a perfect world, should ever have to make.

'Mrs. Owolabi? Did you hear me?'

It was the words 'by her own hand' that had made any response impossible. She couldn't speak. The policeman must have lifted that string of words from a textbook. Yinka was dead by her own hand?

'Ma'am? Hello?'

Her Yinka?

'Mrs. Owolabi?'

She couldn't breathe but only for a half a minute, then the air flushed bringing with it more anger than any world would ever survive. Then, as quickly as the emotions had flooded her body, something began to set — stiffen — in her veins. She could breathe again but there was no feeling in her chest. She'd been in the kitchen doing dishes when the call had come through. Now she needed to get away, go away, but she would have to go far — she needed to run from the news, run from a moment when Yinka Owolabi could be dead by her own hand.

*

Hunger wakes Mojisola before daylight. Yinka's fridge carries four eggs, a dish of butter and there is half a loaf of bread in the freezer. Mojisola fishes out a frying pan and cracks two eggs, smelling each one before searching for a spatula. She should go shopping but she must avoid Zelda Petersen. Perhaps there is a back way. She makes a note to explore. She could escape, buy groceries, think of the next step. She is here to see, to untangle everything. There is the laptop with its question-mark password. She feels dangerous in her freedom, but, of course, it is all held in a tight bag of anguish.

What sounds like footsteps come to the door and Mojisola can almost see, through the hard wood, Zelda Petersen raise her hand to knock. But nothing happens. And then a phone rings. She ignores it. Titus has always been persistent. When he courted her it was useful but ever since it's been a nuisance. He thinks she's sick again, that's why he keeps calling. Thinks 'acute stress' is the explanation for their entire marriage and for her struggles with Yinka. The ringing stops but starts up again, and it is only this second chance to listen to the chime that makes Mojisola realise it is not her ringtone. She starts about the flat, looking. It is Yinka's charged-up cellphone that is ringing and as Mojisola picks it up the sound goes dead. She waits for the phone to ring again but several minutes pass and it does not. The name in the window for the missed call says 'PM'.

Mojisola goes to flip the eggs. She remembers the curl of hair from the previous night, checks the pocket and it is gone. Looking for it reminds her of a programme she would watch on days when she didn't care about the laundry or was too tired to think of preparing dinner. Each episode had a police detective searching, sifting through prints and smudges, locks of hair, drops of blood. Mojisola turns off the stove. She eats the eggs, slightly overcooked, tasting each unremarkable morsel — she forgot the seasoning. When she's done, she reaches for Yinka's phone, presses the button and the window gives her a face of dots.

'Aah,' she exclaims. More passwords; our lives are coded, nothing ever given in the clearest of terms.

The grid of dots. Mojisola understands she must make a figure without lifting her finger. She first draws out the letter *y* — a *v* on a stick — imagining this to be the obvious code Yinka would use. *Y for Yinka. Y for...*It doesn't work. *For 'yes', for 'yesterday'.* Mojisola next tries *m. For 'me'*, she thinks, but secretly she is thinking, *For Mojisola. Mummy. Mama. Mine.* It doesn't work. Now, with neither *m* nor *y*, Mojisola decides that somehow the code must be random. There is no real logic to this decision, but she feels it instinctively and despairs. There are 26 letters in the alphabet, two of which she has eliminated, but surely she will not be given 24 more chances to guess. *Is the code random or deliberate?* she thinks again, feeling less certain than only moments before.

She gets up to wash her hands although she couldn't explain why. She decides at the faucet, returns to the phone and draws a *1* or an *I* down the centre of the grid. Strangely she is angry when the phone greets her; annoyed with life, with phones, with her daughter dead, with herself, for the flush of success that comes up in her cheeks, for a sense of excitement in playing a game she's lost anyway. Nothing she does henceforth will bring the child back.

She scrolls to find the missed call. PM. The necessity for covertness assails her and she instinctively chooses to dial the number from her phone, not Yinka's.

'Hello?...Hello?'

'Hello.' She hasn't spoken since Zelda's unwanted visit the previous evening — her vocal cords are stiff. 'Who's this? PM? Is this PM?'

'What the — who the fuck is this? How do you...?'

'It's...it's, ehm, a — a friend of Yinka's. She gave me your number.'

He pauses then, cautious, 'Yes? Okay.' He sounds uncertain. 'Well, how can I help? Where is she? I've been trying to reach her. Can you please tell—'

Mojisola drops the call rather than relay the news. PM calls back several times but she doesn't pick up. She stands apart from the phone, unable to look away, unable to answer. She stands and watches the calls come through. Eventually they stop. After washing the dishes and making the bed — duty follows her even here, even now — Mojisola goes back to Yinka's phone and scrolls through 'Contacts'. The flow of names has a meditative effect. There are three Carmens. There is a Demita. Mojisola pauses on names that really are not names. Hot Stuff. Jam Again. The Wood. She is tempted to dial a number, open a page of her daughter's life, like a diary, and collect answers to all her hanging questions. But something keeps her scrolling. There is a King and she passes quickly through L M N O P (Piano-tuner) to check if perhaps there is a Queen. There isn't. Q. Quinta. Quinta. Remi. Ridwaan. Uriel.

By the time she gets to Zolile, Mojisola has a headache. What is she to do? Phone everyone on Yinka's list? And say what? Interview them? When PM (is that a name, a time of day or a physical condition?) asked, she'd said she was a friend. That was instinctive. She knew. She knew that if she were to come and see, to check, to insert herself into a life she should have known but didn't, she could come as neighbour, as friend, as classmate; she could come as teacher, as gym-buddy, as enemy, but she could not come as mother. So what? So she presents herself (friend) in front of these names. Quinta. King. All the names. Line them all up and question them?

She puts the phone down for half an hour, spends that time looking for the other blue slipper. *What would I ask them?* Mojisola thinks, as she bends, with some difficulty, to look beneath the couch. No slipper. She'll say...she'll say... What? They'll see through her, smell the guilt. See that she is the mother and come around finally to the same question everyone else has: 'How did you let this happen?'

*

Titus had been on campus at the time of the news. Later, in relation to Mojisola's reaction, the physician would say acute stress disorder, a label Titus would memorise and proceed to use on her like a weapon. At the time of the call however, it hadn't crossed Mojisola's mind to phone and tell Titus, or to ask him to come home so she could tell him face to face. These were not the kinds of thoughts she was having. Suddenly she wasn't even thinking about her daughter dead, the policeman, she wasn't imagining a body, a mortuary, a funeral. Her brain was fighting, fighting for a different universe and the best way to fight seemed to be to run. She was assailed by a desperate need to get away — from the house, from herself, from the pain waiting to pounce. But first the house.

It was just after midday and the roads were busy. Mojisola thought people were probably hungry. She thought, they either have food or want it. They are either about satisfying their appetite or suppressing it. Her steps were shaky, as if her legs were new, as if the road was polished black ice instead of rough tar. She walked away from the house — from the call — up Harfield and, after a cursory glance at the Arderne Gardens, turned right onto Main. As she walked Mojisola noticed that a man was gesticulating at her from across the road; he was shouting something at her, his mouth ajar, violent. She stopped abruptly; the woman walking behind, a baby to her bosom, swore and sidestepped, sending Mojisola a look of annoyance before walking on with her child safe in her arms. Mojisola stood staring at the man for a few seconds, the time it took for her to realise something was wrong — she could not hear a word he was saying, she in fact could not hear anything, she'd gone deaf.

The man's mouth was still wide open. He was standing next to a white minibus taxi. Still unable to hear, Mojisola reasoned that he was probably trying to get her to climb in — maybe he thought she was headed to Mowbray or Woodstock or the Foreshore. Maybe she should head to the water. If she plunged in, her whole body (nothing left back), the cold unforgiving Cape Town water might jolt her blood. Maybe then she'd awaken back into the correct universe. Mojisola started walking again.

She headed down Main Road, her steps suddenly certain, ten kilometres of road between her and the Atlantic. She didn't feel the need to run just then or get into a minibus taxi or think of the train and the train tracks heading into the city. She needed to walk. She tried not to think of the sergeant at the other end of the line asking if she'd heard him. She struggled to excise from her mind that Yinka was gone, by her own hand, that was what he'd said, that while she'd been on her way, just a little late but coming, her baby had died.

She passed Wilderness Road, studying the Claremont library, thinking innocently of when last she'd borrowed a book. There were men at the side of the road, to her left, selling bitsy things, cellphone chargers, minuscule batteries. They called out to each other in French, to prospective customers in English and Xhosa. On her right she saw a man bent almost double trying to fetch something off the ground. His pants were falling down and she could see his brown bottom, the dark valley demarcating one buttock from the other. As he straightened up, she saw he had picked up a dirty coin and that he was propped on a wooden crutch, that he had only one leg. Ahead, the woman and her child were way in front; she would never catch up with them and, of course, there was no reason to. Within reach was another woman, whose head was covered with a pink scarf. She was wobbly. Mojisola looked at her feet and noted she was wearing unreasonably high heels. She looked like she might fall at any step — she could barely stay on the pavement. 'Take off those stupid shoes,' Mojisola felt like saying, but she merely made a wide arc around her, walked on.

Then, as if in punishment for her lack of solidarity (woman-to-woman and in full knowledge of societal pressure to wear unreasonable shoes), Mojisola's bum was on the pavement. She'd slipped on wet garbage and the strap of her sandal had broken. Someone tried to help her up, but she batted him away and, after staring a while, he let her be. People walked around her while she collected her thoughts. She still needed to walk but could not do so without shoes. It was decided, she would pop into Cavendish, pick up a pair of shoes, and get back on the road.

The minute she entered the mall, her hearing returned, assaulting her with noise — she wished she were deaf. She navigated the bustle. Each time she passed someone languidly sipping a cup of coffee she fought the urge to punch them. Fought the urge to stomp up to them — somebody with designer glasses, someone who got their teeth fixed, someone wearing underwear as outerwear, using cleavage to flirt — and land a punch into their guts. (She thought of the gun she didn't own.) They were obscene and ugly. People had shopping bags, so many they didn't have enough fingers to hook (ten weren't enough); they hung them on their legs, dragged them along the shiny tiles, laughing, stopping to answer their iPhones. It had been a bad idea to come into Cavendish because nothing is more detrimental to the mourner than commerce. Mojisola felt enraged and simultaneously exhausted, resisting her anger, trying to quell the impulse to strike out. Finally, at a sports shop, she sat on a cushion and sank her feet into a pair of Nikes.

'Are you preparing for the marathon, ma'am? That's an excellent choice.'

Mojisola remembered the famous Cape Town marathon that claimed the streets each year. 'Yes,' she said, dazed.

'Well, good choice. Let's check here.' The woman bent over and felt the tips of the shoes. Good choice! She'd gone for the first thing she'd seen and now she looked doubtfully at the bright pink. She didn't wish to talk, though, to argue about colours, she didn't even wish to be inside this shop. What she wanted, needed, to do was walk.

'So — will you take them?'

Mojisola couldn't ask if they had a different colour, such a question fraught with sin. She nodded. The salesperson appeared amused but happy for the quick purchase, the lack of indecision.

'Keep them on,' she offered. 'I'll put these in the box. You can pay over here.'

At the counter there was the problem of money. Both Mojisola and the clerk realised the same thing at the same time — that she had none. That was where the unity ended. The clerk assumed Mojisola was some nut from off the street or a chancer. Mojisola alone knew that her only error was to have run away without her purse. She left the shop, too preoccupied to be embarrassed.

Back outside she threw her sandals (one with a broken strap, the other functioning but useless) into a blue bin. She took huge gulps of air then headed back to Main Road. Right. 'Are you preparing for a marathon?' the saleswoman had asked. And with that Mojisola worked her stride into a gentle jog. She ran amok all over Cape Town. She ran for upwards of three hours and would have gone on running if Titus hadn't sent out a search party. Mojisola was picked up by a patrol unit along Beach Road, her clothes soaked through, feet bloody, heart broken.

*

The idea to check Yinka's last dialled numbers comes when Mojisola is wondering whether to fry the last two eggs. The idea and what she is doing at the time have no obvious connection. Just that she is sufficiently distracted for the idea to surface. Surely there will be something significant about this number, the last she dialled. There'll be a date to it, maybe even a time. There was no investigation, there was no need for one, but Mojisola suddenly feels she is in her own crime movie.

PM's question about Yinka's whereabouts had taken her by surprise. She'd assumed, naively that anyone on Yinka's phone would know more than her, not less. She'd set it up wrongly, introducing herself as a friend. This time she will be neutral. She will be a company with a parcel maybe. An insurance salesperson, someone from the insignificant spaces of life, someone in an office with Yinka's name on a list of thousands. 'And why are you calling me?' the last-dialled-number person would ask. Quinta or King. She would say, 'Yinka gave me this number, gave you as a friend.' Friend. Mojisola would not recognise her daughter's friends in the street. Yinka had always made it that way and they, as parents, had never insisted either. And now she's confronted with all these unfamiliar names on Yinka's phone. Mojisola experiences, not for the first time nor the last, a measure of her failure. Her own mother had been so diligent about Mojisola's friends. 'Who are you sitting next to in class?' she would ask at the start of each school year, and she once went so far as to request Mojisola change seats. It turned out the girl her mother had disapproved of was the daughter of a politician who Mojisola's mother had referred to as a thief.

That was it: parents were meant to be obsessively interested in their children's friends. As are the proportions of life, the friends would eventually take up more room than the parents, so while you still had a greater fraction you were to influence the nature of those friendships, calibrate them, take out the bad influences and introduce the good. Mojisola had resented her mother's intrusions and thought it best to give Yinka much more room. Was that an excuse or a reason? Was her daughter dead because of it?

Mojisola leaves the uncracked eggs on the counter and goes once more to Yinka's phone. What was on her child's mind the morning she died, who did she phone and why? Maybe King knows. Or Quinta. Or Remi. A whole life Mojisola has no access to. She has no way of deciphering who means what and why. What can they tell her, really? Can they explain what happened, precisely and in detail?

Mojisola scrolls to the call log till she hits the date she has memorised — Yinka's last day alive. In the morning a phone call to a Cape Town number, a landline. She dials it from her own phone. It rings and rings — no answer. She makes a mental note to come back to it, thinking she ought to write down all the clues, like a good detective. She ought to get a notebook. She continues to track through the dialled numbers. There are several in the preceding days. There is one with no title. Mojisola dials.

'Hello, Blessed and Bounty.'

'Hello, where is this, please?'

'Blessed and Bounty, how can I help you?'

'Pardon?'

'We're a beauty parlour, ma'am.' Bored. 'How can I help?'

'I…I'm just following up on an…an appointment.'

'Yes?' Drawn out as if speaking to an idiot. 'Name, please.'

'Yinka. Yinka Owolabi.'

'Okay. Just a…What did you book, Mrs …Mrs…?'

'Owolabi.'

'Yes, what did you book?'

'No. I…it's not…Check your books or something. Maybe—'

'Just a second, ma'am.'

Mojisola moves around the apartment. She has her phone to her ear, and she is holding Yinka's phone in her other hand, pressed against her belly.

'You said first name?'

'Yinka.'

'Spell that, please.'

She does.

'Yes. Ah. Sorry, ma'am, we cancelled your booking when you didn't show up.'

It makes Mojisola so sad: 'when you didn't show up.'

'Ma'am, you there?'

'Yes…yes, I'm here. I'm…sorry about the appointment.'

'No problem. Most people don't even bother to check back.'

They hang on the call for a few seconds of distant civility and then the beautician rings off.

Determined not to lose momentum, Mojisola dials the next, also unnamed. A clipped voice assures her that the number does not exist. The third is another business location, We Do Boards. When the man announces the company and asks how he can help, Mojisola drops the call. She goes back to the kitchen counter and the flyer is still there — We Do Boards and an address beneath. She phones the disgruntled taxi driver, whose number she'd kept. He says he'll be there in 15 minutes but arrives in 40.

*

Mojisola is out. She is feeling triumphant because she put on Yinka's sneakers (she's always relished the fact that they wore the same size) and did precisely what such shoes are named for

— she sneaked out of No Cove No Crescent without so much as giving Zelda Petersen a reason to sneeze.

We Do Boards is a large shed at the top of a rise surrounded by what look like smallholdings. Mojisola has the mapbook she'd bought at Cape Town International tucked into her handbag. It makes her feel safe, but she wonders at this. When the taxi drops her and pulls off, a small panic comes up. Now what? She's here on what can only be called a whim. Even more than that, on the spectrum of motivation, she's all the way irrational. She'd come out here so quickly as if she still thought she could erase time, go back and find her child sitting at the entrance grinning, saying, 'What took you so long, Mummy?'

Yinka is not at the entrance. Instead a fading gnome greets her in Afrikaans, holding a blackboard sign against his plaster-of-paris red shirt. Perhaps Mojisola stares too long at the sign because a man just inside the entrance says, his English laden with Afrikaans mother-tongue, 'It's supposed to have the specials. Let me put them.' He comes with chalk. Mojisola wanders into the shed and he follows behind.

'Can I help you, ma'am?'

'I was just....' She is out of excuses. She has proven herself useless at being covert. 'I...I think my daughter was here.' She says it like a confession. Something scratches her throat so she must wait a few seconds, clear her larynx, before continuing. 'I saw a flyer in her house. Her flat. One of your flyers. And then I — I saw she'd made some calls to this place. This...' she looks around hoping for a more specific word '...place.'

The man has been looking at her intently. He is incredibly large and his face is pink, his cheeks the pinkest. His hair is in a permanent condition of static, short strands standing up, as if trying to flee from his scalp. His eyes are kind. Mojisola wonders if she is transparent.

'Your daughter, ma'am?'

'Yes, my daughter,' Mojisola says, feeling foolish. 'I mean I think...I mean maybe...'

'What's her name?'

'Yinka Owolabi.'

Mojisola is lifted by the recognition in his eyes. She feels rewarded. She has found something.

'Yinka...Yinka with the...Yes, she came in.'

'She was here? She came here?' She feels the ridiculous satisfaction of tracking a ghost.

'We have her order, ma'am.'

'Mojisola.'

'We have her order. In fact, if I'm not mistaken, we were just about to cancel.' They are standing in the double-volume space, the sourness of curing pine in the air, stacks of cut wood in all shapes and sizes surrounding them. The man walks to a desk with a mountain of papers from which he extracts a clipboard. Mojisola watches him, temporarily absorbed, an old habit, deciphering his character from the rhythm of his steps. 'Ja,' he says, flipping through the sheets of paper. 'Here. Yinka Owolabi. We received full payment and then no response. She wasn't returning our calls.' He looks at Mojisola. 'Thank goodness she sent you. And just in time too. We'll need an address — she hadn't decided between the house and the studio.'

Mojisola is just standing. The more the man speaks, the closer she feels to her child, as if finally she is reaching her. The more the man speaks, the more estranged she feels, the more she comprehends just how far there is to go. She clears her throat.

'Studio?'

'I presume she meant her artist studio.'

'And is this a...this place it's a...a...'

'We sell all your moulding, different profiles, matting, your framing equipment, glass, your glues. Of course, we do boards.' He smiles, but the joke falls flat so he continues unperturbed. 'We cut here; we can also assemble, although I believe,' he consults his clipboard, 'ja, she wanted to do her own assembly. I was impressed, not many opt for that.'

Mojisola is nodding, although her understanding is less vigorous than her head movements suggest. 'And she's assembling—'

'Frames. For her drawings, her sketches. All the wood is here, Mojisola, cut and ready. An address, and I'll get it to her within the week.' He signals he'll be back and moves off to attend to another customer. Mojisola is grateful for the gap. She ducks out and walks some distance away from We Do Boards, away from the man (he might come after her). Once sufficiently removed (as from the scene of some crime, she cannot work out what), Mojisola calls her taxi-guy.

Yinka's drawings. She had forgotten about Yinka's drawings. But not forgotten-forgotten. Only forgotten in the way that we forget on purpose those things we do not dare remember.

*

From early on Mojisola owned her own Bible and any spare time not spent studying was to be occupied reading what her mother simply referred to as 'The Book'. Scribbling and messing around with crayons was not encouraged. While she grew up tagging along with her mother's visits to the sick, the line was drawn at funerals. Some presiding law dictated that children and death remain quarantined.

On those occasions, Mojisola was left with her aunt, her mother's younger sister — a woman who shared her mother's high cheekbones and arched brows but very little else. Not that Auntie Modupe wasn't religious. She was known for dancing on Saturday nights, then sitting to attention — back straight — for Sunday-morning service, right in the front row, reserved for the most devout. Auntie Modupe was known to have miscarried two eggs and would never bear children because her womb was misshapen. After rumours spread that Modupe was consulting Ifa, buying offerings and making sacrifices, her sister stopped entrusting her with Mojisola. The aunt came by to complain, to beg, but the sisters fought and Mojisola was never allowed to visit her aunt again. In Mojisola's five-year-old mind, the relationship — her wild auntie — receded into a murky, unremembered place.

Decades later beads of fluid leaked into her mother's lungs and killed her — pneumonia, the doctor said. Auntie Modupe came to the funeral. Mojisola, by then a young woman, soon to graduate, soon to marry, didn't recognise her.

'Ah-ah, you don't know me? Ah-ah, nawa o.'

Mojisola bowed her head and a nearby cousin was forced, not without embarrassment, to introduce her to her maternal aunt.

*

On the drive home from We Do Boards Mojisola thinks of the life she has left, her life in Cape Town where she would normally be cooped up, not out in the streets, questioning large pink men in their workshops or utilising the services of mysteriously available taxi drivers. In Cape Town she is mostly at home and in the supermarkets; she is in her large kitchen cooking and she is instructing the men how to apply the polish to the wood; she enjoys fixing things so she doesn't call any handymen when the bulbs in the standing lamps falter, then stop working altogether; she figures out what is wrong with the sockets in Titus's study. She concedes and gets a tiler because mould is becoming a problem in the guest toilet, but she stands over the artisan and issues a continuous stream of corrections — he is careless in the placement of his spacers, he does not seem to understand the proper use of sealant. When people come to the house, when Titus brings colleagues home, she sees how they shake her hand. Housewife, like a jail sentence, a twenty-first-century swear word. She is used to the judgement, from her own daughter who, when she turned 18 and discovered feminism, pummelled her with the same derision. And yet she understands the pipes, the joints of the house. It is a machine she has mastered. It is her domain. But here she is cut loose of all that. Suddenly jovial, she asks the driver how he is, questions him as to the origins of his name.

*

John, Titus's colleague, had helped with the funeral arrangements. He'd asked, 'Is there anyone among her friends you'd like me to notify?' Mojisola had wished very much to avoid the funeral. In Yoruba custom the parent does not bury their child; it is anathema. But they are not in Yorubaland; they are so far away, so scattered. Titus wore a black suit and, in the morning, as they prepared, she'd looked at him, barely able to recognise her husband but unable to tell if that was because something was wrong with her or him. Or both. Or just life itself. Yinka gone, everything henceforth is mangled. She still hadn't cried.

'I want to go away,' she'd told Titus when he'd asked her to knot his tie. 'Did you hear me? I need to leave.'

There was another funeral happening in Nigeria. Many months back an aunt had died and the arrangements were nearing completion; any day now a date would be set for the burial. But that was not the kind of place Mojisola wanted to run away to. In Nigeria, the funeral of an elder is almost always a reason to dance and celebrate, to give thanks for the long life. Mojisola needed to run somewhere much darker than a dead old woman's ceremony.

Yinka's funeral was held in Maitland, the hall too big for the few that had gathered. Titus had been raised by a nun; Mojisola's mother was an extreme Christian. They'd never joined a church, but had gone to one when they married, when they conceived, and now when they'd lost. The pastor kept mispronouncing Yinka's name, putting an *m* where there was none. Not because he was evil. Perhaps an idiosyncrasy of his speech, that soft *n* in Yinka's name would trip him up in any word. Tongue. Want. Gaunt.

If she had felt more conscientious, Mojisola would have spoken to him after the service, attempted to get to the bottom of his 'Yimka'. But in those early days of grief there was no room for such detective work. Mojisola had sat in the front next to Titus, her eyes shut tight and her hands on her belly.

'I need to leave,' she'd said again to Titus after the service.

*

To Mojisola's surprise, her cellphone receives an SMS from the bank; a payment has come through from Prof. Owolabi. It is the 25th of the month and Titus has forgotten to stop a debit order. It is the money that, were she in Cape Town, she would use for the household: groceries, repairs, upkeep. Should she feel guilty? Is she stealing?

She goes to a nearby ATM, the Cove Crescent guards greeting her when she walks past. She deposits money into one Zelda Petersen's chequing account. On the way home, she stops at the grocer's. When Mojisola returns, she walks around Cove Crescent with her head up high. She lingers in the rose garden. She has food and she's paid her rent; for the moment she's afraid of nothing.

*

Having been settled, Zelda Petersen has, while not a look of contentment, at least the beginnings of cherubic leanings in the apple of her cheeks. It could be that she is smirking but Mojisola simply cannot tell — her glasses are on the bedside table. Only when the front door is fully open, and nothing stands between them, does Mojisola notice that the woman is carrying a cat.

'Oh,' says Mojisola, startled.

'I thought I should return her.'

'Return?'

'To her rightful home.'

'It's Yinka's cat?' She accepts the bundle of warm fur from Zelda even as she stands perplexed. She doesn't like cats. 'Then what was it doing in your flat?'

'Inanna is her name. Your daughter named her Inanna.' Zelda's expression does not hide her disapproval of such a cat name, but she also seems bound by some law to observe whatever name a cat has been given. 'She comes to me for comfort.'

'Since...' Mojisola stops.

'Even before the incident.'

Mojisola is momentarily distracted by the word 'incident'.

'...terrible, simply terrible. Your daughter, I'm afraid to say, was not very kind to animals.'

Mojisola has missed the bulk of the assault but she picks up the tail end and is amused that Zelda Petersen feels positioned to lecture on kindness.

'I meant to ask, did Yinka rent any other space here? A... studio kind of space maybe?'

'Studio?' Zelda shakes her head. She's only half listening, playing with the cat, talking in short whispers as if to a human baby. 'By the way I wouldn't walk anywhere if I were you,' she says. And then, 'Leave your bedroom door cracked open, I recommend. She sleeps on the bed but also likes to wander.'

'But I don't have anything to feed it,' says Mojisola.

'Ag.' Zelda brushes this aside, turns to leave. Over her shoulder she says, 'Anyway, she'll eat the rats.'

Rats? Mojisola does not sleep that night, partly because Inanna the cat keeps busy night hours, coming and going, and partly because, as if she didn't have enough to make her anxious (drawings, Yinka's drawings), she is now worried about rats.

*

Somewhere in the night Mojisola falls asleep. In the morning she expects to see rat carcasses littering the floor, blood and carnage, but instead Inanna is asleep on her paws. There is a dead ladybird by the door (whose death could well be accounted for by natural causes), but nothing else. While taking her first cup of tea, a wave of anxiety comes over her. A quiet foreboding (but surely the worst has already happened?) — the drawings.

Soon after the funeral, Titus's colleague, John, had sent them the number of a bereavement counsellor, Thembi Minyuku. Mojisola called once but didn't show up for the appointment. And then they'd had one other conversation when Thembi called to follow up. Mojisola had said she could not use the counselling, that it was not for her. Minyuku had suggested she write in a journal. 'The memories,' she'd said, 'you might want to start writing them down.' The idea had seemed absurd to Mojisola, fit for television programmes but too romantic for real life. And yet here she is in Yinka's flat, thinking back on the drawings. Counsellor Thembi seems to have been right.

'I'm trying to come to terms with the death. I can't get into the memories just yet,' Mojisola had said, a note of impatience in her voice.

'I understand. But in fact, to get over there — to come to terms — you must pass through your memories. There are many ways to come to terms, Mrs. Owolabi, and this is by no means the least painful but in my many years of practice—'

Mojisola had sighed.

'Is something wrong, Mrs. Owolabi?'

'No.'

There were some seconds of silence.

'I suppose all I'm trying to say is that...often it's not about getting to the memories. They find you.'

Mojisola hated to admit it, even if only to herself, but the woman was right.

*

They met as students and, on the completion of his doctorate, Titus's mentor, Professor Hussein Gbadebo, found him an appointment at the University of Ile-Ife. After a small wedding he and Mojisola moved into House 11.

At Ife, Titus taught several first-year courses. Gbadebo travelled frequently; within Nigeria, to Lagos for instance, but also to Ivory Coast, Libya and Ghana. He was involved as an advisor to a continent-wide project, trans-continent committees telling the complex stories of Africa's past. Fond of the young man and usually within reach of travel grants, Gbadebo was always keen to take Titus along with him, as research assistant but also acolyte. From Gbadebo Titus cultivated a persona that would serve him well into the peak of his academic career. He learnt to be public, to have an appetite; he was charming at dinner tables, well-versed in world politics, by necessity conversant in all histories; his French was good, his Portuguese passable.

Mojisola graduated cum laude. Her mother had passed on a year before and she was trying to hold Auntie Modupe at a distance, disturbed by her somehow. So neither of the women she had known as a child was present at her wedding to Titus Owolabi. His guardian was there, an imposing woman despite her age and frailty. Mojisola had met her once before: they'd taken a trip to Illesa to receive the nun's blessing. The woman had glanced at Mojisola and there had been a distinct look of disapproval on her face. When Mojisola had raised it with Titus he'd said she was sick, a slow-creeping emphysema that made her look permanently displeased. "Don't mind her jòó," he'd said. On that visit Sister Immaculata had spoken very little. Kemi, Titus's aunt, explained that the old woman was too tired to speak. Speaking and smiling take up energy. A small nod was what Sister Immaculata had used to grant approval and, having said nothing the entire afternoon, when Mojisola approached to bid her goodbye the Sister turned her cheek to be kissed and said, 'I'll pray for you,' the words more recrimination than benediction.

*

The day Mojisola found out she was pregnant she couldn't believe it. Not because she didn't understand biology, after all the long classes with Miss Daxon, the textbooks with pictures that looked unfamiliar no matter how she held the book, how far or close the page was from her nose. It surprised her that she was pregnant. The kind of surprise she could not admit to her husband. Why should she have been surprised? There hadn't been anything specifically called sexual education, but there had been those biology lessons. Mojisola had grown up under her mother's religious eye, kissed no boys, met Titus, and married him. As a married couple, they'd been regularly copulating. That she was pregnant was a mere feature of natural science. And yet she was surprised. Not even because she'd been using pills to stop a pregnancy or her rhythms or his withdrawal to hinder nature. They hadn't discussed having a child but neither had they discussed not. She a virgin, Titus with his dubiously proclaimed authority on love-making, they had explored themselves and each other with a curiosity set loose and legitimised by the priest who'd pronounced them man and wife.

In the 20th week of pregnancy, on a Tuesday, Mojisola took a while to get into the magenta Volkswagen. A strange dawning had come upon her body and she'd stood by her car, struggling. It was not that she couldn't fit: she carried the pregnancy in her back, sometimes it felt as if her womb was behind her abdomen instead of beneath it.

'Can I help you, Ma?'

The university students were cute. Often she was only a few years older than them but they insisted on calling her 'Ma'. Many recognised her as the wife of Dr Titus Owolabi. Some addressed her as 'Dr Mrs Owolabi' and, never having been quick with quips, Mojisola was always too slow to ask that they should not do that. In Dr Mrs Owolabi, she found nothing resembling herself. If life would slow down a bit, she'd say something like 'No, just Mojisola is fine.'

'Ma, let me help you.'

She couldn't bend. In the time since she'd risen from her office desk, collected her things and made the short walk to the car park, something in her body had changed. On arriving at the car she had attempted to enter it but a fierce objection had shot through her bones, as if her body was saying, 'What's wrong with you? Are you mad?' She was standing in the embrace of the open door. Just step up and sit, grab the steering wheel. The young man offering help looked distressed; perhaps he had a late afternoon class to get to.

'It's okay,' Mojisola said. 'I'm just...waiting for a moment.'

She was a bad liar, but it wasn't a complete lie: she was waiting for the moment when her body remembered how to bend. The young man didn't seem completely satisfied with this. Someone called to him from a group that was headed towards the law building.

'Mò ń bò, jòó!' he shouted, and then he told her the same. 'I'm coming.' He dashed off, with a concerned backward glance and no real intention of returning.

Still standing beside the driver's seat, Mojisola placed her palms on the roof of the car. She looked around, nervous she was being watched, but the car park was near empty. Her boss's powder-blue 504 was still there. Oguns liked to convey a sense of being overworked but, as his main administrator, she understood this to be a cover. In fact, she knew it was his intention to request a promotion; that he used the appearance of being hardworking in order to seem most deserving. He deliberately ignored letters: anything that arrived and was urgent he ignored for several hours. It was especially critical to ignore those that were pressing because it made him appear even more important, too beleaguered even for the urgent.

After much prodding — Oguns was not one to support his staff without first being begged — Mojisola had been assigned an enviable project for the department, the task of surveying and recording all the flora of the campus. The project, this new lens, had coloured her vision. Suddenly the campus they'd lived on for years signified itself through trees and flower buds. Just that afternoon she'd begun to work on the car parks — there were several, well planted, and sprinkled around the university.

Looking around, Mojisola noticed a group of university drivers standing beneath the shade of what she now thought of as her trees, passing the time. A young girl, with unshelled groundnuts balanced in a glass box on her head, walked past and the drivers called out to her; she stopped to sell her wares.

'Afternoon, Ma,' a young man walked past Mojisola.

She nodded, recognising him as her boss's driver. Oguns would be out in a few moments and he'd want to know what was wrong. Not because he cared but because it seemed de rigueur that he be the last to leave. If he left her standing in the

car park, how would that look? Spurred by a desperate need not
to encounter Oguns, Mojisola attempted for the second time
in just under 20 minutes to enter her car. The stiffness was
still there but less, as if it too was chastened by the thought of
an unnecessary encounter with her boss. Thank you, Mojisola
said, to her finally cooperative joints. She settled the cushion
to support her back and turned the key.

Trees lined her way home. Large ones with broad leaves,
a deep green; the familiar almond tree, several of which had
grown in the yard when she was a child. The almond fruit had
sour flesh and a large seed that could stain your tongue. It was
June: the rainy season was gathering itself. Mojisola drove up
Road 2, past the conference centre and the staff club, mostly
obscured, she noticed, by a verdant grove of Yeye trees. They
were almost out of hand, free things that would climb through
the entire campus if no one came with a cutlass or axe. She felt
a sense of quiet wonder at this, that way of nature, the way it
just continued.

Mojisola turned right up Road 9 and spent the rest of the
journey with her fingers loose on the steering wheel. She
reached home and didn't realise she was breathless until she
called from the yard, 'Titus!' His silver Peugeot was badly parked,
leaving little room for the Beetle. 'Titus!' She saw the Achiote
by the door. She remembered this plant from childhood, red
and spiky. She'd painted her lips with the sap and her mother
had cautioned her. When Titus didn't come out, despite her
calls, and unsure if her body would co-operate, Mojisola held
onto the roof of the Beetle and hoisted herself out. She stood
with her hand to her breast, steadying her breath, and only
then did she see that a woman was sitting on the patio.

'You really should not be working at this stage. I told the
same thing to that husband of yours. At 12 weeks your mother
was off her feet and, mark me, it saved both your lives. Ah,
well. Óyá, come,' she rose off the patio with ease that belied the
age in her voice, croaky and tired in a way that no earthly rest
could soothe. 'Óyá, now!' she shouted over her shoulder when
Mojisola did not immediately follow.

As Mojisola stepped into the house, Titus appeared.

'Moji,' he said, but the woman cut him off.

'Let her sit down first o, hábà! Óyá,' she led Mojisola, now a guest in her own home, into the lounge, rushing to arrange a footstool and remove the day's newspapers from the seat.

'But, Moji,' Titus continued, a familiar note of annoyance in his voice, 'do you know this person?'

'Auntie Modupe,' Mojisola said quietly, almost to herself. She took the seat on offer, allowed her feet to be placed to rest.

'Correct,' Auntie Modupe said.

Mojisola's mother had referred to her as Jezebel in hushed tones. Auntie Jezebel was famed, in her youth, for dancing on stage with nothing but a string of cowrie shells and some (discreetly placed) yellow feathers.

Satisfied with that as introduction, Auntie Modupe moved swiftly into the kitchen. 'Ọmọ,' she called. 'Kí lo fẹ́ mu?' The fridge door was opened, the clink of glass and the sound of water.

'Who is she?' Titus gave Mojisola a look. He wanted some kind of explanation, but she had none. She was enjoying just sitting, her head was aching. It's true the pregnancy had been difficult but Oguns had made one comment that woke her up each morning and made her drag herself into work. Two words he'd said when she mentioned she was pregnant: 'You women.'

'Moji!' Titus snapped, realising his wife had gone into a daze. 'Who's Auntie Modupe?'

'Don't you remember her from the funeral? My mother's sister,' Mojisola said.

Over the next few days it was revealed that Auntie Modupe had heard of Mojisola's pregnancy through some cousins in Akure. She took exception — 'You should have told me personally,' she chastised, stabbing her open palm against her chest. She'd aged since her dancing days, but it was only visible in a slight swelling of her joints. She walked slowly to disguise pain, wore face powder to hide fatigue. On the matter of children Auntie Modupe said an assortment of contradictory things depending on the time of day, how much gin she'd drunk, how convivial she felt. 'It's hard, Moji,' she would say. Mojisola wasn't sure how to take this, considering what she knew of Auntie Modupe's history: she'd never raised any children.

Nonetheless Auntie Modupe seemed to have a wealth of knowledge to impart. 'It's frightening,' she said. 'It's natural, it's normal, it's not normal, it's easy, it's not easy, it's proper love, men don't know, men can't know'. Sometimes Auntie Modupe said nothing.

Mojisola meanwhile wasn't coping. The bending episode was one in a string of bodily concerns. She got headaches. Her bladder wouldn't cooperate, and each day she marvelled that she didn't just dissolve and sink through her water-laden feet. On Auntie Modupe's urgings (and relinquishing any push back against Oguns' derision), Mojisola stopped working to wait out the final months. Auntie Modupe stayed on. Titus grumbled. Auntie Modupe went to the market on days she felt enterprising and came back with dark green leaves, prepared them, said, 'Drink.' She squeezed Mojisola's hand, winked, smiled, cried, prayed. Auntie Modupe prayed for a quick birth, a clean cut, a steady push, much breath; she prayed for a whole child, an easy child, a proper sleeper, a good eater; she asked for fine looks; she asked for a boy. Sometimes she asked for a girl. Sometimes she asked Mojisola, 'È wo lo fẹ́? Girl or boy?' Mojisola didn't respond, stunned as she was that anything was coming at all.

There she was with a pregnancy that had been neither planned nor unplanned. A pregnancy that made sense to her husband ('At last,' he'd said and kissed her hand). The pregnancy made sense to science but not to Mojisola. And even her surprise was a surprise. It was a moment where she saw her naïvety her capacity to live in an unreal world. In Mojisola's world, her aversion to children should have been contraception enough. In fact, after five years of marriage and nothing, she'd felt justified and relieved to conclude that she was unable to conceive. And yet, January, dawn time of a Friday, a pain hit but not only pain. Also a sensation they have not yet named, a thing that wakes all the senses, the sinews, all the jelly in the life-giving body, wakes it up and says, 'Let's go.'

*

'Moji?'

She'd answered automatically, without thinking. She'd seen his name in the window and simply picked up. As if her hands had forgotten what her brain had set in motion, a coming away, a peeling away.

'Moji?'

'I'm here. I'm here, Titus.'

He exhales. 'How are you? How is it, how's the apartment?'

The weariness in his voice somehow touches her. Is it fair, really, for her to keep all the grief to herself? Mojisola straightens her back as she realises she has spent very little time considering his pain. She clears her throat and looks around the lounge, the cardboard box, the character-less curtains.

'It's…it's.…' She thinks. 'It's clean.'

Titus grunts.

'Everything is very clean.' She doesn't really wish to speak with him but reserves of patience suddenly surface and she has the space for it. 'I've been trying to find the drawings.'

'Drawings?'

'Did she ever mention that to you?' She wants something from him now, which means very soon the call will be over — their relationship has always worked best when she'd muted desire.

'Drawings? No. Never.'

He is so clipped in speech she is driven to ruffle him.

'Do you miss her?'

'Moji, what kind of a question is that?'

'I'm sorry.' And she means it.

'I called that woman.'

'What woman?' She assumes he is talking about his lover but he is quick to clarify.

'The therapist John recommended.'

She can't pretend, she is surprised. For the first time in almost 20 years her husband has surprised her. Even his cheating wasn't a surprise.

'You're seeing a therapist?' She can't keep mockery out of her tone, but she tries.

'She asked me to journal.'

The scoff escapes, a life of its own. Titus says the word 'journal' as if it's of a foreign language, new and opaque.

'Don't make fun of me.'

'I'm not, Titus.' She thinks for a few seconds. 'Did John insist, is that it?' Just like Titus to end up seeing a therapist in order to keep up appearances. 'Did you tell him I've moved out or would that be too embarrassing?'

'Have you moved out? Is that what this is?'

They don't have to say much after that, the call has taken a momentum of its own, will propel itself, like their marriage, like most, towards a logical conclusion. For them that conclusion is a heavy silence. Mojisola is about to drop the phone when Titus speaks.

'Can I share it with you?'

'Wh—'

'The journal.'

'It's supposed to be private. It's not a calling card, Titus, it's meant to be intimate and personal.'

'Can I?

She doesn't know what to say. She feels a twinge of envy but who is it of and for what? Is she jealous of Titus and his journal, his capacity — however vain — to visit and sit with the therapist? Is she jealous of Minyuku who has obviously convinced Titus of the efficacy of writing down his feelings, very Oprah-like and American.

'When she was five, I took her into class one day. Introduced her to my students. It must have been no more than 10, 15 minutes. Remember?'

'Hmmm.'

'I'd picked her up from school or something and you were busy. The students loved it. And...her being there changed something.'

'How?'

'It was a new class, a new course, something had been dragging. I was young,' he laughs. 'There had been some struggle, some tightness and then there was Yinka, five and shiny. Ernest. I sometimes wondered what it was. Did I teach differently because she was in the room? Did the students listen better in the presence of real innocence? Whatever it was, it became something. I started bringing her to class. Like a—'

'Mascot.'

'Talisman.'

Mojisola remembers Titus's ritual of inviting Yinka to his lectures.

'Now I'll go on teaching classes, teaching students that will never meet Yinka. Students who will never meet my daughter.'

'What was it? What did—'

'They saw me differently after that. The students. After she came. And somehow or other seeing me differently made them listen differently, newly, do their assignments differently. Felt like my entire career changed.'

Mojisola is part-wonder, part-cynic at this suggestion of some kind of Yinka-juju. She is careful not to scoff though, enough ugliness has happened already.

'I'm almost 70 years old, Moji.'

It takes her some time to realise he is crying, so seldom has she been confronted with her husband's tears that this is utterly alien, even comical.

'I'll live another 20 or so.... Do I miss her? I don't just miss her now, I miss her for the absences that are still approaching.'

Mojisola, contemplating this, doesn't hear Titus's question.

'Can I?' he asks again and she is confused. She knows her husband, she knows this must be a performance but there is an appeal in his voice that is cracked and raw-like...he is begging.

'Moji?'

'No, Titus. No, I don't want to read your journal.'

*

When the day of Yinka's birth arrived, Mojisola had experienced a miserable 41 weeks. She'd imagined she'd be relieved to bear down, to surrender to the ripping of her tender passage but just when the midwife ordered that she push, Mojisola, with every intention to do as commanded (at this dark point in the process of birth no other action would be logical), discovered a resistance within her bones that seemed not of this world. Something stronger than her was at work.

'Push, now!' the midwife repeated, a touch of panic in her voice. She repeated it three times, louder and louder, until Mojisola once more mastered her bones. Holding her new sticky child, she'd felt ashamed for having possessed this will (greater than her will to mother) to resist, to fight and hold the child in limbo, rather than push it out into motion. And yet it was undeniable. Lying there, the nurse screeching, 'Push,' on the sidelines, Mojisola had had brief seconds of hope and ecstasy. She would experience the very same, but in reverse, many years later when she heard of the death of her child, but in that moment on the birthing bed, Mojisola fantasised that she somehow had the ability to reverse time. The fantasy that the child would go unborn, that she could reverse the irreversible and return to a simple existence that had gradually, over the many weeks, disappeared.

For all the prayers, Yinka turned out to be a queer baby. Crumpled up somehow, and creased. Her eyes seemed to take up most of her face which was unsettling, the staring child. Mojisola knew it was a bizarre thing to do but if they were alone and Yinka was staring she looked away, broke the gaze. Hers, in the end, was a serious face. None of the cuteness babies require as armour for their most vulnerable years. A serious, staring face. Her cheeks were round but her lips were straight; she didn't gurgle. She seemed to be conserving all her energies for some later time when she knew she would need power and would have to draw it from within. *What a strange child*, Mojisola thought. *What a strange, strange child.*

As if hearing her thoughts: 'This one. This one sha,' Auntie Modupe kept saying.

'This one what?' Titus once shouted. It was a tired household. He later apologised.

'This one,' Auntie Modupe whispered, as she collected Yinka from her mother after the day's first feed. 'She will make you suffer.' She laid the baby between her jaw and shoulder, rubbing her back. 'Moji,' she snapped at Mojisola, who was already dozing.

'Hmm?'

'This one will make you suffer. Wait and see.'

The child was a wonder; an endless crying, eating, pooping creature held together with skin and seams. Sometimes Auntie Modupe would catch Mojisola and say, 'Be careful. Don't love her too much.' Was it love, though? It felt more like being overrun, being colonised, at once complete and irreversible.

Yinka had come out baying and wouldn't stop. She bayed and bayed and bayed and bayed. Soon after the incessant crying ended, she developed colic and a new kind of crying began. Mojisola could not sleep for three uninterrupted hours. Titus was at work most of the time; he was being encouraged to publish his doctoral thesis and it meant long hours in the office. He would come home and ask his wife why she looked so haggard: what was the matter? And then she'd scream at him. This was new. Up to that point in their relationship there had been no shouting. It took the birthing of a child for Mojisola to discover that there were things about her husband she didn't like. He tagged the word 'understand' behind almost all of his sentences. It had been endearing and a not unfamiliar word twitch, until one evening a colleague of his stopped by. Mojisola was breastfeeding, unwilling to be gracious with unexpected company so she sat in the adjoining room. After the colleague left, she approached Titus, Yinka asleep but firmly attached to the teat.

'How come you didn't ask him if he understands anything?'

'Moji, what are you talking about now?'

'How come you didn't ask him if he understands anything?'

Titus had developed a frown for such interactions with his wife.

'How come? How come you ask me all the time if I understand? Do you think I'm stupid, Titus?'

'Where is all this coming from, Moji?'

She hated the fact that his breasts were not the size of cushions, his nipples were not cracking. His bowels didn't oscillate between two available modes, constipated and diarrhoeic. Regular and solid, well formed was Titus. To be fair, he slept almost as little as she did, but it didn't result in black welts beneath his eyes.

She breastfed till Yinka was two. Nothing else agreed with the child so, while the paediatrician looked for alternatives, Mojisola's breasts worked. 'Second child,' Titus whispered, one night, after some rare coitus.

'What?' Mojisola said, pulling herself away while Titus was still anticipating more sex. 'I need another two lives to recover from the first.'

*

The memories are a drug. Mojisola moves through the house, doped. On occasions when she doesn't come forth, Mojisola finds herself looking for Inanna the cat, under the couch, in the cupboards. Despite herself she wants to lay the cat in her lap and stroke it. Yinka's cat. Yinka's laptop. Yinka's cellphone. Yinka's clothes. Yinka's drawings. It's a bizarre inventory, the belongings of the departed beloved. The ordinary that would warrant no second glance suddenly heavy with meaning. Mojisola finds herself trying on her daughter's clothing. There is a towel hanging on the back of the bathroom door. It is bone dry but still Mojisola intends to take it to bed with her. Half bottles of cold cream; unpaired earrings; a box of tissues; one tablet left in a blister of Panado; an empty suitcase, the one Yinka had left Cape Town with (full). Amidst her things the absence — complete, absolute — of the person herself is so unfathomable. Mojisola glances at the front door, she cannot help it. She imagines Yinka walking through any moment: 'Hello Mummy, sorry I'm late.'

*

The months after the birth were a blur. Auntie Modupe moved in. Sometimes she even slept in the bed with her and the baby, Titus in the spare room. For a spell that was how things were, Mojisola in a kind of stupor — the baby had come and shifted her. This lasted almost a year and then, slowly, she began to feel like herself again. Auntie Modupe moved out but would visit from time to time, usually on weekends, bringing with her special condiments from Akure or some grasscutter she'd purchased on the Illesa road. She had no need for invitations and came whenever she felt like it, claiming to have dreamt something, to have seen something in the bush behind her house.

Just like that, much to Titus's chagrin, she would arrive unannounced, and instantly commandeer the kitchen to make what she called óúnjẹ gidi. She seemed to think neither Titus nor Mojisola possessed the necessary skills to cook proper food, turning her nose up at whatever leftovers Mojisola inevitably offered her as proof that they were not starving. Within days Auntie Modupe would go to market to select yams (no one — especially not the young woman who cleaned and cooked for the family — was as skilled as she in selecting the perfect tubers) and would then return home determined to pound the meal herself. Here Mojisola drew the line, reminding her of her age. It's true that they ate better during those visits so Mojisola withstood the criticism that came her way when Auntie Modupe scrutinised Yinka for evidence of neglect. On an almost daily basis during her visits, the old woman would pore over the child as if looking for cause to take her away from the parents. She never found anything sufficiently indicting. Occasionally Auntie Modupe asked that they cut Yinka's nails: 'Or she must first pluck out her eyes àbí?'

Mojisola envied Auntie Modupe the space that she took up in the world. It felt as if she'd missed out on some birthright, some metaphysical connection to ancestral strings and pulleys constantly directing knowledge and behaviour. Her mother had been the same. Expansive except, because of her devout leanings, she'd thrown it into the service of God, allowing it to reveal itself only when she prayed. Mojisola's mother prayed with the intricacy of one who was on intimate terms with the Bible and the Lord. Her prayers were not so much prayers (beseeching in tone) as instructions, precise and even tinged, just that little bit, with impatience. Mojisola's earliest memories are of the sound of her mother praying. And for some years — perhaps until she was five and growing in understanding of Christ and Afterlife — Mojisola had always thought, in praying, her mother was addressing a subordinate, some stubborn person who never learnt and constantly had to be appealed to to do the correct thing.

Auntie Modupe had that same air of superiority: she carried herself in a certain way and addressed you as if every second she spent doing so was a grace she bestowed. There was a poise to both women that Mojisola was certain she had not inherited. Further proof was how flummoxed she was by motherhood. She could not imagine her mother becoming undone by her entry into the world. How could a child — a simple small being — have come and shifted her so?

After Yinka's second birthday, Mojisola tried to return to work; she still dreamt of being assigned back onto the team documenting the biome. But there was a lot of noise in her head when she thought of her job; her rotund greasy-faced boss (nastier now his promotion had been denied), her astute colleagues, and she felt queasy, felt it would be impossible to walk a straight line much less arrive at work and be productive. She struggled to reach the mental composure her job required and so eventually she gave up. How easily it had happened. How easily everything can be sitting as it should, the layers in order, up is up, and then suddenly she could not feel herself, would never again feel that Self. She had a desire to be in the world, to venture, but on some days it was too hard to cross the threshold. In this way she and Titus were a cliché: the birth of their child had sent him hurtling into the wide world while it shut her in. She travelled tight trajectories away from the child and towards her as if they were joined by a rubber band with only this much give.

If she was in the habit of collecting appellations and had asked, medicine would have told her it was anxiety, post-partum, schizophrenia, mental illness. But something prevented Mojisola from seeking diagnosis. It was, declared the dark corners of her mind from which came determinations, to be a disease of one, something to suffer and bear alone. She could not talk to Titus about it and yet he was exasperated at what he called 'this your behaviour'. Her rash flared up: for that she tried to find new doctors, new creams.

Once a senior colleague of Titus's invited him and Mojisola to his daughter's wedding. Titus, sweating with ambition, saw this as a chance to break through. Mojisola tried to bow out but he would not allow it. They'd get a babysitter and he'd arrive with his wife, he in agbádá, she in bùbá and ìró and appropriately tied gèlè. It was the gèlè that unravelled her. Mojisola had never possessed any skill in tying. Her mother had schooled her in church and God but not in cultural dress. While she and her mother wore starched church uniforms, as a young woman Mojisola had observed with envy the other girls and women in her community, thought them formidable in their head-ties. There was the right-handed left-hander problem and on top of it all the baby had come and shifted her, producing an impatience that was of especially no use when it came to tying gèlè.

On the morning of the wedding, Mojisola fussed with the starched àdìrẹ, planted in front of a full-length mirror, her arms on fire as she fiddled. 'Ask the neighbour,' Titus offered but her pride wouldn't allow it. The fabric would not sit as was required of gèlè. Each time Mojisola finished a tie (she knew three and went through them over and over before giving up), instead of it holding form, commanding obeisance, it flounced, shivered, threatened to fall at the slightest turn. Titus, a different kind of animal in his green and brown agbádá, checked his watch, walked out from their bedroom down the corridor of their bungalow, walked back into the bedroom, checked his watch.

Mojisola gave up. At the function she noted the eyes cut her way, felt anew the obscene nature of an uncovered head at a prestigious Yoruba wedding.

*

Mojisola is knocking on Zelda's door. As usual there is no light inside, at least none that she can see from the hallway. But the woman must be home: as far as Mojisola has observed, she goes nowhere.

'Mrs Owolabi, Mojisola, how can I help?' Zelda is dressed completely in black.

'I had to ask.'

'Yes?' She is half turned away, as if Mojisola had interrupted her and she is keen to get back to whatever it was.

'Are you sure there is not somewhere a storeroom, perhaps, a garage?'

'I don't follow.'

'Yinka was an artist. She…she was…framing things, buying wood. She had a studio. I know she had one. Perhaps just a room somewhere. Did she have a car, a garage where she could have stored stuff?'

'Oh, my God,' She turns fully to face Mojisola. 'I forgot about the car. Oh, goodness.' Zelda raises her hands to her mouth. 'Yinka had a car. God, how could I have forgotten? I'll show you the garage. Wait, let me put on my shoes. I'm so sorry.'

They retrieve the car keys from No. 81 — hiding in plain sight in a bowl on the kitchen counter — and Mojisola walks behind Zelda, who takes big strides. She walks as if at any moment she will break into a run, not because she is in a hurry but rather because someone is chasing her.

'The garages are back here.' Zelda leads Mojisola round the side of the building. 'It's number 81, same as the flat.'

A man in blue overalls walks past. He greets Zelda but she ignores him. When he is out of earshot, Zelda hisses, 'That's the building manager. Hateful man.'

When they reach No. 81, Zelda hangs around. Mojisola jangles the keys, stalling. She does not wish to open the garage in the landlady's presence. It feels too delicate a task, requiring a tender presence and sanctity, neither of which Zelda has exhibited in the short time Mojisola has known her. She clears her throat.

'Oh,' says Zelda, feigning sudden comprehension. 'Oh, let me leave you in peace. Call if you need me.'

Mojisola watches her go, then bends down and unlocks the padlock. When she pulls on the lever it doesn't budge. A sense of dread comes over her as she thinks she might need Zelda's help after all.

'It's stiff, ma'am,' comes a voice from behind.

'You scared me,' Mojisola says. She looks at the boxes in his hands long enough for him to give an explanation.

'I gather the recycling.' He sets the boxes aside and comes up close, tugs the garage door open.

Mojisola stands back. 'Thank you,' she says, when the large door hangs above them like an awning. The 'hateful' building manager nods and leaves. She is alone again. She goes to the car. A silver Ford. The engine starts with no hesitation. Mojisola revs it for a few seconds. The petrol gauge is halfway; the mileage suggests it was bought second-hand. The car is clean. There are no bills, no mud on the mats, no change in the pockets, no CDs, not even some lint on the fabric of the seats. It's as if, just before she died, Yinka laundered her car. *All plausible*, Mojisola thinks, as she switches off the engine. She feels an absence, not just of the child but of something much less tangible than a physical body.

*

From when she was two, Yinka had a predilection for pencils
and pens. She seemed to conclude that anything long and
slender ought to be applied to the walls, ought to be used to
make marks. Mojisola often found her with a carrot, a stick, a
ruler, always attempting to draw. By the time she was three, she
understood what a pen was, distinct from other long similarly
shaped things. No pen was safe in the house. Yinka hoarded
them in her bedroom, was known to go to bed with one or
two in her grasp. Initially Mojisola did not notice anything
particular because there didn't seem to be anything to notice.
By the time Yinka was about three years and a few months
old, Mojisola was accustomed to being handed little squares of
paper. 'A sun,' Yinka would say when asked, as if there were
several and this was the one she'd drawn on that specific day.
Other times she'd say, 'A moon. A round thing,' and Mojisola
would laugh.

'What are you drawing today?' Mojisola once asked.

'I'm drawing me,' the child said. 'What are you doing?'

Mojisola was making a grocery list. 'I'm writing,' she said.

'Are you writing you?'

Mojisola smiled and continued with her list. When she
looked up again Yinka was making squiggles and chanting
softly, 'A B C A B C.'

'What are you doing now?' Mojisola asked.

'I'm writing me.'

When Yinka turned five she became fascinated with
charcoal, dismissive of crayon. She was leaving behind the
circles and drawing lines. Once they were sitting together in
the living room, Mojisola on the couch, Yinka crouched over
a stool. She'd commandeered her mother's ruler, fascinated by
it, as only children can be in thrall to the ordinary. At some
point Mojisola turned from the magazine she was holding and
looked at her child. Yinka's concentration was palpable: two
bars shooting from the enormous holes of her eyes onto the
page. There seemed something unnatural in how the child was

staring at the paper although Mojisola could not quite place it. Disturbed she'd cleared her throat and asked Yinka what she was doing.

'I'm making lie-ands,' Yinka said, without looking up, without pausing, as if she'd been waiting to be asked. Sheer reverence in her voice, in the way she attended to the word 'lines', the way she awarded it two syllables instead of just one.

As she grew older the drawing seemed to become more obsessive. Mojisola would find her six-year-old in a daze, a piece of paper before her and a pencil in her grip so tight you could not pry it out.

'Yinka? Yinka?' Mojisola nudged her gently and the child would snap back into consciousness, finally taking notice of her mother, blinking rapidly and looking around her as if in need of a reminder as to where she actually was. After a few more instances of this, Mojisola took her child to the doctor. The man was kind and listened to her concerns but even she could hear the absurdity of what she was saying.

'A daze you say?' the doctor asked as he moved the stethoscope along Yinka's narrow chest.

'Well, she…she isn't focussed. As if she's somewhere else.'

But he found nothing wrong and counselled Mojisola instead on the nature of the developing brains of children, the tendency to drift off. 'Harmless,' he said. 'Totally harmless.'

And yet it didn't seem harmless. Once when Yinka emerged from one of her dazes, a series of papers in front of her, she asked her mother where she was.

'What do you mean, where are you? Is something wrong? What happened, Yinka? Where did you go, tell me?'

But Yinka could never explain what had happened. She often needed a few reminders: You're at home, it's time for lunch; it's afternoon, it's time for a nap; It is bedtime, put down your pen and paper.

The decision to take the drawings away, along with all her implements, came the day she fell off the high stool and cut her head open. She'd been drawing and in her fugue-state had fallen off the chair.

'I'm taking everything,' Mojisola had declared, mowing through the house, Yinka whimpering behind and Titus putting in the occasional plea: 'Come on Moji, I think you're exaggerating.'

But that was it, drawing was banned. To better implement the law Mojisola collected all of Yinka's pencil colours and papers into one shoe box. Yinka's playgroup teacher was instructed to let the child play with blocks during drawing time.

Yinka begged. 'Mummy, I want to draw.'

'No. You can't.'

'Let the child draw,' Titus snapped.

Later, they argued.

'Moji, give her whatever she wants. She loves drawing. What's wrong with you?'

'No.'

'No what? Why not? Because—'

'Because it's not good for her, can't you see? And I know what's good for her. You can't just get whatever you want in life, Titus.'

Yinka cried in protest but slowly over the years she both acquiesced to Mojisola's will and resented it. A small hole grew in the space between mother and daughter — it would never close.

As Yinka understood she couldn't fight her mother on the drawings, she fought her on the small things instead; what ribbon to tie into her plaits, what underwear to put on. Often Mojisola felt Yinka was fighting for fighting's sake. The arguments came from a place of instinct, as if a small, unconscious part of Yinka still remembered being six years old, being defeated. It had been too small to fight back then but each new year, as the child grew, this small part of her became hungry for battle. Unable to reverse time, though, to win the fight that really mattered, she fought with her mother about blue stripes or red, resisted eating all the food on her plate, shouted when a whisper was appropriate, whispered when clear speech was necessary. This was now the board on which they would play out the remainder of their relationship, the squares marked out, the rules established. It was Yinka's role to struggle against, and Mojisola's to keep firm.

*

She starts in the kitchen, searching through the cupboards, although the chance of Yinka having stored her drawings in here, among pots and pans, is unlikely. They must be somewhere, though, the drawings she was planning to frame. It is a comfort to look, to rake her hands through Tupperware and scold her daughter's ghost about the dust on the top shelves.

She finds a cupboard full of heavy-duty equipment. These must be the framing tools the man at the framers had mentioned. There is even a blow torch. When she moves into the sitting room, she thinks again of the studio. It could be anywhere, although sense dictates that perhaps it is close to home. There are no clues in the house as to some other location, no extra set of keys, no piece of paper with an address helpfully scribbled. Mojisola pushes aside the thought of a studio: it is too far beyond the realm of what she can deduce from the few bits of evidence she has garnered so far. She once again embraces her detective role, her earlier failures forgotten. For now she will tuck away the existence of a studio, pretend she hadn't heard him say it.

There is nothing underneath the sofa except Inanna.

The cat regards her coolly but says nothing.

In the bedroom she senses that something will reveal itself. She prepares as she checks underneath the bed (just dust and a forgotten sock), as she checks the chest of drawers (her daughter's underwear, all black except for a few pieces of colourful lace), as she checks the closets. She is ready for the drawings. She is also ready for a diary, a confessional that would explain it all, even (and this she only thinks of for a second) a note, a goodbye note.

She is ready for all of this but what she actually finds, in the bottom of the cupboard, is an envelope with some writing on it. Inside a folded piece of lined paper protects four neatly rolled joints. Mojisola knows what a joint is, of course she knows, even if she has never put one to her lips. *Marijuana*, she thinks, frowning. She looks back at the envelope, now interested in the lettering. It's Yinka's name and a price but Mojisola is more taken by the handwriting. She knows that handwriting. Quickly she goes to her suitcase. She has unpacked most of her things but in the little pocket is the letter. She takes it out and puts the two samples of writing side by side, then marches to Zelda's door and knocks, this time so hard she bruises her knuckles.

'Can I help you?' Zelda says, before noticing the envelope Mojisola is holding up, like a conductor's baton. 'Oh,' says Zelda, and then, 'Why don't you come in, Mojisola?'

They are inside the room where Mojisola sat that first day, still only one chair. Now that she is here, she is uncertain what the exact nature of her accusation is. She'd felt propelled by a deep anger, a need to extract penance. And explanation. Sitting, Zelda standing by the door, all the fight in her is suddenly gone. Instead she sees Zelda standing and says, 'For God's sake, where's all your furniture?'

'What furniture?' says Zelda.

'Exactly! Your chairs. Your...seats. Where do your guests sit when they visit?'

'What guests?'

But Zelda goes into another part of the house and returns carrying a dining chair. When they are both seated, Mojisola feels the words come back to her.

'Is this what you were afraid I would find?' The envelope with its contents is in her lap.

'I suppose, yes. I confess I searched for it myself. Not hard enough, apparently.' She looks regretful as if she would have preferred to avoid this whole situation, whatever is about to unfold. 'I thought maybe she had...smoked it all.'

'You sell these?'

A pause.

'Yes, Mojisola. I sell.' Her face is tight, until suddenly, she spills. 'But this was the only time I sold to your daughter.

Someone must have told her...I mean, I don't go around advertising, if that's what you think. A tenant must have told her. We weren't really on speaking terms, Yinka and I. She just caught me in the hallway once, and asked.'

'What do you mean?'

'Once!'

'No no, what do you mean you weren't on speaking terms?' It has never occurred to Mojisola to question and interview the landlady, that she might know something useful. 'What — you argued?'

'I wouldn't say argued.'

Zelda remembers Yinka. Skinny, too skinny. She says this and looks harshly at Mojisola because, no matter how long past the age for suckling, a mother is always responsible for what her child does or doesn't eat.

She came jumpy, with a large suitcase. She was alone. After some time, Zelda noticed there was a cat.

'Animals aren't allowed in the flat,' Zelda had told her.

'It's not an animal,' the skinny girl had replied.

Zelda hated these types. Clever artistic folk. Which is to say, stupid.

'It's a cat. A cat is an animal.'

'Inanna.'

'Pardon?'

'Her name is Inanna. She's a goddess.'

Over the months Zelda would find the cat in her own flat.

'She'd come in through the flap. Sort of agitated? Then she'd calm down, then leave...then return.'

For all her rules Zelda had softened on the cat, felt sorry for it.

'I don't understand what the problem was?' Mojisola asks, motivated by a maternal, if futile, urge to defend her child's behaviour. 'Are you saying she was abusing the cat...hurting it in some way?' She is distressed at the very suggestion.

'I don't wish to go into the details.'

'Oh, no, no — you brought it up. You need to go into the details, Zelda. What was she doing to the cat?'

Zelda struggles to form the words. 'It's not that I think she was doing anything physically.'

Mojisola frowns.

'All I'm saying is the cat was frequently...distressed.'

'I don't understand. What are you? A cat psychologist?'

'Actually,' Zelda is triumphantly smug in the face of Mojisola's sarcasm, 'I ran a very successful pet shop before I retired.'

Mojisola is stumped. She hasn't wondered what kind of life Zelda had lived before she became a landlady and cooped herself up in No-Cove No-Crescent day-in day-out. The thought of her herding fluffy rabbits and selling guppies to six-year-olds is strangely comforting. 'I didn't know that,' Mojisola says softly, before she gets a handle again. 'And now you sell marijuana.'

'Well—'

'So did you fight? You and Yinka? About the cat?'

'I asked her to stop distressing the cat.'

'And what did she say?'

'She didn't say anything. We stopped talking. She paid her rent on time. We had no other reason to interact.' After some silence, Zelda says, 'I don't have guests. I try to avoid that.' As if having company was a kind of virus.

'When did she buy the thing? When did you sell it to her?'

'I don't remember specifically.'

'How many did you sell?'

'I sell ten a pack.'

'Ten?' There were four left. Mojisola is disheartened. She knows perhaps she is being backward. She knows people smoke this; it's common. Some even believe it is harmless, yet she is shocked. 'Do you think...that she smoked one on the night? That night.'

'Oh, Mojisola, I'm...oh, God, I'm so sorry.'

'What?'

'I'm sorry.'

'She did, didn't she? How do you know? Did you see? Was it you who found her?' In all the details she has chased, Mojisola has avoided this. In the days after the news came, she simply wasn't ready. Titus's colleague handled all arrangements with the undertaker, moving the body, a coffin, everything. 'Tell me.' Mojisola's voice is soft: her lungs contracting.

'What? What do you want to ask me?' Zelda sounds nervous.

'How did you find her?'

'Find who?'

'Zelda, please. How did you find Yinka? Tell me.'

As seems regular for Cove Crescent, a couple's lovemaking starts up somewhere in the building. Zelda speaks over the noise, slowly, deliberately.

'Okay, I'll tell you. But first I want to clear something up. Yes, I sell weed. I take it myself, for my arthritis, and I sell it to a few people in the block, elderly folk. Let's get something straight. I am not a drug-dealer.'

Mojisola nods. Zelda takes a big breath before continuing.

'You have to understand that I had no reason to suspect anything.'

In her tone, Mojisola sees that Zelda will try to be kind in the telling; she relaxes a little. Zelda will tell her something difficult, but she will take care of her while she does so.

'Occasionally I'd hear her go to work in the morning. And sometimes, if I had my programme on low volume, I'd hear her come home late but, really, it isn't, has never been, my habit to listen out for my tenants. If they are late in payment, I accost them but that is all. Otherwise I let them be. In particular your daughter and I....Well, as I said, we had our differences. She was dead to me.'

Zelda puts a hand to her mouth but the words are out already. Mojisola is amused by the look of horror on her face. Zelda Petersen has horrified Zelda Petersen.

'I am so, so sorry.'

'Please,' Mojisola waves a hand. 'Slip of the tongue. Continue.'

Zelda takes another big breath. 'It was the cat.'

Mojisola frowns.

'It was the cat that found her. I would never have known. I would have had no reason to...suspect anything.'

'Yes but, how did you...? Oh.'

'It was just some red on the otherwise bright white fur.'

Mojisola knows she doesn't like what's coming.

'Okay, a lot of red. It frightened me. I thought Inanna had hurt herself or that your daughter had finally done something to her. But after I cleaned her and searched her coat, I realised there was no wound.'

'So you...'

'So I left it but then again, she appeared, red on her coat, some on her whiskers. I went to knock on Yinka's door. I knocked for a long time. I left, assuming she was out, and knocked the next day. And the next.'

Mojisola has now understood.

'It was just a finger, Mrs Owolabi.'

She feels furious. That's what life has come down to — angry at a cat.

'Just a little bite. In fact, what a blessing!' Zelda is suddenly high in spirit, chuckling and sounding like a pastor. 'If the cat hadn't taken a little nip we essentially would not have known. Yinka could have stayed in that tub for weeks. Now surely that would have been infinitely worse, don't you think?' She is high on relief — she has said the worst, done her bit.

'You called the police?'

'I have a spare key. I knocked one last time and then opened up. Well, I knew immediately. The smell.'

Mojisola raises a hand to indicate that enough has been said.

On the way out, she remembers something.

'Yinka owned a piano? Is there one somewhere in the building that she played?'

'No, not to my knowledge.'

Back in the apartment it is difficult for Mojisola not to feel a complex set of emotions towards the finger-eating cat, whose appetite nonetheless saved her daughter from decomposing in the bathtub. She sleeps with her door shut and late into the night hears Inanna scratching to be let in.

*

When Yinka was old enough to be left with the nanny and Mojisola was feeling a bit like herself again, she took drives through the campus. The biome project was long complete, her job beyond dormant. She knew, despite a pretence she kept up with Titus, that she would never go back to work. She could often be spotted, her car pulled up on the verge, squatting by some plant or other, camera slung around her neck, magnifying glass focused on the branches or the leaves. She had no training as a botanist but shored up her poor knowledge by reading an extensive amount. She learnt the descriptors. Dense. Leafy. Shrub-like. Perennial. She was imbibing new vocabulary, a delicate sort that bothered with millimetres and the fractional difference in colour shades. Grey-mauve, pink, yellow and brick-red. Texture: woody, velvet, hairy, hairless and needle-like. The language was sensual, almost forbidden: tongue-shaped sessile leaves that bent backwards when mature; erect shrubs with swollen glands, sticky, birds arriving to suckle. She took a secret pleasure in touching the letters on the page or, when she was in the field, writing slowly, curling the lines in her eternally wonky right-hand cursive.

In bed at night Titus, overcome with a fit of sneezing, blamed her pollen. She liked how he said 'your pollen' as if the spores were her own real estate. Otherwise he ignored her growing obsession, only occasionally asking, 'Where is this going? What are you going to do with all that?' in reference to sheaves and sheaves of notes. She didn't know yet. Whatever she was doing didn't spring from anywhere she could explain. She felt right when she was out in the forest. Felt it imperative to record the exact circumference of the branches of a Moringa. She tracked fungi. Went hot in her cheeks each time she dissected a mushroom. The bulbous cap was innocuous enough but when she got down to the membrane out of which the stem had grown, when she had to jot 'volva' in her notebook, those were the days she could barely wait for Titus to switch off his bedside light. She'd grab him in the dark, and if he was frightened or startled, he never let on.

Then, just when it seemed like all would be well, Mojisola fell ill. She couldn't come right, by each turn she was blocked; each turn she took, her life telling her 'no, not this way'. The sickness came imprecise. She suffered from pain. She couldn't describe it to Titus ('Is it malaria?' he asked) and he was too impatient to offer any help. He dismissed her winces, her cries at night. The pain was always in pinches, short bursts but so electric that each time it happened she thought a knife had cut her open. Finally a sickness came, it manifested itself in a way that couldn't be ignored: the left half of her body refused to move. They sat through a series of comments from the doctor they'd travelled to Lagos to see; Yinka trailing, moping, unsure why the sudden trip, Mojisola regretting they hadn't just left her with the neighbours. The doctor had no name for it, but it could be described. This felt palliative. Not a cure to the mystery illness but a poultice on the sting of Titus's accusations that Mojisola had been inventing her condition. A real doctor examined her, himself puzzled but unable to deny that something was actually wrong. Soon, though, it progressed beyond her feeling one-up on her husband's smugness. She was actually sick. One late afternoon, several weeks after the visit to Lagos, they were at the consulting room of Dr Hussein; grey hair along his jowls, slow to get the words out, plodding in his walk but one of the best at what he did. He spoke and, with no grace, Mojisola's mortality arrived.

'What?' Titus looked winded. He sat up in the chair beside his wife. Bad news required that you pay attention.

The latest tests had shown a new development. Dr Hussein said development and then retracted, realising the uselessness of that word. This was a set-back.

'I'm so sorry, Mrs Owolabi.'

She was fine for a few days but then, as he'd cautioned, a profound weakness settled upon her and she was admitted to hospital.

Yinka asked many questions about her mother and Titus, determined not to lie, rehashed catechesis, and spoke, for the first time, to the child about death. Auntie Modupe disapproved, suggested he simply tell Yinka that her mother had travelled. But Titus thought: *And what if her mother dies? What do we tell her then?*

Titus relayed all this to Mojisola when she was safely returned to them, alive and healthy. There was a wistful way he spoke about her time in hospital even though Mojisola knew he'd been terrified. Dr Hussein had spoken clearly and Titus had been convinced he would be a widower. And yet, so soon afterwards he was calm again, boasting about how he'd stood up to Auntie Modupe. It made Mojisola sad. Titus had these moments of profound earnestness, sparse moments that reminded her of why she loved him. He'd really believed she would die, and he'd been frightened. More afraid, he'd said one evening at the hospital, his honesty brought about by proximity to mortality, than he had been of anything he had ever experienced or would ever know. He had said this with a face that made Mojisola wish they could live their whole lives in just that moment, going neither forwards nor back.

But the moment did pass. And as Mojisola was to find out, when you confront your mortality, you're never quite the same again. After she returned home, there would be a few minutes in a day when she'd find herself in a daze, lost, thinking of her impending death and then she'd come to and have to remind herself, *You're well now, you're not dying any more.* It marked her. It got so it didn't matter that she was well again, what mattered was that she'd been considered so close to death, she'd been asked to prepare, to ready. And she had, without disappointment or ire — she'd been ready.

When Mojisola returned from hospital, Yinka was drawing again. Freely, with no supervision. In fact, when she entered the house after many weeks of absence Yinka had given her mother a hug and handed her a stash of drawings or draw-wings, as Yinka called them at the time.

'Did you know she started drawing again?' Mojisola asked Titus, when they were alone.

'Ehn?'

'Yinka.'

'Oh,' he said, sounding guilty.

The first drawing in the pile was simple. A horizontal line (almost the width of the whole A4) with the liquid blue of the biro. A circle shape at one end of the line ('That's the head,' said Yinka) and two shorter lines splayed at the other ('Those are the legs.') And a body in between.

'What is it?' Mojisola asked.

'It's a Dead,' said Yinka.

Some days after her return, Yinka asked, 'Mummy, what is dead really-really?'

Mojisola had been prepared for this. 'It's a long kind of sleeping.' She'd fought death and won.

'Sleeping? Like normal sleeping?'

'Not normal, Yinka. But you're very still and quiet and you're far away, the way it feels when people sleep.'

'Sleeping?'

'Yes.'

'And normal, like dreaming?'

'No, not normal. Sleeping, not waking. Just sleeping, not dreaming.'

*

After raking the entire house and finding nothing, no drawings, not even a pencil stub, it is desperation that brings her back to the computer. She turns it on. There is the red hibiscus. She clicks the screen, and a box appears prompting her (goading her) to fill in the password. There is also something she had missed last time. Underneath in fine lettering: 'Password hint'.

Mojisola clicks on this and her heart balances halfway up into the sky: 'What is your mother's maiden name?' She can't help herself, she smiles. The first time she'd written her own name, she'd done so instinctively, then felt stupid, selfish. But here, now, she writes out her maiden name. 'Incorrect,' says the screen. Mojisola is now at a loss. Unless Yinka has some other mother she doesn't know of, or perhaps Yinka did not know the correct Yoruba spelling for Mojisola's surname before marriage, or maybe it is all some cryptic game, which Mojisola will never crack. She remains on the outside of the computer. She has not qualified to read her daughter's documents, decipher her emails and pore over her notes. A simple wicked test and she cannot pass it. Password. The word takes on appropriate meaning. Mojisola is looking for just that. She is looking for a word, which, if given, would mean she has passed. She is looking for a word to let her pass through, let her saunter past the boundary and into her daughter's graces. She feels desperate and useless.

Inanna comes by. Since Zelda's revelation they have not been on the best of terms.

'Do you know it?' Mojisola asks. She doesn't care that she is slowly going insane. If only the cat would look at her and give the code, pass her the word, the password... 'Well, do you?' but Inanna moves away and is gone.

Mojisola sits with the computer. It seems she must sit with it, screen exposed, battery draining. Sure enough, at some point the machine lets out a squeak and she goes in search of a charger. She finds one at the bottom of the cardboard box, decides she has about one guess left, and returns to the menacing screen. She capitalises the first letter of her maiden name where previously she had written the whole thing out in lower case. At the end of the word she adds the number 1. The screen disappears for a millisecond and suddenly Mojisola is looking at the desktop of her daughter's computer. It is a much-desired intimacy, however mechanical, and the exhaustion of coming so far overtakes her. She falls asleep on the floor right by the cardboard box and open laptop. Sometime in the night she moves to the bed.

The following day she returns to the laptop. What she finds is unexpected. She had braced herself for pornography (after the marijuana-reveal this seems the worst thing she can imagine), but instead she meets FireBabe, Yinka's bombastic moniker on her online dating profile. The application opens itself up to her, having no way of knowing that she is not Yinka/FireBabe. She is an intruder; she can scroll through whatever she wants — there it all is, open on the screen, delicate and susceptible, like the insides of a soft fruit.

Yinka's profile has no photographs. Just two short sentences, as revealing as if she'd written nothing at all:

I'm new in the city. Would be nice to meet friendly people.

The first and only time Yinka told Mojisola she was depressed, it had taken her by surprise.

'I'm unhappy, Mummy.' Yinka was 15, maybe 16 and it had come from nowhere. She'd simply launched it onto Mojisola like a runaway rocket.

'What happened?' Mojisola had been chopping tomatoes methodically. She'd worked out how to cut them so the juice didn't leak and the whole thing get messy. On top of it all, her rash had sprung up that week. She'd scratched in her sleep and the skin had broken.

'No, that's not what I mean.'

'Pass the…pass the colander.'

'I mean…I'm…sad.'

'Thank you.' She collected the diced tomatoes into the colander, set that aside for the stew. 'Tell your dad dinner in 30.'

'All the time.'

Only then had Mojisola understood that a conversation was happening but the words had been bouncing off her ears.

'All the time?'

Yinka nodded. 'I don't feel well. I want to but…I can't.'

And something in Yinka's tone had reminded Mojisola of a time when she'd stood in the doorway one night and asked her

fierce praying mother if her body was all right, if it would hold
up in the world, would it do?

'Mummy?'

Mojisola went to Yinka and held her face in her hands.
Their relationship had never been tender. She has no other
memories of holding her daughter's face in this way. She'd
looked deep into Yinka's eyes and something had passed
between them or, at least, Mojisola would like to think so.
That a message crossed from woman to woman.

Mojisola stroked Yinka's face then.

'Cover it,' her mother had said but not with any meanness,
mostly just clear fright in her eyes which conveyed to Mojisola
that without the necessary covering, the world out there would
devour her.

'I'm sad, Mummy.'

And Mojisola had not known what to say. 'Cover it' was the
wrong instruction, she knew that much but couldn't form the
words for the right one. She held her daughter's face, wiped the
tears that fell. At some point Yinka had pulled away. Mojisola
heard her enter her father's study, telling him about dinner.
Just then a heavy knowledge came into Mojisola's chest; she
knew she'd failed, that she ought to have said something and
she'd failed to do so. After that night, she looked for a moment
to open up the talk again, to ask about this all-the-time sadness
her baby was having. Often Titus was around but even when
she found herself alone with Yinka, the texture of the moment
was never right. Desperate, Mojisola would ask, 'Are you okay?'
and always, Yinka's quick response, 'Yeah, yeah, I'm fine.'

*

Mojisola observed Yinka; the child was drawing again and
appeared to be perfectly fine. A few times Mojisola would come
upon her drawing and, as if testing, call out to her, 'Yinka?'

'Yes, Mummy,' Yinka replied, eyes glued to the page but
clearly there and alert.

'You're okay?'

'Yes, Mummy.'

Drawing returned to their lives but regardless her child had been made strange to her. Sometimes, watching Yinka draw, Mojisola noted with alarm two uncompanionable emotions. Pride at the child's intensity, her strong marks albeit indecipherable. She drew consistently, daily, as if in her little body she understood the act of drawing was a ritual or way of life. Six, seven, eight, nine, she drew. She drew with a hunger Mojisola could not dismiss; a mature appetite, a commitment to see and to seek. She pulled half trampled snails from the garden, placed them on the floor and drew; she stood in front of her mother's cupboard, doors flung open, and drew; she asked her father to hold still and drew; she looked behind things and under, unplugged things dug up things. No one had taught her this, the child just seemed to have come from the womb filled with her own intent to search and uncover, to find. It scared Mojisola not because she still feared for Yinka's safety. Clearly the doctor and Titus had been right and she, Mojisola, had been wrong. Drawing was just drawing, not some practice that turned her child into a zombie. No, it scared her because it was the opposite of who she was. Her daughter's mission to turn everything over cast her own life into relief; her timidity, her right-handed letters, crippled and small. Beside Yinka's rude works, Mojisola's careful sketches of leaves and stamens seemed tight and too precise for passion. So there was pride in her daughter but Mojisola also felt a sting, a feeling of envy so misplaced between mother and child it made her dizzy. And whenever she experienced that sting, a third and final emotion would settle — profound shame.

*

Mojisola returns to the dating site. Despite the absence of a picture and the minimal profile statement, she is surprised to find how popular Yinka is with men. And women. There are many threads left hanging, people waiting to hear back. Mojisola goes to fetch her glasses from the bedside table and settles down to some reading. If the profile itself is sparse, Mojisola is pleased to see how eloquently her daughter interacts. She is self-deprecating and warm, funny. But she also tells people off. In one exchange after she has told the other that she is Nigerian he says: 'Nigerian women have man hands. Do you have man hands?'

Yinka responds: 'You're very stupid.'

Most of the chats, though, are flirtatious. Her daughter delivered from teenage torpor into adulthood. Confronted as she is, Mojisola doesn't know how to feel about Yinka's beauty, her wit and sexuality, slippery and excited with itself. She tracks through the various profiles and chatter. There are so many threads, so many replications of opening lines, she is mesmerised by the spaghetti highways of communication. 'Hey, Gorgeous' and 'Suck cock?' are commonplace. One or two men simply want pictures; ask for them incessantly. 'Of your boobies,' one message reads. 'Of your hairy plug hole.' To which Yinka responds: 'Which one?'

There is a man who seems only to have written to Yinka because she has never been married. His profile has a long diatribe against the divorced and how no one in this condition should dare contact him. With such a disagreeable manner, Mojisola wonders if anyone would contact him at all. 'Marriage is for life,' he declares. 'Till death us do part.' His favourite book is the Bible.

Another man lays bare his adoration of Christ: 'I serve the G-d of Israel,' says he. 'I stand United with Israel, Shalom.'

Others are strident in their good qualities, so strident as to render them unbelievable: 'I am honest and straight talking I don't know lyeing.'

Yinka types: 'Yeah, you don't know spelling either.'

Among the Christians are the philanderers: 'I'm not looking for anything serious. I already have a wife.'

Mojisola opens a chat box with D-Man. She chooses him because no pictures have been exchanged, types: **Hello**.

*

After the rough patch of early childhood, the fights about drawings, Mojisola's sickness and Yinka's eventual return to her favourite pastime, things settled. Yinka was growing (she was nine, then she was 11) and, even as she quietly filed away her conflicting emotions, Mojisola felt emerge between them the gentleness of a truce. The child had unwrapped from her early years into a well-behaved young person. This felt like a triumph, although Mojisola didn't feel she could take any credit and she certainly couldn't ascribe any credit to Titus for Yinka sitting straight-backed, not interrupting adults when they spoke, saying 'good evening' and 'good morning' without first being cajoled to greet, saying 'mister' and 'madam' and 'auntie' and 'uncle'. With his travelling and heavy teaching schedule, Titus had barely been around long enough to issue any instruction. The puzzle of where their polite child had come from was another little shameful bite. Mojisola's mother had ground all her manners into her, laboured and threatened and punished and yet here was a child requiring none of that. Right-handed, well-behaved, and wild all the same.

Mojisola sought refuge in her small projects. She no longer harboured ambitions to return to work at Capital Projects. She found something else that, however humble, gave her something to do with her hands. One day, looking through her collected data, Mojisola decided to publish a thorough compendium, *The Definitive Guide to the Flora of Ile-Ife*. She'd even, at a Zonta meeting (she was a member but seldom made the gatherings), approached one Dr Okpanum, a botanist, and asked if she could send her a letter detailing the work she'd been doing. She was hoping to get some kind of partnership going with the botany department: perhaps they could endorse her work, or she'd even be willing to share it with one of the scientists, so long as they secured a book deal. Okpanum had been enthusiastic but there was much still to be done. Mojisola applied herself to this with fervour and there was a kind of happiness in the household.

But then Titus announced to the family that he was considering work in South Africa. There was talk of a position, the offer was not imminent, in six months to a year, but he made it plain that when it did come, he would go for it. Yinka asked some questions about South Africa (that place where they hate black people). Despite an alarm in her belly, Mojisola attempted to ignore the whole thing, hoping naïvely that it would go away. But sure enough within a year Titus was offered a post at the University of Cape Town. It carried a lot of prestige — he would take up a chair at the Department of African Studies. He was ecstatic; Mojisola devastated.

By now she had become known for her work on the campus, even if only among a small group of botanists. On account of her dedication, she had managed to document a few unclassified plant species. In truth she had turned into a quiet celebrity. They called her The Flower Woman.

'Well, you can stay back,' offered Titus.

But Mojisola knew this was a ridiculous idea. He and Yinka starting life in Cape Town without her? For one thing they'd starve.

'Or work from there.'

But the trees were in Ife, not Cape Town. What did he expect — that she move the biome?

*

One afternoon, just before the move to South Africa, on the way home from a day at the library, Mojisola picked Yinka up from school. She was determined to work like a maniac and complete her project before their departure but, each day, this goal seemed more and more impossible.

'Belt,' Mojisola said, when Yinka got in at the back. She waited till she heard the click, then joined the traffic out of the car park.

'Mummy, did you get my pencils?'

'What?'

'Pencils.'

'Yes. Yes, I got the pencils.'

At home, the dishes. Housegirl sick, no replacement. The kitchen was in a state of congealed anarchy, a sink at something past 5pm that was full of 8am crockery. The smell of ripening food pervaded. There'd been an evening lecture the night before and Titus had come home with an entourage. This was the ruins.

'I'll help, Mummy.'

'No. Go and do your homework.' She felt tight, as if the slightest thing would spin her into a stratosphere of sorrow and rage.

Mojisola mopped the floor. Feeling ready to burst, she thought of her mother, who often prayed aloud while doing housework. Mojisola had grown up to the soundtrack of her mother's prayers. She prayed and all her beauty shone out. She prayed in a way that was singular and distinct, as if prayer was her own kind of making. Her speaking voice was deep but sometimes, in prayer, she could make it go really high. Mojisola remembered listening to her mother pray and expecting any moment her voice to break, to hit a top note and shatter, but it never happened. Her prayers always contained her, contained them both.

Her mop strokes widened, slowed to a rhythm, like rowing through gentle waters. She finished mopping the floor, then cursed herself as she dirtied it again when she started the dishes. A tray with glasses, some wine dried at the bottom, some orange liquid lipstick marks. Plates with bones in different states of gnawed. Napkins, smeared. She found the source of the stench — a pot of assorted meats she'd forgotten to pack away at 1am when the last body had upped and left.

Mojisola emptied the sink of its casualties. Stacked up the array of dishes. Filled the sink with water. She plunged in her hands, sweating but liking the heat throbbing underneath her nails. A man she didn't know walked in.

'Sorry, Ma. Good afternoon, Ma,' he said.

It took Mojisola several seconds to work out that he hadn't broken in. The man was an ex-student she remembered vaguely from a few graduations back. Titus was famous for hangers-on — he encouraged it, as far as Mojisola could tell, but protested if she ever suggested this.

'Prof was looking for cold beer.'

Mojisola stared, initially uncomprehending. She hadn't heard the front door but now her husband's voice came through along with other murmurs. A twitter, the laughter for women. A deep chortle, the laughter for men, for people who have a sense of humour and are allowed to display it. Mojisola dried a newly-washed glass, all the while thinking a request for more glasses would soon come. Surely they all lusted for cold beer. Who wouldn't on such a hot day? It was after five: beer was an appropriate drink for such an hour.

'Thank you, Ma.' He ducked back out.

She washed the other glasses, her hands burning.

Titus came in. 'Hello,' he said.

'Afternoon.' She didn't turn around.

'I didn't realise you were in here,' he said. 'Where's Yinka?'

'Her room.'

'Are you okay?'

'I'm fine.'

He was silent for a while. She still hadn't turned around. She'd stabbed three knives and a spoon into the dish rack.

'Well, Professor Gbadebo is here…if you want to say hello.'

After pinching some nuts from the cupboard, Titus slipped out. Mojisola stayed in the kitchen and did not go out to greet Professor Whoever. The kitchen steamed. Asymmetric sweat stains spread from beneath her arms, all along the sides of her starched linen jacket. She began to smell herself.

After the dishes were done and balanced to dry, she thought of food. Soon hunger would be announced, and the people must eat. She remembered being chided by a neighbour for having only one housegirl and an eyebrow raised to go with the rhetorical question, 'And no driver?' The last thing she felt like doing was grinning at visitors she hadn't invited. She was prepared to not leave the kitchen, to go to bed on the floor if she had to. Or even to sneak out and sit in the backyard.

She couldn't drive anywhere because her car keys were in her handbag, placed, as she'd left it when they came in, on the dining table.

A pot was bubbling when Yinka peeked in. 'The pencils, Mummy.'

'In my bag. Bring it here and I'll give them to you.'

Yinka returned and Mojisola rummaged in her bag. 'Don't touch that,' she said, but it was too late. All the carefully balanced crockery crashed down.

'What was that?' Titus shouted, from the living room, and there was a muffled laughter.

Mojisola turned on Yinka, who was trying not to cut herself. She lunged at her and Yinka danced out of the way, side-stepping until she stood in the open doorway, her face both amused and scared.

'Close that door,' Mojisola said.

Yinka shook her head and moved further out of reach, deeper into the open doorway, staring at her mother. Mojisola could hear the guests, sitting just paces away.

'Come. Here.'

But Yinka shook her head again.

Mojisola took the coloured pencils and snapped each one, Yinka looking on. When she finished, she reached forward, this time not to hit Yinka but to shut the door in her face.

*

D-Man responds: **Hey. I thought youd fashied me Long time o. Youre back**

Yes.

*

After they moved to South Africa, after they settled Yinka into a good school, Mojisola went back to Nigeria for a short period: Auntie Modupe was dying. She didn't take long.

Mojisola had packed enough clothes for three months; Auntie Modupe died within weeks. During that time Mojisola sat by her bedside, tried to remember her aunt's recipe for fishhead pepper soup, although by then the old woman wasn't eating much. She complained that her tongue was paining, lay supine, eyes tightly shut, jaw slack. She had no energy to speak. Mojisola sat beside her alert in case she needed anything. Often she called for water or to be helped into a position. Up, down, side to side. The sight of her aunt helpless left something swelling at the base of her throat. All that power draining out from a woman she had always revered. Theirs had never been a relationship governed by physical affection. Mojisola could not recall ever hugging her aunt although she understood her love to be fierce. Auntie Modupe loved with a scrubbing motion, leaving you in no doubt of her affections, if somewhat a little bruised. After a few days Mojisola took to reading the *Pacesetters* her aunt had always had an affinity for; several sat dog-eared on the book shelf. Entranced by the sticky romance Mojisola sat for hours beside a sleeping Auntie Modupe.

'If only life happened that way, eh?'

She hadn't spoken for almost two days, and her voice came out thick.

'Auntie.'

'I'm okay, I'm okay.' She signalled for Mojisola to sit back down, not to fuss. 'Óyá, explain the story.'

Mojisola turned the book to study the sleeve. 'It's just…you know.'

'Explain the story, jọ̀ọ́.'

Except, when Mojisola tried, Auntie Modupe kept interjecting, adding further details she felt were being dropped. It was good to see her enlivened, castigating the characters as if they were people she had known all her life. As they neared the end of the story, as narrated by Auntie Modupe, she suddenly said. 'Put it down. I want to say something.'

Mojisola put the book aside, unnerved by the tone of her aunt's voice, the sudden straightness of her face.

'Come a bit closer.' She indicated for Mojisola to sit right beside her on the edge of the bed.

The closeness was unfamiliar and Mojisola could smell the menthol rub her aunt insisted be massaged into her joints, daily.

'You know,' she began, looking off into the distance. 'When you were born Wunmi said the right thing should be done.'

In all the years since Yinka's birth, the topic of her mother (the estranged sister), had never come up. This had never seemed a problem to Mojisola; she'd assumed there was nothing really to talk about, found herself totally uncurious and had assumed Auntie Modupe felt the same.

'The right thing.' Auntie Modupe went on talking, her voice steady, looking away from Mojisola, telling an old story, a secret one, explaining the things Mojisola had always simply accepted, first mystifying them, then laying them bare. 'I'm sorry, Mojisola.'

'You didn't want me?'

Auntie Modupe still would not look at her but Mojisola had her face turned full on this woman who, with a simple confession, was now her mother.

'I was not in any position to know what I did and didn't want, ọmọ. Please...please try and understand. Jọwọ. I'm so sorry.'

All the questions from her childhood rushed up; her mother's sternness, the fights between the sisters, the distance.

'Did you ever...' she tried to separate the questions, get them to line up obediently, she couldn't ask anything if they all bunched together like that. Questions must behave. 'Did you...did...' Tears came instead but Mojisola, determined to push through, kept stuttering the beginning two words of a thousand unruly questions, 'Did you...'

Auntie Modupe finally looked into Mojisola's face, held her eyes and reached out with a feeble shaking hand. 'Every day. Every single day.'

*

You there Yinka

Yes

Dont go quite on me again o

She understands the appeal of this, the anonymous intimacy.

*

She sat through the flight, her body in full shock, the numbness occasionally abating to let in waves of feeling. In between a quiet mind analysed, searched through the same material but with new eyes. She saw looks that passed between the sisters, what had been simple gestures to her young eyes she now understood. There had been an argument about a dress, a bright purple colour with a large pink sash. Auntie Modupe had arrived with it, fresh from the tailor. She had collected Mojisola's measurements in secret. Finding excuses over the months to check the exact length of the little girl's arm, the size of her waist, the breadth of her torso. Sitting at her window seat, eyes tightly shut, Mojisola remembered the intense delight in Auntie Modupe's face, delight at the secret she'd kept hidden and now the birthday gift, a dress that fit perfectly.

'See how fine you are?' Auntie Modupe had said after fitting the dress onto Mojisola, who'd twirled and twirled.

Wunmi had found them like that in front of the mirror.

'Ẹ̀gbọ́n, isn't it beautiful?' Auntie Modupe had asked her sister.

Mojisola recalled her mother's tight lips. She'd known even as she'd let her aunt zip up the dress and tie the sash that these were not church colours. Her mother had nodded and told Mojisola to thank her aunt. She never saw the dress again. This was the fate of many of Auntie Modupe's gifts over the years despite the fact that she made an effort to adjust them to suit. A specific book was too indecent, an empty notebook not really suitable for a young girl still forming — what will she write there, Wunmi had asked her sister. Once, not long before her aunt disappeared from her life altogether, Auntie Modupe had visited and shoved something small and hard into the palm of her niece's hand, closing the fist around it, suggesting with only the most subtle of winks that this was a secret. Later in her room five-year-old Mojisola had dug the rock out of her pocket — black and smooth, indecipherable. The gift had confounded Mojisola at the time but indeed it proved the only one she was ever allowed to keep. She set it on top of her cupboard; at some point she must have forgotten it, the same way she forgot Auntie Modupe. Years later when they were reunited at Wunmi's funeral it was the one question Mojisola had found the courage to ask her estranged aunt.

'The stone you gave me.'

'Ehn, yes. What about it?' The woman had needed no extra information for her memory to be jogged.

'What was it? I didn't understand it.'

'That's exactly right. Neither could I.'

Her mother was her aunt, and her aunt was her mother. She understood newly her sense of anxiety about being good, the need to behave, some subconscious part of herself that dared not be more of a burden than she already was. Wunmi's intention to devote her life to Jesus, somewhat hampered by her sense of responsibility towards her niece born to an errant younger sister, addicted (on and off) to ògógóró and devoid, as far as big sister was concerned, of the moral rectitude required for child-rearing. Mojisola imagined the negotiation and finally a decision. She found room to at least fathom Auntie Modupe's suffering when her sister decided she was not fit even to babysit her own child. Mojisola raced through the years, Auntie Modupe's indignation at her mother's funeral and her use of the death as an entry back into her daughter's life; the way she muscled into her life with Yinka's birth, fixing herself with an unashamed sense of proprietary. Auntie Modupe's funeral had been one of celebration, much dancing and long speeches, as was appropriate for an old woman. But on the plane home Mojisola wept, she cried so hard her eyes turned red. By the time she landed, without any clear moment of decision, she had slipped naturally into a commitment to maintain the secret. When Titus picked her up from Cape Town International Airport he assumed her tears were for the death of an aunt, not a mother.

One day some weeks after her return Mojisola could not get up off the toilet seat, Titus stood on the other side of the door hearing her tears.

'Are you okay?'

She could not control herself.

Titus had remained patient at the door (Yinka had been out), not forcing in but not wandering off either, one of his rare moments, tender. Mojisola understood, but could not explain to Titus right then, that she was not grieving who Auntie Modupe was, who she'd known her to be; she was grieving the Auntie Modupe she hadn't known, the secret identity that had been folded away. She cried from anger towards the sisters — the irreparable damage a lie can wreck. She cried from fatigue. She cried for herself too, feeling mangled somehow, half of something. She'd sat and thought the tears would never stop. When her eyes finally dried up, she washed her face and hands. At the door, in response to the question in Titus's eyes she'd simply said: 'I'm fine now.'

Over the years Mojisola would forget the truth of her childhood and then stumble upon the story like a detail in a book she hadn't put to memory or had misremembered. 'Oh,' she'd say wherever the memory found her — washing dishes, looking for a specific brand of cereal, waiting for the green light. 'Oh.' Oh was in place of a longer sentence. Oh, that was my mother. She was my mother and I never knew her and now she's gone. Oh, that happened, that was my life not someone else's. Oh, I really don't know myself. I'm lost. Where is my place?

Here she was many years on, sitting in Yinka's apartment, having a moment of 'Oh.' She sits on the couch, defeated by her past, wishing never to get up again. As each generation adds their poison — what chance could anyone have? What chance did Yinka have?

*

Loud knocking startles Mojisola. She doesn't want to get up. 'Who is it?' she shouts.

'Open up,' comes the sharp voice of Zelda Petersen.

'No!'

'Mrs Owolabi, would you open this door right away? Or… or I will bash it in!'

The threat is so preposterous — the image of Zelda Petersen stomping the door down, like some kind of post-menopausal superhero, that Mojisola gets up and opens it. She wants to perform her flabbergasted laugh in Zelda's face.

'You're very ridiculous,' says Mojisola.

'Well. Let me in. You've been cooped up in here for days. What is it you're doing? Nothing crazy, I hope?'

'What? Did you think I—'

'Well…how was I to know?'

'You think it runs in the family?'

Zelda looks unsure of how to respond. If it is a joke, it is macabre. If it is serious, then it is tragic. To avoid making a mistake she does nothing but gently edges her way past the threshold. Mojisola does not resist: she lets Zelda in, closes and bolts the door behind her. Zelda settles on the couch, sizing her up. Mojisola is aware that she must look a sight. Neither woman speaks for a while. Maybe almost 15 minutes of silence pass, as if someone finally pressed the pause button.

'Why are you punishing yourself?' Zelda asks, and Mojisola, who was beginning to doze, straightens her clothing.

'Punishing?'

'Why are you sitting here? Where's your husband?'

Mojisola scoffs, 'Where's yours?' and when Zelda looks injured, 'Can husbands do anything?' Softly, 'What can husbands do?'

'I didn't mean it like that,' says Zelda. 'I just...What are you looking for here?'

Mojisola hears Zelda asking, *Why did you come, why do you stay, what is it you hope to find?* But surely underneath she must be asking the only question there is. Surely underneath she is really asking: *How could you let this happen?* Mojisola gets up and makes them each a cup of tea. She doesn't ask Zelda how she takes it — there is no milk or sugar in the cupboards.

'Why are you always wearing black?' she asks, when she settles back, happy to be the inquisitor for a change.

'Funerals. I go to funerals,' says Zelda.

Mojisola takes some time to digest this. Her mind has been still for so long she feels, suddenly in Zelda's company, that she is now arriving from fog.

'The funerals of friends?'

Zelda considers this, the corners of her lips turned down. 'No, they are usually strangers.'

Mojisola waits for a few seconds, but then can resist no longer. Her face crumples into utter confusion. 'Why?'

'It started by accident.'

Several years ago someone close to her died. Zelda doesn't specify but Mojisola wonders if it was a man, a male companion; she cannot tell for sure, but it seems to her that it was probably a man, the missing husband? Perhaps she thinks this simply because she wishes for a world where even a woman like Zelda — so indefatigably solitary — once had bright, intimate love in her life.

'I went to the wrong funeral.' At the memory she laughs. 'I don't know, I got my churches mixed up, my Sundays, my hours.'

Mojisola frowns.

'It was a difficult time that year,' says Zelda. 'I...I had...What do the Americans say? I had fallen off the wagon.'

Mojisola thinks that you can never really know a person.

'Yes. It's another life, my Cape Town life, before I moved up here. I haven't had a drink in 1,825 days. Anyway, that isn't the point. The point is I was back drinking, and I made a mistake and went to the wrong funeral. Arrived to bury a dearly beloved and ended up standing with strangers.'

If a person can transform in just a few moments, this is what happens to Zelda Petersen. Whatever Mojisola knew before of the woman does a somersault and just like that, she is looking at someone she has never met. As she talks, Zelda looks hypnotized by her own memory. Mojisola tries not to move, afraid to startle her.

'I'd been drinking. Of course. I found a seat at the back, shaky, and the woman next to me pulled her child close.' She laughs. 'I remember that one.' She laughs again then comes down, somehow, from the spell.

'I don't understand.'

Zelda gives a small shrug. 'I dunno if I can explain it...That first one I sat through almost the whole thing. Hymns. I was really in a bad way but I stood for *Abide With Me*. I stood for "where is death's sting?" I wanted to stand for that. And then...' she starts to giggle. 'You know how I figured out I was not at the right funeral?' The giggles are getting out of control. Zelda pounds her thigh. 'The priest says, "Does anyone want to say a few words?"'

Mojisola catches her breath.

'Oh, yes! Oh, yeah...Zelda Petersen, that's how I go out, with aplomb.'

'What happened?'

'I got up. People were whispering but alcohol — do you drink?'

'Not really.'

'Alcohol has this ability to make you...to give you the feeling you ought to be dancing on the table — I don't know if you get my meaning.'

Mojisola did not but she nodded.

'I went up, stumbling, and started talking. I said four words. I said, "My relationship with Reginald", and the entire church was suddenly making a noise. The priest came and gently convinced me to sit down, right next to him. He held onto my hand as if I were a five-year-old who can't be trusted to behave in public.'

'My goodness.'

'So I sat there, the alcohol leaving my body, the whole thing dawning on me. I wasn't at Reginald's funeral. I was at the funeral of a woman called Fiela. Cancer, a long illness, her mother there in the front row comforting the nine-year-old. My God. I wished it was my own funeral. I went on my knees afterwards. Begging forgiveness.'

'But you went back?'

'Wouldn't you? I mean...they were nice to me, they gave me food. I think they just felt sorry for me, actually. They, the family, the mourners, they looked at me and they saw what I was. They took pity on me. And...back then anyway, I — I confused pity for love. I went back. I used to check the *Tatler*. Check the funeral announcements. It became a habit.'

'Zelda...I don't—'

'I know it's a little shocking. Listen, Mojisola, it's shocking for me too. But...initially I just kept pretending I'd made a mistake. "Sorry."' Her voice is suddenly theatrical. '"Wrong funeral!" But then I guess I got tired of that. Then I started to say I'm an old friend. So-and-so and I worked together. Always I said, "worked together". For a while this passed. Most people have worked something or other in their life. Except this one time I walk in and there's a box the size of a crate of beers. I didn't say anything that day. Went home, called my sponsor.' She takes a final sip of her tea, sets the mug down, not without a sense of drama. 'I didn't drink that day and not a day since.'

'But you still go to the funerals.'

Zelda gives a big shrug.

'What's it like? When you go?'

'Quiet. Together.'

Mojisola nods.

'What was Yinka's funeral like? Oh don't answer if you don't want to, I'm sorry I asked I—'

'It...it was...cold.'

Zelda frowns.

'The day I mean. And...the pastor got her name wrong. And no one really was there. Even me...even I wasn't really there.'

Zelda shifts in her seat.

'Well,' Mojisola looks around. 'I'm here now.'

After several minutes of silence Zelda makes a soft sigh and extracts a long, solid zol from her pocket.

'Is that—'

'Yep! I don't drink but I do do this. I don't overdo it, though. And, yes, I sell it.' She gives Mojisola a look as if to say, *Come down from your high horse.* 'I sell mostly to old people. People like me. It eases away the pain in my joints.'

She lights it, leans over, offering Mojisola a pull but she doesn't accept. 'I sold it to your daughter once. Only once. And I told her not to return, that I wouldn't sell to her again.'

They sit quietly. After a long pull Zelda offers it again.

'Too much is bad for you,' she whispers. 'Too little useless. Somewhere in the middle lies a cure.'

Mojisola is reluctant.

'Take it,' says Zelda.

The night unfurls.

*

'Tell me.' The reefer has loosened her.

'What?' Zelda prefers to smoke in silence, she is not used to company and there is an edge to her voice.

'Tell me about her. What was she like?'

'Who? Yinka?'

'When she died, we hadn't seen her for almost six months. She took my calls sometimes but—'

'Oh dear. I'm sorry, I hadn't realised.'

Mojisola has the zol. She is on the wingback, attempting to keep her back straight. Zelda reclining on the couch. Mojisola takes in a deep pull. Zelda watches.

'I never really knew her, Zelda.' Zelda accepts the zol. 'Children.'

'She was…she was quiet.'

Mojisola nods, her back curling, her bones acquiescing to stimulant.

'I hardly ever saw or heard her. We squabbled over Inanna, but she seemed to get on with the neighbours. There were never any complaints. As I say I really didn't see her that much. We didn't speak I told you. We...I—'

'Did she have friends? Were there people that came?'

'I don't remember seeing anything like that. She...she was actually very quiet. Apart from the cat stuff, she was polite. I saw her chatting to the guards occasionally, joking.'

'Did she seem...sad? Lost?'

'Mojisola, really, I...No, no, she didn't seem sad. But, really, who seems sad? I don't know. I don't know who's sad. Did she seem sad to you?'

It's almost as if Zelda was there that day, in the kitchen. All the time.

'I...made a mistake.' The phone starts ringing. Initially she's tempted to answer, assuming he would only call at this hour if it were serious, but then she remembers his occasional insomnia. 'He's calling me because he cannot sleep.'

'Your husband?'

She nods.

'You're Nigerian, right?'

She nods again.

'I knew a Nigerian family. Back in Cape Town when I still had the shop in Lansdowne and my drinking was...I guess it was never under control but let's just say I wasn't confusing funerals.'

Mojisola cracks a smile. 'I wonder if we knew them. When was that?'

'Oh, long time now. They'd come in '91, sometime then, just before. As if they wanted front-row seats.'

'We got here soon after, in fact. Maybe we knew them. I don't remember another family in that time. There was a doctor at Children's Red Cross. And the husband was a journalist. I think he was with Reuters or something. But no kids.'

'No, no, this was a full-on family. The parents were scientists, and they had these two little boys, twins.'

'Hmm. I'm racking my brain. There were so few families. Not like now, there really were...Are you sure they were Nigerian?'

'Why do you think there were so few families?'

'It was speculation. South Africa, I mean. No one knew what would happen. People didn't want to experiment with their loved ones. They came alone — some came in pairs. But now you say—'

'Well, maybe I was wrong, maybe they weren't Nigerian.'

'Even so. Whatever happened to them?'

'I'm sorry, it's a sad story.'

'What?'

'The boys died in a car crash. The parents got a divorce, and the father returned to Nigeria or wherever. They'd been in the middle of applying for citizenship and he cancelled his application, went back. The mother said she could never leave. She said, I remember this, she said, "Nothing binds you to a country quite like grief." I saw her on and off over a few years. She held onto that grief...like a life-raft. One day I saw her and she was laughing like a maniac. Said thank you Jesus they're both gone, imagine if he only took one?'

The phone starts again.

'I should go,' Zelda says.

Mojisola presses the red button long enough for the phone to shut down.

'You think I'm holding on?'

'Oh, no, I wasn't really—'

'I'm not holding on, Zelda. I made a mistake, see? It's my fault. It's my fault she's dead.'

'Everyone blames themselves.'

'No, no, no, no — this is real.'

Zelda looks about to rise. And then Mojisola starts speaking fast.

'How did she do it? Tell me. Please explain it to me.'

'Oh, God.'

'Just tell me straight, Zelda. Just say, please. I need you just to say it.'

'I... I can't.'

'I know she drowned...the police told us, but...I need you to describe what you saw. Tell me. Just straight.'

'No.' Zelda is on her feet. 'This is crazy.'

She has her teacup in her hand. Mojisola rises too.

'Tell me. Straight.' Her voice is climbing: she has moved from asking to begging and finally to screaming. She grabs Zelda and the cup falls but doesn't break. 'Tell me, for God's sake.'

'She cut her wrists. She cut her stupid wrists. She cut them. She sliced them with a knife, a kitchen knife, a small fucking knife with a...with an orange handle. There, look in the cupboard.' She gestures. 'Maybe I washed it for you. Go look, try and find it, go. Go!' She pushes Mojisola who is now calm, whose face is clear and relaxed, as if she was spot on, as if this was all she needed to hear to restore equilibrium. Zelda looks shocked to see her so still.

'Was there blood?' Mojisola asks, now down to a whisper.

'Yes.'

'A lot?'

'No, a...normal amount. After the police, after...everything, I cleaned it myself. I didn't want somebody coming through to do that. Didn't seem right.' Zelda picks up the fallen teacup and sets it down on the kitchen counter, her back to Mojisola. 'Reginald found a rope strong enough and a tree branch that wouldn't break too soon.'

'I'm sorry.'

'I'm sorry, too. I'm sorry this happened to you, Mojisola. But you need to cry long and hard, then carry on. Go home to your husband.'

'My husband cheats on me. He's not phoning out of any kind of love or devotion. He's phoning because this looks bad.'

They stand lost until Mojisola asks, 'Do you have any more?'

Zelda pulls half a zol out of her magic pockets. They settle down again. Instantly, as if she'd been called, Inanna enters through the flap, winds towards Mojisola, hops up onto her lap and stays there. Since discovering that the cat had bitten off a piece of her daughter, Mojisola has avoided the animal — she does not know where she sleeps but certainly not beside her. For her part, Inanna has maintained a cool air but now she seems to be attempting to make amends. Mojisola, the cat's belly warm upon her thigh, acquiesces to feline wisdom, strokes the flank. After a minute of this, satisfied with the truce, the cat climbs down and wanders off. With each puff of the zol Mojisola sinks several centimetres more down into the soft chair.

'You know,' she says, 'I found out that in Uganda they beat the corpse.'

Zelda nods. A seasoned weed-smoker, her back is straight but her green eyes are glassy. Mojisola wants more of a reaction.

'Of the suicide, Zelda,' she says, raising her voice. 'They beat the corpse of the suicide.'

'I heard you.'

The conversation disappears, and there is only the sound of Zelda re-lighting the blunt, the two women toking, the cat scratching, three beings breathing, in and out and in.

'Have you cried yet?' Zelda asks, as if she's been quietly scheming, debating solutions to alleviate Mojisola's dilemma.

'No, but I ran really far.'

Half an hour passes — maybe it is already another day, except it is still dark outside. The love paroxysms of the most sexed woman in Cove Crescent start up. But there is also something plaintive in her calls. She is no doubt in pleasure but maybe she is also in pain.

'Jesus Christ,' says Mojisola, shocked to blaspheme but stoned enough not to care.

'I know,' Zelda says, droll.

'Is it like that all the time?' Mojisola suddenly looks scandalised, dropping her voice, needlessly, to a whisper. 'Do you think she's a prostitute?'

'Tch tch.' Zelda is disapproving. 'It's not prostitution anymore, Mojisola.' She beckons with her hand and leans forward conspiratorially. It is an effort for Mojisola to bend forward but Zelda won't speak until she's done so. 'It's now called sex work.'

*

It takes Mojisola a while to fall asleep. She cannot work out if that is because of the weed she has smoked — it must be. All those deep inhalations, watching how Zelda toked and copying. Her brain is soup — any moment it'll leak out of her ears. The incessant thinking ... Her mind will not shut off. She's thinking of Yinka's drawings: where could they be? The ones her daughter had wanted to frame. Or maybe she hadn't drawn them yet...or maybe...Her mind can't quite settle on anything. She blames the weed, imagines Yinka smoking, then lying in this same bed. She imagines her sketching. She imagines her taking a bath. Mojisola does not believe in ghosts but she sits upright in the bed, surrounded by darkness. She turns her head to the left, wishing to address a corner of the room. When she opens her mouth, she doesn't know what to say.

Mojisola dreams she owns a restaurant, something she could never imagine for herself. She spends the days on her feet, but it is joyful. There is a husband and wife, loyal patrons, and they come with their two children. At least Mojisola only sees the two children, toddlers, playing about in the mud. There is mud and rain suddenly. And the parents are languid and easy with their children. Then the wife comes to say goodbye to Mojisola, to thank her, perhaps, for the excellent eating experience. As they are gathering themselves the mother begins to panic. 'My child!' she cries. 'My baby!'

At this point Mojisola understands that there is in fact a third child, a baby boy, and he is missing. The father has gone ahead with the other two children to bring the car around apparently. The mother is climbing towards hysteria, grabbing her head, wringing her hands. Mojisola appeals to her for calm. Mojisola herself is remarkably calm. She appeals to the wife for the same while making her way through the now empty restaurant. 'Baby,' she whispers. 'Baby, baby.' The mother is in the background moaning because although she still breathes, her life has come to an abrupt end. 'Baby,' whispers Mojisola. Her footfalls are soft and deliberate. At each step she swings her head from side to side, scanning with intense concentration, looking wherever a little baby could possibly hide, fall, slip, sleep, get lost. She is even aware she might be looking for a corpse and she readies herself, without any drama (any carrying on), to find a small dead body.

Towards the side of the main eating area she takes tentative steps. 'Baby,' she whispers. 'Baby, baby.' And she hears the very faintest of crying. Underneath the floorboard? She suddenly remembers that, along the side, some floorboards are loose. She goes to this. 'Baby,' she says gently, and again she hears the crying and this time she is certain that the crying is coming from underneath the floorboard. She wiggles a loose board and it gives; she understands how in a second a baby could have crawled over the loose floorboard and, no doubt with great shock, fallen through.

'He's here,' Mojisola tells the mother, who rushes over, flooded with relief. Mojisola puts her hand (it is all that will fit) through the hole in the floor but the child is not only lost he's afraid: thinking Mojisola is an evil witch, he scrambles out of reach and it is another several minutes before he, with his mother's encouragement, allows Mojisola to grab hold of his chubby ankle and pull him out from the dark, dank depths underneath the floor.

She wakes triumphant and sweating. She can hear the cat scratching just outside the bedroom door. Mojisola gets up, switches on the lamp and lets Inanna in. The cat settles on the duvet, content unto itself and only a little indignant (any more would be unroyal) at the past several days of exile. When she gets back into bed, Inanna is looking at her. As if it knows she has just been dreaming, as if it wants to ask: 'Did you get the baby this time?' Because it's a dream she has dreamt so many times over the years. Always, by the time she gets to him, the baby has been eaten by rats, or he's turned into a prayer, or he's disappeared altogether never to be found. This is the first time she has found the boy alive and returned him to his mother.

The cat is looking at Mojisola as if to say, 'Well done.' She switches off the light and they fall asleep, the two on the bed. Mojisola has another dream, the same dream, except this time the baby, as she returns him, is herself. And the mother, as Mojisola hands over the bundle, is Auntie Modupe.

*

Youve gone again
No, I'm here.
She draws comfort from the short interactions with D-Man. She wonders what his real name is, why the aversion to punctuation.
Wuu2
What does that mean?
What are you up to
Nothing.
Any new drawings Or you've stopped
In all the correspondence Mojisola has not considered that D-Man would know any more than she about Yinka's life as an artist.
Yes.
Yes what
Yes, I'm drawing.
The sketches again The portraits
Yes.
Trying to be detective she writes: **Which is your favourite?**
Of your new stuff I don't know
He doesn't know.
But the one you told me about with the faces that sounds cool
Mojisola is scheming what to write when his next message comes through.
Did you get the framing thing sorted
At the mention of framing, Mojisola reads back over all the conversations D-Man and FireBabe have ever had. She

kicks herself, considers it a generational error. She imagined
online dating was how-are-you-fine-can-I-take-you-out-yes
and variations of that. In her world conversations, real talking,
happened across from one another, eye contact, body language.
Now she rakes through D-Man and FireBabe's messages. No
photographs had been exchanged over the almost four months
of chatting. There are occasional silences. They speak of their
Nigerian-ness. Share anecdotes on Afrophobia.

D-Man has a particularly harrowing tale of being chased
in Hillbrow by a man with a panga. It was during the riots
and he'd found himself in a place he shouldn't have been.
They salivate over suggestions for where to get good egusi.
'Cresta Mall,' D-Man says. 'Jumi's Kitchen off Corlett,' Yinka
retorts. She writes that she is slowly learning her way through
Gauteng. There is tenderness. Even though they don't share
photographs of themselves, there are a lot of pictures of food.
Come and eat, they say to one another. You're invited. But as
far as Mojisola can ascertain they never exchanged numbers
and, despite the frequent requests from D-Man, made no plans
to meet. He offers to prepare her his own egusi. Yinka ignores
this.

Days pass and he offers a ticket to a comedy show. He
mentions it twice and points out that she is ignoring him. She
is forced to decline with a reason that sounds more like an
excuse. The messages continue but over the course of their
long online courtship (what else can it be?) they never meet.
D-Man makes occasional jokes that he is her Internet-special,
including a link to a recording of a Brenda Fassie song. They
have a joke that repeats itself. 'You don't come around,' his
message would begin. 'To see me off the Net,' Yinka responds.'
'Smiley face,' he replies. He seems a nice boy.

The string of messages peters out, more from Yinka's side.
He writes urging her not to break up with him. When he
presses, she tells him that she is sad, that she cannot write to
him when she is sad. He claims to understand. A whole two
days of silence then Yinka writes: **I'm drawing something.**
Sorry for my silence I was sick what do you draw

Sorry. Flu?

They are delicate somehow. In one rally of messages, Yinka asks after his sister as if she'd met her once and would like to pass on greetings. D-Man occasionally asks about her family in Cape Town. Her standard response is, 'They are fine.'

I collect art What do you draw

You collect art? Wow. Whatever comes to me

He asks to see but she refuses to show him. He nags and nags and then she asks that he send her a postal address. 'Why don't we just meet?' he protests. 'No,' she says. To his credit he seems to understand that she is in charge. He relents and sends her a postal address. She mails him drawings.

Suddenly Mojisola understands that she has been talking to a genie. And, as genies do and must, he can disappear, he can get tired. What do the young people call it? He can ghost. Ghost is the right word, he can ghost her, turn her into a ghost.

Can we meet?

Ah!!!! OMG Finally!!!!!!!! I'm doing cartwheels oooo Big ones

Let's meet she types again, her mouth dry. And his response comes back rapid — **Yes lets.**

*

She phones We Do Boards. She feels her chapter is ending. Get her child's drawings, get them framed, then carry on with her life until it's time to sleep and no longer dream.

'We Do Boards — Wicus speaking.'

'Hello, this is Mojisola. Mojisola Owolabi. Could I—'

'Ah! I was wondering what happened to you, ma'am.'

Mojisola recognises the voice of the man she interacted with the other day at the shop. 'Yes. I'm sorry about that.'

'You just disappeared.'

'Yes. Well…can I still proceed? With the delivery.'

'Excellent. To the Cove Crescent address, ma'am?'

'Yes, thank you.'

*

She'd expected a bakkie to arrive with a few men. She is right about the bakkie, but when her phone buzzes and she goes out to the gates, she is surprised that there is only one man in the car. He drives through, hailing the security guards, and follows Mojisola's gestures for where to park. When he climbs down from the car he smiles, and there are creases in the outer corners of his eyes. He puts out his hand.

'Wicus,' he says. 'Wicus Kriel. We didn't meet properly last time.'

Mojisola is embarrassed but his smile is kind and she sees that he is genuine, not mocking.

*

Wicus Kriel is a very large man. When he first steps into Yinka's apartment, Mojisola has a few confused moments wondering if the apartment is small (smaller than she had initially experienced it) or if Wicus is large. It is Wicus. And yet, she cannot refer to him as fat or overweight. Looking him over (trying to appear as if she is not), there is no 'fat' or 'overweight' that she can point to. There are men like that. She has seen them in the supermarket. They have a distended belly. Fat. Overweight. Their necks have taken on more flesh than the initial design intended and now it sits in rolls and makes funny shapes and lines, holds grime and sweat.

Mojisola has always known of her distaste for such people and, back when she would share this openly, her daughter would tell her off. 'Why are some bodies more right than others?' Yinka had asked. 'Who decided that?' Mojisola had no answer. She'd felt sufficiently chastened, though, and stopped speaking up about her antipathy. Later, when the school suggested Yinka might be anorexic, for a few days (before the family doctor gave the all-clear) Mojisola worried she'd influenced her child, condemned her to a life where, large or small, her body would always be wrong.

'Is she out?' asks Wicus. Mojisola had suggested he come through to see if the wood for the frames could be stored in the house or whether they were better off in the garage. Now he looks quizzical. 'Here's the order form by the way.' He sets it down on the counter.

'Thank you,' says Mojisola. 'Why don't I make you some tea? Coffee?'

He accepts without so much as checking his watch or shifting uncomfortably on his large veldskoen-clad feet, red socks peeping out. He doesn't mumble about any other deliveries but accepts, gracefully, her invitation as if he has already suspected that something will be different henceforth and he is the sort of person with the luxury and capacity (the internal reserves of patience and generosity) to go with the flow.

'Thank you. Coffee, please. Black.'

When they are sitting at the kitchen counter, Mojisola takes a sip of her tea, swallows, draws in breath. 'I'm sorry for my behaviour.'

'Oh, it is not a problem, Mojisola.'

There is a way he says her name that makes her strange even to herself. An unusual care he takes with the vowels. She likes it.

'The thing is...Yinka, my daughter, died almost two months ago.'

'God. I'm so sorry.' He blasphemes with the guttural g.

'I — I didn't.... Back when I came to the shed, I mean the... your shop, I wasn't quite—'

'Oh, my God, I'm so sorry, Mojisola. Please, you don't have to explain anything to me.'

Mojisola can see that, apart from being genuinely sympathetic, Wicus is also, inexplicably, embarrassed. He is uncomfortable, keeps issuing apologies.

'Let me go, let...let me...' He gets up to put his cup of coffee, barely drunk, by the sink. 'Let me...I can always come back or...we can cancel the—'

'No!' It comes out harder than she'd intended and startles them both. The force of her word stops his mumbling and he stands to attention, awaiting instruction.

'I don't want to cancel. It's important. Please, the whole thing must go through.'

Wicus nods. He reaches for the cup he had just placed beside the sink, as if her words, once uttered, have restored a reason for his presence, for them to simply be. He comes back and sits.

'I wish to continue with what Yinka planned.'

*

Mojisola is jumpy. Inanna the cat is jumpy. Zelda visits.

'You can't sit still. Why can't you sit still? What's going on?'

'It's nothing,' says Mojisola.

Zelda sips her tea. It's not quite that they are friends but somehow she came by, and before Mojisola knew it Zelda was sipping tea.

'So who was that man, then? Don't give me that look. We all saw him — everyone is talking.'

Mojisola is struck by 'everyone'. Since the time she'd arrived, she's seen almost none of the other residents. There's a man on the fourth floor who walks with a cane. There is a woman with scars on her face, vacant eyes — Zelda calls her an acid casualty. And there are the guards and Percy the building manager. That is all. The building is large but by some agreement those dwelling within do not cross paths. Some suburban politeness coded into their schedules does not permit this. The odd occasion when they do cross paths there is awkward silence, everyone adopts that special kind of gaze that takes nothing in.

'He's no one.'

Disappointment is clear on Zelda's face but begging for titbits is perhaps beneath her. She finishes her tea and leaves.

As if his ears are burning, Wicus calls.

'Mojisola,' he says, jubilation in his voice, 'I hope I'm not bothering, I thought I could call to find out your progress. With the drawings, I mean.'

Because she is silent, he talks on.

'Perhaps I am pestering you. I apologise. I confess I have been thinking. It's not every day I have a — a situation like this. I'm sorry, I would of course like to complete the job. I'm sorry if I'm bothering you, I could—'

'No, no. You're not.'

'Okay.'

'Thanks for calling. Yes, I imagine this is a little strange.'

'Just a little.' Always, there is mirth in his voice.

'Thank you.'

'It is just my job.'

'I know but…you care a bit and that's nice. Thank you.'

She mentions that everything should be ready in a week or so. She doesn't tell him about her date with D-Man.

'I can help with the assembly…if you'd like?'

It sounds as if he is offering more. 'Yes,' says Mojisola. 'Yes, I would like that.' And it sounds as if she is accepting.

*

Something deeply pleasant and discomforting passes between Wicus and Mojisola on the phone call. She phones Titus as an antidote to this thing she cannot name.

'Oh,' he says. He is angry; it is there in his tone.

'Titus.'

In the silence she feels she can hear his bristles sparking. It is true he has been calling and she has ignored his calls. He has a right to this anger.

'Titus—'

'You don't take my calls. What is this?'

'I—'

'Any day now I thought I'd have an envelope.'

Yes, she has thought about that. And she can't fully decipher why. Because of all the cheating? Because their child is dead so marriage, husband, those words have lost meaning, context?

'Mojisola!' Titus shouts, interrupting her thoughts.

'I'm here, I'm listening.' She doesn't have the energy for counter-recrimination, to ask about his lover, inflict guilt.

'I said what are we doing? What's going on here?'

And then, spurred by his indignation, she suddenly has the energy for it. 'Are you still seeing her?'

Titus sighs. Only then does Mojisola look at her watch, wonders where her phone call has caught him. Still at work, back home? She waits.

'No.'

'Since when?'

'Since you left.'

'And no one else? No one new?'

'Moji—'

'Just answer the question, Titus.'

'No! No one new.'

He hasn't apologised. He's never said sorry. She is acutely aware of this and she fans her anger so it glows. Now they are both angry on the phone call so very little will happen. He asks her when she'll come home and she says she doesn't know. She asks him how long he thinks he can stay faithful. He talks over her. They ring off.

The thing is, she doesn't really care. As soon as the call is over her anger subsides. In some ways she was just performing. She cannot muster any care about Titus and their dull suburban drama. Her energies are caught up with memories. Once, when she was still small, Yinka asked about her grandmother.

'Do you have a mummy?' she'd asked Mojisola, who'd been taken aback, unprepared. It was before she'd fallen ill and explained death to the child. As far as her three-year-old was concerned, people lived for ever and they stayed what they were. In other words, Mojisola had always been a mother and Titus had always been a father; the child had no real concept that her own parents had also once been babies, then young adults with thoughts and intentions, even regrets.

'She's not here,' Mojisola had said.

'She's away?'

'Yes.'

'In another country?' She'd just begun to grasp that there were other places apart from where she was.

'Yes,' Mojisola answered.

'Far away,' Yinka said conclusively.

So conclusively, in fact, that Mojisola felt no need to confirm or deny the assertion. She'd once read somewhere (a poem) about how the mother's amniotic fluids are the baby's first sea. And the girl-baby swimming in her mother's waters has, 20 weeks in, all the millions of eggs she would ever have, all the life she could ever make right there swimming with her. Initially when Mojisola had read that she'd understood, in some way, however tenuous, that if atoms are sentient, Yinka had known her grandmother. They were all wrapped in together, floating, bound in a conspiracy of which no one party knew all the details. And then much later when she found out that Wunmi had never carried her inside her, the webbing, the ties that draw one to another, warped.

*

And now there is the date — at least, that was what D-Man called it when he wrote and suggested where to meet. Mojisola had hoped to avoid such a label but what did she expect? As far as D-Man is concerned, he's been flirting with a young woman for several months and now, finally, she has suggested that they meet. In his energetic messaging, Mojisola can almost smell the mounting desire. Something is enticing. She thinks of her self-possessed aunt (mother), her mother (aunt) a chaste Christian version of the same thing.

*

It's a small thing but at Blessed and Bounty Mojisola signs her name at the reception.

'Yinka,' says the receptionist. Her accent is untraceable. 'That's a beautiful name. Yoruba?'

'Yes! How did you know?'

The lady winks. 'One of my boyfriends is Nigerian.'

Mojisola nods, as if the world of multiple boyfriends is familiar to her, and follows a beautician through to the nail bar.

'Full mani-pedi?' The lady has the kind of skin Mojisola figures you need to work in such a place, poreless and without blemish.

'Yes, that's what I want.'

'Okay, Yinka, I'll be right back.'

Or perhaps it's make-up. Mojisola does not wear make-up. She supposes she doesn't wear make-up because her own mother didn't. She wonders if Yinka, in the time since she left her (this divorce between mother and child), wore make-up. She makes a mental note to search when she is back in the flat. If she finds it, she tells herself, she will put it on.

After extracting monosyllabic answers to a few questions, the lady, whose name is Carmelita, keeps quiet and expertly polishes the nails. Her hands are soft and firm. When she massages Mojisola's feet, she chastises her for the hardened skin and takes a sophisticated blade to it.

She'll never be able to explain this to anyone. They'll say, 'She went to live as her daughter. She went to her appointments.' They might call it a mental breakdown. Is it? Mojisola is not afraid to ask herself this. She is not afraid of the answer, although she doesn't feel broken down, mentally or otherwise. She feels spirited away, transferred by her own hand but also perhaps by the hand of another into a different but necessary existence.

'Yinka?'

The woman has been speaking. 'Pardon?'

'I said, how is the pressure? You were frowning.'

'The pressure is fine, thank you.'

There is Thembi Minyuku, the bereavement counsellor back in Cape Town. Mojisola has her number in her purse still.

'What colour?' Carmelita proffers a tray full of nail polish. Cutex was the brand Auntie Modupe used but there is no

Cutex among the dainty bottles. 'I was thinking this one, to go with your skin.'

Mojisola is taken aback by the colour Carmelita favours: red.

'It's very sexy,' Carmelita says, which does not help matters.

Too shy to speak, Mojisola nods. Her finger and toenails are transformed into the colour of roses, of hibiscus, poinsettia. In particular, as her nails take on the coolness and weight of the layers of lacquer, Mojisola remembers the Chethi flowers that populated so much of the University of Ife campus grounds. And the Achiote she played with as a girl, too red to be decent.

*

She thinks perhaps she'll wear something of Yinka's, then goes to the bedroom to see what there is. She opens the cupboard and, gently parting the dresses, wonders whether the clothes of our dead look different. Will there be anything that fits her? It seems silly even to wonder — they have never had the same kind of body. Mojisola recalls walking with Yinka through the stomach of a shopping mall. 'People are looking, Mummy.' And they were. Yinka had always been tall for her age, taller than average. Her parents had wondered who she took after. There were enough blanks (Mojisola's father and both of Titus's parents) to feed the mystery.

As soon as she'd realised that her child would be tall, Mojisola had taken it upon herself to train Yinka, with a stack of books, to hold her head up high, neck straight. No slouching permitted. They are looking. Later that day Yinka had asked, 'Are we beautiful?' The question had surprised Mojisola. That the child hadn't said, 'Am I beautiful?' or 'Are you?' She'd said 'we'. And as for beauty, what could she tell her? Mojisola had kept quiet, pretended not to have heard.

For days afterwards she'd felt angry. She'd snapped at Titus but, truly, she was upset by something much bigger than her husband. She could smell the sweat of Beauty, an ever-hungry hound in the lives of women. She could smell it bounding about her girl, felt keenly her inability to protect the child from all this, and the whole thing had made her mad.

Mojisola lifts a hanger with a sequined top. Too elaborate. She replaces it. She has spotted something red but she ignores it. She looks out of the window. Beyond the garden, over a low vibracrete wall, she observes a little boy on his bicycle: he is wobbling on two wheels. There is no one else in sight but Mojisola somehow knows that his mother is close by. The invisible but discernible cord of the guardian's gaze some paces away. Or, in the case of lost children, severed. Sure enough a woman soon comes into view. Mojisola purses her lips and holds the expression as she turns back towards the closet. There is a black jacket, long but too severe. A series of grey outfits, suits. A few summer-looking dresses in adire and ankara fabric. Shoes, but nothing with heels except the red ones by the door. There are some evening gowns. Mojisola cannot help it: she leans in to smell them.

The red dress is short, it's the same one from the photograph. Perhaps in university Mojisola wore such things. And then she posed for the camera, propped on a stool, her hair in a beehive, her beautiful legs naked from just above the knees. Occasionally Mojisola could look dangerous. For those pictures, she removed her glasses and went without seeing or inserted contact lenses. Her danger (which is a form of allure) relied heavily on her gorgeous legs. She never smiled. The smile that reduced her to a good person.

She fills the tub. Yinka was found in the bathtub. It is a Thursday, late afternoon. It is winter in Johannesburg, and the days, despite the cold, are yellow. After standing, watching the steam move off the surface and disappear, not entering, just watching, Mojisola removes her clothing, sinks in, closes her eyes. She is holding the knife. Zelda may have been jesting (goading) but Mojisola did go to the kitchen cupboards. The orange of the handle is a real defiant orange. A child's orange. Crayon orange. The texture is not quite smooth. For grip, Mojisola thinks, and this deduction is bolstered by the ergonomics along the length of the handle — a series of indentations where the fingers can rest. She checks for a brand name but there is none. Did Yinka buy it specially or, before she took it to her own skin, had she used it to chop onions, tomatoes, careful so the juice didn't leak? Mojisola tries the tip of the knife with her index finger. She applies pressure, wanting to push all the way. The flat of the blade is smooth and gleaming, reflecting light and form. Later, she puts the knife away.

*

How is it that the dress fits her? Yinka was always so much skinnier, more Auntie Modupe's frame — stretched and slight. Mojisola opens the cupboard door for the full-length mirror. He'll be surprised by her age. Might he try not to look at her breasts? So many years since someone had tried not to look at her breasts — that is, so many years since she'd considered herself to be someone that another someone had to avoid looking at too closely for fear of being struck dead with passion.

Her hair is no longer the length it was when she was a young mother. Instead, soon after they arrived in Cape Town, she had cut it short. For many years she visited the salon for a perm but recently she had let the perm grow out, chopped off the stretched hair. Now she wets her fingers at the tap and runs them through the soft curls of her Afro. This will do.

Yinka's make-up, if some powder, a wand and lip-gloss constitute such, is less of a fit for Mojisola's lighter complexion, but she moulds it to suit, her hand shaky with the unfamiliar ritual.

Worried, she double-checks, looking again through the history of the correspondence between FireBabe and D-Man. Once more she concludes that no photographs were exchanged. She can't be 100 percent sure, but then Mojisola's judgement is bolstered when D-Man writes to ask that she describe herself. In making arrangements for their meeting, he'd written: **What will you ware?** Mojisola had scowled at his spelling. She'd written: **No. What will you wear?**

He'd answered that he would have on 'blu jeans, brown suede shoes'. He mentioned that he was bald and that he'd wear a long-sleeved light 'blu' shirt. She didn't know what came over her but she wrote: **Bring flowers.**

*

As she drives to the venue Mojisola cannot shake the feeling, once again, of being in a crime movie. Except now she knows she is both criminal and detective. Perhaps she is even the victim. *But no*, she thinks, pulling up at the venue, *Yinka is the victim*. After all it is always the victim (always, in all the movies — an inviolable rule) who is dead. It is a Thursday. Mojisola is relieved that at least by one day they have avoided the weighted meaning implicit in Friday night meetings. Because although D-Man has referred to this appointment as a date she has told herself over and over again that it is just a meeting. Regardless of what fantasies he has brewed up (fantasies that will surely disappear when he sees her — no doubt she could be his mother), for her this is about the drawings. The drawings, the drawings.

She'd debated whether to reveal herself as a bereaved mother, perhaps rely on his sympathy, but the reality is she does not know the man. He might have no sympathy to speak of. Her daughter may have taken a liking to him (she can't tell for sure) but she, Mojisola, is discerning. This modern way of courting, while amusing, is really absurd. So when she sees him from a distance, standing (nervous?) at the entrance, lit by Ocean Basket's blue neon she must remind herself that really he is a stranger, she cannot trust him, yet he has in his possession the most precious thing. Basically, he is dangerous.

'D-Man?' She feels stupid for not having asked his real name. Hot with embarrassment, she reaches her hand out fast, before he can say, 'FireBabe,' and offers herself: 'I'm Yinka.'

'Jide,' he says, smiling easily, taking her hand in his. In his other hand are the flowers. There are five yellow heads, the plastic wrapping arranged around their long green stalks. She doesn't even have to check whether his shoes are suede. 'So good to finally meet.'

He has surprised her: his height, the fact that he is bald, as promised, but he also wears a not-too-close beard. His eyes are sharp, and he shakes hands as if he wants to pull her somewhere. Together, he a second behind, they walk into the restaurant. The suggestion was hers, once again to head off any romantic notions. But as they sit down she sees her naïvety; Jide is looking at her in a way that translates across time zones, languages and generations. The dourness of a chain restaurant will not dampen his ardour.

'You're beautiful,' he says, straight away, before any waiter has even had a chance to hand them menus.

'Oh...Look, I—'

'No o! None of this shy-shy business, abeg.'

He turns to the waiter and orders something she doesn't quite catch, busy as she is catching herself.

'Now, I'm not sure why I let you talk me into this useless place. Anyway, sha, I've ordered their best wine. Don't judge me, though. I'm working with what I got.'

He is young. Older than Yinka, by a decade or so, but still too young. Surely he must realise she is old. She decides to pretend it is his youth that was unexpected.

'I thought you'd be older,' she says.

'Abeg jọ́ọ́!'

Her attempts at being delicate are ineffective in the company of one so gregarious and unaffected. When he opens his mouth to speak, her country comes out. Apart from when she'd returned home to help Auntie Modupe, they have not gone back. 'There is nothing for us there,' Titus took to saying. As Jide attempts to banter with Mojisola in Yoruba, she concedes that she has lost her traditions; the ache is in her stomach. She tries to recover and receive Jide's play but her language is rusty. Her mother had not encouraged what she termed 'vernacular'. Auntie Modupe's insistence in speaking to Mojisola in Yoruba and pidgin English had always felt like a kind of rebellion against her sister's preference for English. In particular, Mojisola's mother had encouraged her daughter to pray in English. Auntie Modupe had pointed out that it would indeed be a useless God who did not have at least a serviceable grasp of the Yoruba language. All this was around the time the sisters were drifting apart, the only family Mojisola knew splitting in two.

Jide talks a lot which gives Mojisola time to strategise. He tells her about his work. He refers to himself as a 'Money Man', working for a small investment company. She tunes out. She must find a way to introduce the topic of the drawings gently, without setting off any alarm bells. She realises that she can perhaps use his fondness to her advantage. But she must be subtle. If he suspects she wants something from him, and that once that thing is provided, she will disappear, he might... might what? She doesn't know, but he might...something.

'I've started drawing again,' Mojisola says.

'Eh ehn? Tell me about it. I still have the ones you sent me by the way. Very...Well, I'll save that for later. But I was thinking maybe I could commission something from you. I have some clients, remember I told you?'

'Oh, yes, I was wondering.' She tries, very hard, to be normal, casual.

'So what have you been drawing lately?'

'Ehm...actually the ones I sent you were part of a...of a series. In fact I was wondering if—'

'A series. Tell me about this series.'

In his words and his eyes she can see he has no interest in the series. She decides to be direct but thinks it best to wait till after the main course. He asks her a question. Mojisola nods, the prawns are fine. Food at Ocean Basket is always fine, always just what the picture promises, never less or more — that's the art form of a chain. When the waiter floats their plates away and returns with ice-cream, she makes another go at it.

'You're too young for me so maybe we could just—'

'How about if you're the exact right age for me, though?'

'Well, how old do you think I am?'

'To be honest with you, I don't care. I like you.' He sits back and takes a mouthful of wine. 'And I'd like to see you again. Maybe you'll let me cook for you.'

'You cook?' She remembers vaguely his suggestion to Yinka that he make her soup.

'Ogbono. Egusi. Edikang ikong. Name am, I go prepare am for you.'

He slips in and out of pidgin. His accent has peaks and troughs, which he explains by saying he moved around a lot as a teenager.

'I might need the drawings back,' she blurts, in the middle of a story he is telling about his first dog Prince who got hit by an agbẹgilódò.

'Haba! I thought this was a date, not an art class.' He laughs through his teeth, pleased and enjoying himself.

'I may have lost the originals...ehm, of the series, I mean.'

'Okay, okay, so let's do it like this.' He puts out his hand in a fist and counts off finger by finger. 'You come to my place. I cook you dinner. I make soup. I make fufu. And I give you these drawings of yours. How about that?'

They finish their dessert; he pays. When they walk out, she lets him go first, observes his stride as if that is the most accurate means with which to take the full measure of a human being. Once outside and standing face to face, Jide moves in to hug her. She can smell his sweat.

'I now understand,' he says, as he pulls away. His tone is conspiratorial, as if they are in on something the entire world must never know. 'About not sending photographs, the whole thing. I get it, now. And I think that you're nice.'

When she reaches home, despite herself Mojisola looks in the mirror. She leans in to inspect the skin on her face. She feels some embarrassment. She can hear Yinka saying, around the time she started to eschew *Cosmopolitan*, 'Why do women have to preen so much, Mummy? It's the patriarchy.' Mojisola considers this even as she notes her acne scars. Of course her child was right. But what does that make her, tonight, after a

date with a young man, standing in her underwear in front of a
mirror enjoying the fact that her lashes are thick. Is she foolish,
victim to some condition that falls like mist upon the girls and
women of the world?

'Surely not,' Mojisola says to herself.

Her lips are full, brown like Yinka's. She goes in search of
a pair of tweezers and attacks three hairs, spread apart, on
her chin. She puts her hands lightly on her waist and pushes
her chest out. How her bosom has managed after a long bout
of breast-feeding she doesn't know, but there it is. She cups
her breasts. Is it wrong to enjoy this? Would her daughter
disapprove of her sudden delight? Mojisola runs her fingers
along her jawline, scrapes through her hair. For the second
time that day she fills the bathtub.

*

They'd always seemed to have an easy friendship, Yinka and
Titus. One Mojisola noted not without a touch of envy. The
ease of it, the lack of complexity. There was often laughter,
a joke Mojisola was inescapably on the outskirts of. 'What's
so funny,' she might ask but whatever it was brooked no
explanation. In response father and daughter would often
just shake their heads; Yinka might say 'Nothing, Mummy.'
Once or twice an explanation would be attempted, a useless
endeavour since Mojisola would find herself asking, 'That's
funny?', which would only make them laugh more. It was hard
to let go of though. If she'd been particularly irked at dinner,
cold on the outside of yet another joke, Mojisola might corner
Titus before bed.

'What was so funny this evening?'

'Huh?' he'd say, half-absent, only making her more upset.

'You and Yinka were laughing about something. I didn't
catch the joke.'

'Were we? Have you seen my socks? I thought I had two
pairs of these and now I can only find one.'

'Yes you were. Something was funny.'

'It's impossible to keep socks in this house.'

He'd bend to look under their marital bed or wander off into the bathroom. *Leave it,* her mind told her but she couldn't. Around the time of Yinka's confession as to her all-the-time sadness, Mojisola wondered if she'd told her father as well. From her observations, the same jovial lightness that was absent from her interactions with her child were still present between Titus and Yinka. Did he know? Had Yinka told him anything?

'Does she talk to you?' Mojisola asked Titus one night when they were already prone in bed, lights out.

'Hmmmm?' From his voice she could tell he'd been almost asleep.

'Yinka.'

'What do you mean?' Slightly more alert.

'You two are always laughing. Does she tell you when she's...not happy.'

Titus reached and switched on the light. In the yellow, Mojisola noted a furrowed brow and softened, her jealousy melting a bit to make room for something else, camaraderie maybe — was he as flummoxed as she?

'Not happy? What, something happened at school?'

'I...no I don't think so. Did she...I mean has she said anything to—'

'No. Did she say something to you?'

Here Mojisola hesitated. Really she should just have said, 'Yes, our daughter is sad all the time, let's do something about it.' But Titus was frowning so heavily. She liked to see it, see his confusion. And the darkest part of her liked to know that Yinka had not confided in him. Yes, she laughed with him about silly jokes — what else could they be — but it was to her mother she'd entrusted her pain.

'No, she didn't say anything.'

Mojisola wanted to keep something for herself. 'It's nothing,' she said. 'Go back to sleep.' She vowed to try harder at inviting Yinka to open up to her again as she had that one time. She lay in the dark arranging the kinds of words that would encourage Yinka to bring up the topic. And in daylight, when the opportunities presented themselves, Mojisola tried, she really did, but Yinka never took it up. She was 13, then 17, then a young adult, living with them as she looked for her first job. Then one day she was gone. For this first absence — if not the second, more permanent one — Mojisola blamed Titus.

Yinka had left Cape Town in a small fury. She'd visited her father in his office, caught him with his pants down, his secretary on her knees. Mojisola recalls the angry phone call.

'Did you know Daddy is cheating with that assistant of his? The one that follows everywhere like a tail.'

Mojisola had been quiet on the call. Finally, Yinka stopped fuming, said 'You knew? And you didn't do anything?'

Whatever her father's crime, Mojisola was suddenly an accomplice. Yinka called her a coward. Within a few weeks she informed them she was leaving. The next time they saw her, she was in a box.

Of all the things her daughter had accused her of (ageist, anti-feminist, homophobic, to name a few), coward was the worst. Mojisola recalls the disappointment in Yinka's eyes. The sense that somehow, even though he was the cheat, it was her, Mojisola, who had failed. *Wasn't that the bloody patriarchy?* Mojisola thinks, indignant and angry with a ghost. The accusation had been especially painful because there'd been a brief period when Mojisola had tried to insist, fight for her dignity, take a stand; all the things her daughter held so dear. It was during Yinka's fourth year in architecture. The school characterised the year as a time of practical experience and Yinka secured work with a firm in Durban. For the first time, she was out of the house. Mojisola and Titus had to look at one another across the dining table. Within a few days she asked him to move out.

'What?'

'I'd like you to leave the house, please.' She was determined to be polite about it.

'Moji, this doesn't make any sense.'

'Yes, it does. It does make sense. Please don't argue.'

She'd caught him a few times, except he hadn't known. She'd heard the tail end of a conversation that could only have been with a lover. She'd stumbled over a gift that was never delivered to her. At first, a small sting in the corner of her eyes, a heat behind her eyeballs. She searched her emotions, feeling unknown to herself, numb. She was hurt but unsurprised. Had she always suspected he would wander, get bored, look elsewhere? Was that inevitable? She searched for disappointment. In small amounts. The overwhelming thing was a deadness, a real still (sleeping not dreaming) emptiness. There was nothing to fix, she didn't wish to fight or carry on. She didn't wish to go over the evidence in order to convince him, she simply needed him to leave the house — they could make final arrangements later.

'Don't make it difficult, Titus. Please.'

And he'd left, packed a small duffel bag and a box of books and left.

But then the bell rang.

'Titus?'

'Sorry to disturb you. I left my spare buttons.'

'Pardon?' Mojisola hadn't opened the door. They were talking through the grille.

'Moji, would you let me in, please. I left my spare buttons.'

She wondered if he was drunk; something about him seemed reckless.

'Your spare buttons?'

'I know it sounds silly but I'm certain I left them. Remember the suit I bought for the Stockholm conference? Do you remember that? And remember how I liked to keep the spare buttons separate?'

She actually remembered. Titus had this relationship to spares. First, he bought two of everything. Second, if the item he was buying (a collared shirt or a jacket) did not come with a little casing of spare buttons, he would practically devour the shop attendant. How could they sell something that didn't cater for the inevitability of loss, of damage?

She let him in. She'd just finished speaking to Yinka on the phone. Neither she nor Titus had mentioned the separation: they pretended that all was normal.

'May I?' Titus asked, and he went into their bathroom, looked through the cabinet. He found the buttons in a small envelope tucked into a glass jar. Mojisola let him out. Some weeks later, the bell rang.

'My spare cufflinks. Remember the silver and gold ones? You recall Yinka liked them and kept taking them, so I hid them. I hope I'm not disturbing you. Were you about to go out?'

He looked at her in a way she'd forgotten he could. He admired the dress she was wearing.

He found the cufflinks in his study. A neat man, Titus. He'd folded them into a sweet-wrapper-sized envelope and tucked them beneath a corner of the carpet. Like a dog buries bones.

Always he came with a heaviness in his shoulders, a downward look of the outcast. Mojisola resented the implication that he was to be the object of her sympathy. She held back. She opened the door for him so he could pick up whatever trinket he had left this time and she closed it when he was done.

'Have you got everything now?' she asked.

'Yes,' he said, but returned a week later.

Initially when it started Mojisola had felt upset. Each time she got him at the door, and he said, 'I left something,' when what he should have been saying was, 'I'm sorry.' And the thing he had forgotten was her. She felt upset that they no longer had a common tongue; they couldn't speak to one another and say what there was to say. Instead she asked politely that he divorce her, and he came looking for spare cufflinks, tie clips, leather belts. Whisky stones. She'd imagined that there could only be a limited number of things left behind but week after week she came to realise — to know — that it was limitless. *We're pathetic*, she thought. And maybe if they were that pathetic they deserved each other. This was Titus begging without begging. When he came once and asked her if she'd by any chance come across his collection of essays by Diop, Mojisola understood that he missed her (it was her he'd left behind and needed to return and collect) but he didn't have the vocabulary. A wave of sadness flattened her. Because she saw their life together, she saw it stretched behind and far into the future, badly in need of sunlight but too stubborn to wilt. He kept coming back. One day, months into the separation, Mojisola said, 'Just stop it, okay? Stay.' Yinka returned from her year of work experience; nothing was said and no evidence existed that her parents had been separated for four months.

*

Jide Lawal lives in Johannesburg. They have swapped numbers, and Mojisola texts to let him know she's on her way. She drives Yinka's car, the journey from Midrand towards the bright lights of Jide's neighbourhood longer than she'd imagined. The shine and gleam intimidate her, as does the concierge who is simultaneously haughty and kind when he explains the lifts. This time she has tried to underdress; she wants to disabuse Jide of any sense of the romantic. She feels guilty, though, at how hard it was to dress down, to not attempt to show her body through the choice of clothing, not to take even a few seconds to primp in front of her daughter's full-length mirror. She has had to confess to herself just how much every fibre in her body wants the game Jide is offering. It is scandalous to consider this: she, a married woman, an older woman, a grieving woman, a mother woman, a house woman. There are so many angles through which the inappropriateness of her internal longings is being refracted back, causing shame and loathing. But it's there and, unable to resist entirely, she is guilty of wetting her finger on the mouth of the perfume bottle and lightly dabbing along the bulge of her inner thighs. Whatever would be the need to perfume there unless she had certain intentions for the evening? She could fool herself into thinking she dabbed her inner thighs for the simple pleasure of doing such a thing, for her own private and personal enjoyment, for the sensual delight of one, but Mojisola is too tired to tie herself up in delusions. She cannot ignore it: her loins have been stirred by the young (too young) man and a small hunger is alert.

She'd searched for the dowdiest clothes she had in her suitcase. A pair of ill-fitting but warm blue jeans and a large brown sweater Titus bought for her on sale at Woolworths. The incident is memorable because the sweater had been a birthday gift and Mojisola recalls being more impressed with the wrapping, the careful bow, so much sexier than the gift itself. She donned the sweater, at the same time wearing the anger of that occasion, the disappointment.

On the way out of the door, once more victim to her urges, she changed the sensible flats to Yinka's fire-engine red heels; the overall result was confusion. In the lift Mojisola wonders if Hebrew (the concierge wears a polished gold-edged nametag) understands the sordid turn the evening may take. She looks at him but he is too well-trained, too distinguished. His smile gives nothing away, a professional smile, so Mojisola is left alone — for the duration of the ten floors the elevator must ascend — with her hot face and the incriminating nature of her respectable tidy clothing, perfumed thighs and red stilettos.

'Thank you, Hebrew,' says Jide, without so much as looking at the man.

Mojisola steps out from the mirrors of the elevator and by the time she's turned around to give her own thanks, Hebrew is gone.

'Oh.'

'You're very welcome to my home, Yinka.'

He is wearing a white shirt open down the front revealing soft, not unattractive, muscles and a tidy belly-button. He has on what looks to Mojisola like pyjama bottoms and he's covered it all with an unbelted robe. He moves in closer than necessary and Mojisola takes a step back.

'I—' Her mouth is dry.

'What can I pour for you?' he asks, not backing off.

'Water. Water, please. Just water.'

'Three waters!' Jide says with a wide smile and heads off.

Mojisola has some seconds to collect herself, her thoughts. She thinks of her thighs, her stupid perfumed thighs.

'In here!' he shouts, and she joins him in a kitchen the size of a generous bachelor flat.

'Oh, my!' she can't help saying, appreciating the accuracy of his descriptor, the 'Money Man'.

Jide presents her with a glass of water complete with ice-cubes and a slice of cucumber. 'I didn't ask you whether you wanted ice but ...' every move he makes is full of suggestion '... you looked like you could use some cooling down.'

They go into the lounge; the wooden floors are warm. When she comments he smiles again in his way. 'I turned the heating on. I wanted to ensure your every comfort.'

Mojisola does her best to meet his gaze with a look of practicality, a by-the-way, matter-of-fact. She turns her attention to the room, taken by the walls. There is a slender bookcase with large volumes. She cannot read the spines from this distance — her glasses are folded in her bag. There is art everywhere, but one large painting dominates. It is of the skyline Mojisola knows well except, unlike the postcards, this image of Table Mountain seems imbued with darkness and portent.

'Are those supposed to be dead bodies?'

'The artist is very interesting. Kenyan woman. Alas, that piece won't stay here. I buy for some Europeans. They commissioned it. In another day or so I'll have it packaged — I have a guy I work with — and sent through to Nuremberg.'

'Oh.'

He moves in closer under the pretext of explaining the work. 'The artist works with history. Those are slaves, stacked as they were at the bottom of a vessel...there's a whole thing, the Germans love it.'

'Is this part of your work?'

Jide laughs. 'This, Yinka, is my hobby.'

'You mentioned that you might commission me.'

He looks irritated that she brings the drawings up so early on in the 'date' but it is important for Mojisola to keep her true reason (truer than her perfumed thighs?) for being here uppermost in their collective consciousness. They take seats, Jide looks disappointed she hasn't joined him on the couch but she's thankful he doesn't insist.

'Yes,' he says. 'I could commission you. I like your style.'

'Thank you. Maybe if you have the drawings we could—'

'Drawings, drawings, drawings, ah-ah! Your hustle is sharp sha! But the night is young, let's not rush things.'

With hindsight Mojisola will feel foolish, naïve despite her age, and silly. She will tell no one about this incident and hope and pray that D-Man Money Man Jide Lawal keeps that same code of silence. She would eventually emerge from what she calls The Tower at something past midnight, walk past a startled Hebrew and drive home chastened and sombre, her body alert to fibrillations but also in turmoil and ultimately, drawing-less, disappointed. The climax of the night was when Jide, claiming to have the drawings laid out in his bedroom, takes Mojisola into what can only be called a boudoir, a cushioned dimly-lit place trimmed with red lace. It takes a few seconds to notice the camera set upon a tripod and an assortment of frilly things thrown against a red velvet chaise longue. Leather jodhpurs and a golden—

'Is that a — whip?'

'Don't panic. The camera's not on yet. I just set it up. Thought if we got a little more comfortable later we might—'

'But...' Mojisola had been alarmed that her sense of indignation wasn't as substantial as the situation certainly called for, '...this is absurd!' He'd taken the time to lay some outfits on the bed — was that leather? 'This is...this is...' She felt lightly amused, a touch flattered and the worst of the lot — curious.

'Yinka, come on. I just wanted to make sure we could have fun. I...I'm sorry I assumed since we'd...I mean the chats we had.'

'What chats?'

'Well, we had a few...you know.'

Mojisola had looked carefully through the chat history between D-Man and FireBabe. Had she missed something?

'Clearly I overstepped. I'm sorry. I'm not the kind of guy to assume. You'd said you were into kink so I—'

'Kink? Kink?' What was kink?

'You said! Anyway sha...look, relax o abeg — it's not that kind of thing. I thought we were on the same level. Let's just go back and continue having what, up till now, has been a lovely evening, yes?'

Kink. As in kinky? Mojisola felt a wave of nausea. Yinka was into kinky things?

'Yinka?'

He seemed to think (hope) they could reverse and retrace their steps, sit once again in his living room, discuss the lack of dessert options in Nigerian cuisine and ease along as if none of this had happened. He looked earnestly sorry and Mojisola felt a sense of disappointment come over her. Unbidden, the thought was right there: Yinka would do it. She would. The Yinka she didn't know, the one who'd apparently spoken of kinky things with D-Man, she would have done it. Back in the living room, Mojisola walked to where she'd left her bag.

'Oh, please tell me you're not leaving.'

'I...I...' She was shaking, unknown to herself, unfounded. 'I just—'

'But come on, it's no big deal. We won't go that route, that's all. Doesn't mean we still can't...you know...date or wha'ever.'

Mojisola scoffed. 'I'm too old to date you.'

'Says who? I like what I see. A woman your age knows something. I like that.'

Mojisola regarded him, startled to find him once again sincere. What was his crime, really? Once she'd asked herself that question, she discovered it wasn't he who was the criminal. And her offence? To have lied? Impostered? Or maybe to have been someone he thought would be up for 'that route' in the first place. Where, in what she'd presented to him on the Ocean Basket date or today, did he see that person?

'Will you sit with me?' He was waiting, watching her finger the straps of her handbag, the evening at a pivot point.

'Do I look like someone who would be up for such things?'

'Do any of us look like anything?'

'What do you mean?'

'What do we know, Yinka? Tell me, you're the artist. 'Cause I've never understood this fallacy of human nature that just by looking we can know anything at all.'

She left quietly and he let her. Shame, desire and utter confusion prohibited any request for drawings and, besides, something told her he didn't even have them. Maybe he'd had them once, maybe he'd thrown them away, forgotten them, lost them. Maybe they were right there under his pillow, and if she'd consented to lie in his bed, she could have reached out in the night, caressed them. But none of it seemed to matter so much anymore. She was altered somehow, irreversibly. She had been caught out; indeed, she had finally been seen.

*

The excitement of the night isn't over. On arrival home Mojisola parks the car and walks up two flights of stairs. The door to Yinka's apartment is open. The lights are off but even so Mojisola can tell that someone has ransacked the place. Not quite thinking, she heads straight for Yinka's room, as if expecting to find her daughter asleep, dreaming. The room is in turmoil, its contents strewn around.

Instinctively Mojisola moves to pick up something off the floor and hears a noise coming from another room. She freezes.

'Inanna?'

There's no response, as expected of a cat, but where is the soft padding of paws? Mojisola turns, willing the cat to appear, sheepish, in the open doorway. This does not happen. Again she hears the rustling. She doesn't know how she knows this but it seems distinctly human.

'Zelda? That you? Hello?'

Now Mojisola looks around for a weapon — her heart begins to throb. She thinks of her husband. Of her safe home in Cape Town. Her safe life. And because she is anticipating pain and death, she thinks of her daughter.

'Who's there?' she hisses, and walks slowly into the darkness of the passageway.

She reaches for a light switch but has a vague and sudden memory of being advised to keep the lights off if ever you suspect there is an intruder. Your house is familiar to you, lit or unlit, so the darkness is to your advantage. While she is thinking all of this someone comes up from behind, covers her mouth and the lower part of her face with their large hand. Mojisola can feel her upper lip pressed against her gums and she must have bitten along the meaty side of her tongue because she tastes blood. She struggles. She kicks but he — it must be a he — has a much larger body than she does. To curtail any further struggle, he keeps one hand on her mouth and wraps the other, constricting her torso.

Mojisola stops kicking when she runs out of breath. His biceps digging into her breasts, her chest is on fire. Only seconds must have passed but that's still too long for her not to know what the intruder wants. Surely those are the rules. There they are, in Midrand, No Cove No Crescent. He's broken in, found her alone and vulnerable and he's rendered her immobile by the sheer strength and heft of his body. She's struggled a bit. And now what next? What does he want? On cue he whispers right against her ear.

'Where's the money? Where?' he says, jerking her.

It is comic. His hand is over her mouth. Even if she were mute and communicated through sign, her hands are pinned. How precisely does he expect her to respond? Finally understanding this (understanding the reason for her silence), he starts to give her instructions: she is to behave, to remain silent. In a smooth move, as if his day job is ballet, the man suddenly has a cloth and very soon the fabric is cutting into the corners of her mouth, another over her eyes. He has cord: he winds it around her wrists and then her ankles.

At this stage she is compliant. Too tired to fight. *Go ahead*, she is thinking. *Tie me up.* He manhandles her (she suddenly has a new appreciation for the word), and she realises he wants to store her in the bathroom. Another bout of fight wells up in her. She bangs about with her bound legs and knocks against the side of the bathtub achieving little, other than hurting her foot. He eventually manages to set her in a crouch beside the toilet basin; her head against the cistern, she cannot move. He locks the bathroom door. She hadn't answered his question about money, but she hears him rustling around for a while. A while could be five minutes. Her face hurts. A muscle in her neck is in spasm. The cloth with which he tied her eyes is loose and she has shards of vision. If she turns her head 180 degrees, there is less pain. She can see a side of the bathtub, then nothing at all.

*

Unknown to anyone, a gang had been living in the building, organised and stealthy. The night Yinka's flat is burgled, so are five others. The thieves make away with jewellery, money, a glut of cellphones and no. 23's Nespresso machine. The police come and there is a whole production with fingerprints and statements. When they leave, it is the last anyone hears of the case. Mojisola takes several days to recover from the jitters and a few bruises. She buys a padlock. She sleeps with a knife (orange handle) under her pillow. Yinka's phone and laptop are gone, as if the thieves have done her a favour, taken with them her endless and unanswerable questions. Zelda's courtesy goes as far as not saying, 'I told you so.'

To make matters worse, Inanna is missing. Zelda has a picture she prints off. Mojisola makes copies and sticks them up around the neighbourhood with a number to dial and a small reward.

She texts D-Man:

I am not Yinka Owolabi. I am Mojisola Owolabi, Yinka's mother. My daughter is dead. I have lied to you but only because I am in desperate need. Please understand those drawings are all I have (don't have) left of who she was. Please post them to this address. I hope you do.

She sends the address. Several hours pass, there is no response.

*

One evening, about a week after the burglary, Mojisola calls Titus. He answers after one ring.

'Moji? Moji, is that you? Moji?'

'It's me.' Her voice is hoarse: her throat still hurts from being roughed around. Her foot is swollen and bruised.

'My God!'

'I was burgled.'

'What?'

'Someone robbed the flat.'

'What? Where are you? Have you called the police?'

'Yes. I mean, it didn't just happen. It was last week.'

'And you're only calling me now?'

Mojisola is comforted by the tone her husband's voice has taken. He is furious but he is also scared. She, too, is scared. She realises that she misses him.

They'd married and spent their first night in their new home on the university campus, Road 20c, House 11, a long bungalow with louvres and a medium-sized rubber tree in the yard. Their first night a weary snake had come down the trunk and slid through one of the gaps in the windows.

That night was more difficult than Mojisola had anticipated; Titus proved more hesitant than she'd imagined he would be. 'Am I hurting you?' he kept asking. It had taken them a while to drop their clothing but at this point they were horizontal on a straw mattress not much raised off the floor, their skins pressed up together.

'I'm sweating,' she said occasionally, surprised. 'And you're sweating too,' she observed.

'Sorry,' Titus said. 'Does that hurt?'

'Just push, don't worry, just push. Darling,' she whispered, 'push.'

It was the first time she'd ever addressed him as 'darling'. She would go on to use it often, enjoying the memory, the power she had in offering permission. Perhaps the use of the word worked. Up till that moment Titus had seemed hesitant to break her, which, she thought, exasperated within the confines of her virginity, was exactly what the moment required. 'Just push, darling, push.' Perhaps the newness of the word between them, something, offered the extra titillation necessary to have him become sufficiently urgent to do the thing she'd requested — he pushed. She cried out only once in anguish, then remained silent as he worked up towards finishing. Mojisola had awoken exhausted, eager to launder their sheets, the stiff ashen snake outside their door. When Titus woke up, she suggested he bury it.

'Moji?'

'I...I wasn't hurt too badly. I just...I'm calling you now, that's all I can say.'

She hears him take a deep breath; she imagines he is moving with the phone. Perhaps she caught him sitting down in his study and now he is pacing.

'Well, are you okay?'

'A little bruised, nothing serious. I just needed to talk to someone.'

'I'm sorry this happened to you. I'm glad you called.'

They are quiet for a few seconds. Mojisola searches for her anger but it's not there right now.

'So,' he clears his throat, 'when are you coming back?'

'Sometimes I think I'll wake up in her bed, and she'll be there, right beside me. I can smell her.'

He says nothing for a while, and then, 'Will you come back?...Moji?...Moji, are you there?'

*

Mojisola is writing a letter.
Dear Yinka,
She stops.

*

D-man sends a note:
Come back. I'll give you the drawings in person. On condition.

*

Zelda brings over the weed. She does not mention arthritis. It is clear that they are smoking the weed because it untangles, and they are women who have gotten tangled.
'Where could she have run off to?'
No one has responded to the posters, except a man who called claiming he'd seen Inanna and asking if the R100 reward could be wired. Zelda looks gaunt.
'She'll show up, Zelda. Cats are wild things, are they not? She will show up once the adventure is over.'
Although hard to admit, Mojisola misses Inanna: her company at night, the smell on the pillow of her paws that have trampled the soil. The cat has a way of pausing at thresholds, for just a few seconds — you'd miss it unless you knew to look. Mojisola had become aware of this behaviour a few days into their acquaintance. It is a stately thing to behold, although a touch unnerving to observe in a cat.
'I was thinking about the funeral.'
It takes Mojisola a few seconds to realise Zelda is talking about Yinka's funeral.

'Did you cry? The crying is important. Did you?'

'Well—'

'Because that's the whole thing. Trust me because I've seen it funeral after funeral after funeral. You need to cry. You need to—'

'I didn't—'

'Release. You need to cry.'

Mojisola is silent.

'I see it over and over again.' In between speaking, Zelda makes perfect rings of smoke, aiming her lips like arrows towards the ceiling. 'Some people don't cry. They stand stiff and strong. Often, they are the ones who are tasked with... giving the thanks. Or maybe they do the eulogy. They always look...locked up. I never see them again so who's to tell? But the ones that cry, those are the ones. They are sad, yes, but... they are loose somehow, they are—'

'Wait! Can you just stop blowing those and—'

Zelda straightens up. 'Free is what I mean. Free.'

'So...'

'You need to cry, Mojisola. That's all I'm saying. You must cry.'

Mojisola wants to respond — she's gathering her words. She wonders if she should tell Zelda about D-Man and the drawings, about Yinka. But Zelda moves on abruptly.

'Regulation boards have it all wrong.'

'What? What do you mean?'

'With this thing.' She indicates the spliff. 'I mean instead of full-on ban they should just put an age limit to it.'

Mojisola frowns.

'Teenagers don't need this. 20-year-olds. 30-year-olds. None of them need this. Sure, hard times come at all stages of life but...I'm talking of when things actually start to heat up.' She takes a long pull and exhales before proclaiming, '58!'

*

Dear Yinka,
I am sorry.

*

D-Man: **Well You coming You'll get the drawings back**

*

When Wicus Kriel makes an unexpected visit, Mojisola offers him weed. It is early evening, the sun is falling. The security guards call her on the intercom to say she has a guest.

'Who is it?'

Since the burglary, Mojisola is untrusting and downright rude towards the guards. She suspects them all, even though the consensus is the thieves were people who lived in the block so their presence and planning had by and large gone disguised as the activities of regular tenants. Still, Mojisola is aggrieved. Where before she was polite, now she walks past the guards without greeting — it is the sharpest kind of insult (misguided or not) she has in her arsenal.

The guard gives the name. She is already in her flannels. They'd made no arrangements. He had called once but, with the burglary, Mojisola has not had the strength to call him back or make any plans regarding framing drawings that, despite all efforts, she still does not possess.

She's not sure where she gets the boldness from, but she stands and watches him walk down the hallway towards her. He walks straight, which is a rare thing. She knows; she has made a study of walks. He doesn't veer. Somehow, in the fading light of the day, his shoulders look plated in armour.

'I know this is unexpected, Mojisola,' says Wicus.

Closer, she sees the shine on his shoulders is due merely to how the fading light catches the suede patches of his woollen sweater.

'I actually was in the neighbourhood yesterday making another delivery and I thought of you and our project.'

As usual, he is jovial. She lets him in.

'Well, I thought I should pop by — what's wrong with your leg?'

Which is how come they are sitting so close together on the couch, Mojisola recounting what she can recall of being marauded. Which is how come Wicus listens intently, his face pained and full of sympathy. How come he reaches for her hand as her story comes to its natural end, and how come Mojisola finds it appropriate, somehow, to ask, 'Do you smoke weed?'

He coughs out his shock before saying, 'Pardon me?'

'Do you smoke weed?'

'I thought that was what you said.'

'I have some. That's why I'm asking.' And then, in reaching for a final explanation as to the absurdity not just of the question, the scenario, her person, but life itself, she adds, 'My landlady gave it to me.'

'I...I don't...'

'It's very good. The quality, I mean. You should try some. You're over 58, aren't you?'

The man is clearly confused but also there is intrigue in his face, in his eyes that crinkle at the sides. When he hesitates one last time, Mojisola ups her sales-pitch: 'You should do things sometimes, Wicus, that make absolutely no damn sense.'

After he has taken several puffs, he seems to remember himself.

'I have smoked before, just not for a very long time.'

Mojisola nods as if she is the same.

'I won't say,' Wicus is loosening, 'that this makes no sense, it is just...completely unexpected.'

He passes the zol back to her. There's something in the way he watches her draw...her groin heats. She thinks of D-Man and the perfume she rubbed onto her thighs but now without embarrassment. Rather she is amused at herself. She smiles.

'What's funny?' asks Wicus.

'Nothing.'

She is vaguely aware of flirting with cliché. Scorned wife embarks on love affair with unlikely Afrikaans carpenter. But Titus, too, had fallen into a cliché. The older professor with the young administrative assistant, the protégée sex kitten. Surely you're allowed at least one cliché per lifetime. Mojisola is feeling free and dangerous: she has smoked weed. When she leans across to kiss Wicus, he offers up his warm lips.

*

She shuts and bolts the door behind him, goes to the bed and lies on her back. She takes her hand down the side of her thigh. Even through her flannels, she feels the warmth and weight of her own touch. She allows herself the longest of breaths. She eases off her pyjama bottoms. She's had a few puffs of the spliff so there is a lovely sense of heaviness in her limbs. She finds her vulva — such a word that, vulva. The strokes are slow and even. Nothing and no one has taught her this and yet everything has brought her here. She finds a way to hold herself, all her parts. There are so many bits to her, many without names, without labels, beyond Biology, beyond explanation. And yet here, now, she can hold them all, she has found a way. Her insides begin to grow. They swell and just when she thinks it's finished, she realises she's wrong, that it can continue. Suddenly they are swollen all over the bed, and then all inside Yinka's apartment and then out into the passageways, down the stairs, out beyond the rose garden, towards the boom gate, past the guards. It is a hungry swelling that will quench but hunger again, quench but hunger. It just continues, takes up all the roads, all along the traffic-laden Midrand highways, past everything and throughout and through. Really, really big and soft and full.

Strong too.

And very soft.

*

Okay.
Okay what
Okay, I'll come.

*

Before she liberates the drawings, Mojisola takes a long bath. She checks the simple facts of herself — woman, mourner, scorned wife. She dresses to undress. *This is ridiculous,* she thinks, but feels calm on the drive, calm returning to The Tower. She'd packed the orange knife in her handbag; she's a housewife after all, she knows all about knives.

Once Hebrew has said goodnight and the lift door closes, without giving Jide a chance to say a word, Mojisola slaps him across the face as hard as she can. He jerks back at the force.

'Fuck!' he shouts.

'That is correct. Don't you threaten me. I'm not here on your conditions, young man. I'm here on my own.'

He holds his cheek and she stares at him. She knows what he is seeing, and she knows that whatever he is, she is bigger.

'O-kay,' he says, dropping his hand. 'So—'

'Show me the drawings.'

'But—'

'There is something else I want.' She changes her tone, talks slow, churns it out, like butter. 'I need to see the drawings first, though.'

Perhaps because she raises an eyebrow — or maybe it is the subtle hint in her tone of voice, an unspoken promise — he acquiesces.

There are ten drawings. Jide spreads the sheets of paper on the kitchen table. While she looks, he shuffles his feet, clears his throat. 'I didn't give condolences.'

Mojisola raises a hand to silence him. The images are in blue and red biro. Some are in charcoal, others watercolour. And there are a few with all four. On these, as if burdened by the quantity of medium, the paper has dried in crinkles and she runs her fingers along the contours. There is an image of a woman squatting: she is naked, pulling a red, dripping mass from her own vagina. Mojisola looks closer, wondering, *Is it a child?* There is a quick sketch of Inanna, although Yinka's shaded in her pelt, given her two magnificent breasts and fingers. There is an exquisiteness to the lines, the marks. There are portraits. Mojisola recognises herself. She has two eyes but both are on one side of her face, like a flat fish. Yinka has put a crown on her head made of cowries and beads. She has painted the beads lapis blue.

'Who's that?' asks Jide.

'Yinka's father.'

Titus is drawn with his eyes closed. His mouth is larger than anatomically comprehensible. She hasn't given him any ears.

There is a drawing of a man's groin. 'PM' is the caption. In one, Yinka's face looks back at her, covered with a rash that creeps up her cheeks and along her forehead. Stretching the bounds of logic, Mojisola half expects the image to address her; she waits and nothing happens. Finally, she collects the ten drawings and carefully puts them in a plastic sleeve by the door next to her bag.

'I'm sorry I said that in the message. "Condition". I — I wasn't trying to—'

'Sssh.' Mojisola puts a finger to her lips. 'Stand over there,' she says to him. She is possessed, finally, by herself. She has repossessed her own Self. She moves to the kitchen.

'Can I get you something?' Jide asks, making a move.

'No! I said stand over there.'

She drinks a long glass of water, momentarily slaking a thirst she knows will return. She burps.

'So, what are we—'

'Sssh.'

Standing some way from him, she drops her clothing. She does it as a favour, to humour, to entertain. She does it to dance without the encumbrance of fabric, to expose her skin to man-made light. She sits back on the kitchen table, drawing herself up. She can feel the fine grain of wood along her ass.

'Stay there,' she says again.

At no point in the night is Mojisola required to use the orange knife. Still, she manages to cut Jide up, to consume him in her swell, to obscure and obliterate, to devour.

*

'They found Inanna,' says Zelda.

Some cats know when they are going to die and, in service of the most gracious of graces, they excuse themselves from daily living, find a quiet place to sleep.

In a departure from the norm, the developers of Cove Crescent chose to equip the building with a service basement, a place Mojisola has never had cause to visit. She and Zelda manoeuvre past strange-looking pipes, some slender like twigs, some as fat as the head of a baby. As basements go, it is dark but for a sliver of light coming through a line of slat windows. Occasionally Mojisola sees a pair of feet go past.

'What are all these pipes? Where do they go?' she asks.

'I don't know, I never come here,' says Zelda.

Neither says anything more. Once they move deeper in, away from the slat windows, everything goes dark. Eventually there is room only to walk in a single file. Mojisola is behind Zelda, who wields a torch. Zelda walks like a soldier who knows she has lost, knows they all have.

'How did you find her?'

'I didn't.'

'But—'

'Percy, the bloody building manager, found her. He kept calling and I didn't take his calls. So then he sent me a message, said "Your cat's in the basement."'

'So—'

'So that's how I knew. That's how he tells. What kind of person does that?'

They are silent again, then Zelda says, 'Thanks for coming. I didn't want to see her alone.'

And there Inanna is, sleeping, not dreaming. It isn't awful. By some magic she is intact. She is lying on her side, limbs heavy. Zelda has brought a towel but first both women stand awhile. Zelda switches off the torch, but it is too dark. She switches it back on.

'It's too bright. I should have brought a candle.'

Her voice falters. Zelda is finally at the right funeral: that of a friend not a stranger. Mojisola puts a hand on her shoulder. She is wondering what comes next when the torch is off again and they, Mojisola, Zelda and Inanna, disappear into a thick blackness. So much black that maybe, thinks Mojisola, they have ceased to be. It's silly but she finds herself checking her own breathing, checking she's alive.

From nothing comes Zelda's shaking voice: 'You should cry, Mojisola. You still haven't cried.'

Nothing scurries. Inanna has killed all the rodents. It is purely silent, and the world is patient.

'Now,' Zelda says, her voice in tears. 'Now is a good time. Please, Mojisola. Please do it, now.'

2

The Argument

Zelda acting off. At first Mojisola ascribes it purely to grief. She has noticed a change in her since Inanna's disappearance. A change Mojisola recognises in herself, the woman mourns the cat as if it were a person.

'Everything okay?' Their friendship is ritualised around leaves — tea leaves, marijuana leaves.

'Hmmm,' says Zelda, but remaining distracted, less talkative than Mojisola has come to expect.

'I'm thinking of returning.' There, Mojisola has said it.

'Oh,' Zelda is present now, startled. 'I see. You...found what you were looking for?'

Has she? Not really. Yes, she has Yinka's drawings, the closest thing to having the child herself — she has what she produced, what she laboured over. So many of her questions remain though and Mojisola has been thinking it will be her lot to live out the rest of her life massaging these questions, working them with her thumbs like a knot in the shoulder.

'Not really,' Zelda passes the spliff and Mojisola accepts. 'But truly, Zelda, what am I looking for here — absolution? There's nothing that will save me here — I'm guilty. May as well go home and...get the divorce underway, get on with living.'

Zelda makes a face.

'What?'

She shakes her head.

'What is it, Zelda?'

'There's something I left out. About Yinka.'

All the hairs, grey and black, at the nape of Mojisola's neck come to attention. She also feels betrayal.

'I'm sorry Mojisola, it's not that I lied to you. First, I forgot, then when I remembered I thought, why bring it up now, why upset things? Besides, it's probably nothing.'

'What?'

'I heard something...the morning of...I heard Yinka shouting.'

'Shouting?'

'On the phone I presume. Arguing with someone. I'm sure it's nothing though. Why should that mean anything?'

'What was she saying? How come you could hear?'

'Well for one thing it was a very loud conversation, I'm sure I'm not the only one who heard but...yes I was walking past and...I suppose I eavesdropped a little.'

There are too many other things to interrogate. The landlady's nosiness has never been in question. 'What was she saying?'

'I...now I really don't want you to—'

'What was she saying, Zelda?'

'She was shouting.'

'Yes, saying what dammit?'

'Please!'

Mojisola is initially confused.

'Begging. She was begging. Saying, "Please, please."'

*

Mojisola will not let Zelda rest. She takes a piece of paper and pen and insists Zelda remembers what she did not put to memory in the first place.

'I can't Mojisola.'

'Can't or won't? Come on, what was the gist of the conversation, the argument as you say? Did she mention a name?'

'I would remember a name. Of course, I would remember a name if she'd said one.'

'So she didn't?'

'I knew I shouldn't have told you anything.' Zelda is standing at her front door, Mojisola in the corridor. All their meetings — filled with familiarity and cannabis — are at No. 81; here instead they are back to formalities, as if the quality of a space is what engenders intimacy and not much else.

'No, you were right to tell me. Only mistake is taking so long to do it. This is exactly what I needed.' She is a detective again, heady with the task, with the fake hope, the endorphinic exhilaration. 'I'm going to call a meeting, like a honey trap.'

Zelda blinks, uncomprehending.

*

'I'm holding a memorial.'

She phones to invite Titus, craving a doppelganger.

'There's no point to a memorial.'

She notices he sounds disappointed. He may have had the thought that she was phoning to say she was coming home.

'Yes there's a point. Yinka argued with someone.'

'What?'

'The morning she...died, she argued with someone. Loud enough for Zelda, the landlady, to hear. Shouting. Pleading.'

She hears in the silence him digesting this. And then, 'So the memorial—'

'I want to see who comes. I'll know...I'll know who it is just by looking at them.'

'Moji, nobody hurt her; Yinka took her own—'

'I understand that, Titus,' her voice quavers. 'That's not being debated but...don't you have questions? Did you ever think the Yinka you knew could do such a thing? Don't you have questions, Titus?'

In the silence on the call Mojisola decides only to mention the divorce when next they see each other in person.

'Did you get what I sent you?'

She'd hoped he wouldn't ask. 'Yes.'

He waits on the line as if one word cannot be her complete sentence. Eventually he says, 'I'm assuming you didn't read it.'

'I've been busy,' which was a lie. 'I mean I've been...unable,' which was true.

'Will you—'

'Why?' She feels somewhere in this journal business of Titus's is a trap. She hadn't even bothered to open the parcel. She'd left the DHL packet on the kitchen countertop. Just that morning she'd seen it and thought, *This belongs in the cupboard;* she'd put it away.

'Why what?'

'Why is it so important, this thing you've written.' She hated the word journal, it carried a self-importance which, legitimate or not, felt ridiculous in the context of Titus. Journal made him more pompous, not less.

'I'm trying to...to communicate.'

'To whom? Me? Just tell me, you don't have to write it down.' Having decided she wants a divorce, whatever few strings of tenderness may have existed have curled up. She gives him the details of the memorial and they end the call, Titus sullen.

His insistence does give her pause; she judges his fight for their marriage as an act of vanity on his part. But maybe there is something to save? Although she still doesn't open it, she goes and takes the parcel out of the cupboard; it's back on the kitchen counter. She'll read it later, she has a memorial to plan.

During what she now thinks of as the first investigation — finding Yinka's drawings — Mojisola had scribbled some of the numbers on Yinka's phone down. These are the people she calls and invites; some don't know who Yinka is, one doesn't believe in memorials, two don't pick up. A handful are shocked at the news (one cries — guilty?) and take down the details of the event, agreeing to spread the word to as many friends and acquaintances of Yinka as possible.

*

When the doorbell goes Mojisola feels relief; Zelda with some spliff she thinks, going to the door in little but a t-shirt, feeling loose already even without the assistance of substance.

'Oh!'

'I'm sorry, I thought it could be a surprise. The landlady let me in at the gate.'

'Titus you should have told me.' Three days early. Great.

'Will you let me in?'

She has been standing, barring entry, as if protecting a tomb. Mojisola opens the security gate, stands aside so Titus can wheel in his carry-on. There will be no weed-smoking tonight. She settles him in the guest room, assuming a business-like demeanour even as she notices him looking for little openings, opportunities to "communicate". After the short separation, being under the same roof with Titus makes her anxious. She wants the time to pass quickly, she wishes him gone. There is something unnatural about them, husband and wife. She cannot tell why they are wrong. Because their child is dead? Or were they never quite alright, so revealed by time? Is that what it is to marry, to begin with the best intentions and, the way flesh must disintegrate over time, to dissolve, dematerialise?

*

She has decided to frame the drawings — Yinka's drawings. She wants them at the memorial, hung up on the walls of the flat. She has not seen Wicus since their kiss. He's called occasionally but she's ignored him, terrified at the notion that he desires more kissing. Or more weed. Or both. She wants nothing more from him than she has already extracted, a catalyst for a small, gorgeous fever, a piece of tinder set alight. When she phones to say she has the drawings, his voice is neutral. That's good she thinks, they can do business now and no awkwardness need prevail. She drives to the shed smiling, pleased with herself somehow. But there she encounters a sulky Wicus and is amused by the thought that he likes her after all and is miserable that she has not been taking his calls. Men are suddenly comic, and someone else's problem to solve.

Wicus takes the envelope. Ever since Mojisola took the drawings from D-Man, she has stored them in a large envelope, taking them out occasionally to look, then placing them back; careful.

She follows Wicus to a glass office at the back; he lays the drawings out and catches his breath.

She stands close. She can smell what kind of soap he uses and that he's been drinking coffee.

'These are...they're...'

'I know.'

They stand looking. He turns his back on her to retrieve some documents from his filing cabinet, continues speaking. 'I have all the measurements here, everything...they're not quite a match but...at least you have drawings. We can work with drawings.'

'I'm married, Wicus,' she says to his back.

He stands stiff, doesn't turn around. When he speaks his voice is hard. 'How long do we have?'

'I...I...'

He turns towards her. 'I mean, by when must the job be done?'

She swallows, tells him the date for the memorial.

He nods. 'That's fine. None of this is too much.' He moves in such a way that she understands the conversation is finished. They walk back out into the cavernous workshed. 'Should be done in a few days, Mojisola. We'll call you; payment for assembly on collection.'

On the way home D-Man buzzes, pleading that she come and tie him up. She doesn't know whether to laugh or cry. She'd spent her forties and fifties having bi-monthly mechanical sex with a cheating husband. Now, as she climbs into old age, she's beset on all sides: puppy-eyed penitent husband, sulking Afrikaans carpenter would-be-lover and (not to be outdone) BDSM maniac toy-boy.

*

By Sunday 9am, all the furniture in Yinka's Cove Crescent living room has been pushed up against the sides of the walls. The bedroom doors are locked.

'Ah-ah, is this really necessary for God's sake?' says Titus, when he has to fetch the key for the guest room for the third time. He doesn't lock behind him and Mojisola goes around checking the doors again, locking up then slipping the keys on the top of the cabinet in the toilet, out of sight, reachable only if you stand on your tiptoes.

She'd slept badly, worried. There'd been a problem with the frames (she's tried not to think that Wicus was deliberately being sloppy) and now the delivery is only due at 10am. 'Cutting it fine,' she'd told him, feeling he was punishing her. But he'd sounded so apologetic on the phone and she'd had to realise, as she always did, how every bone in his body was filled to the brim with good intentions. In the days leading up to Yinka's memorial he'd called a few times seeking clarity, a question about the sizing, about varnishing and so on.

Mojisola is dressed. Has been since 6am. Titus keeps changing his socks. He grumbles, performing his old-age, vulnerable, lost. Mojisola takes the keys down and unlocks both bedroom doors.

'Not sure why you locked them in the first place,' says Titus.

She's not sure either, just some instinct to guard.

Who will come through those doors? Maybe no one will come. Except look at all the flowers. They have laid them out on top of the furniture. There are enough to cover everything and give the room a palpable sense of being garlanded. Mojisola likes the smell but Titus had complained so the windows are open and a gentle breeze is working through the apartment. She is scared of the people who will come. Today she will meet people who knew her daughter, knew her daughter's life. She anticipates judgement. She and Titus will be together; he in a white shirt and jeans (she dissuaded him from going out to buy black trousers) and she in her brown sweater and jeans, her thighs unperfumed, her feet in flats. They will stand together but people will look at her. That's the mother. And our Yinka killed herself. And they buried her without telling us. That's the mother.

10am. Wicus is late. Mojisola has not mentioned the drawings to Titus. She doesn't know how to. He must just see them when they come and know they exist. That's enough.

'Knock knock!' Zelda is cheerful.

Mojisola sees her take them both in. She knows they look pathetic. Zelda's face softens.

'I want to bring the trays in, Mojisola. I think we can arrange them here? What do you say?'

Mojisola nods. The kitchen counters have been cleared for this very purpose.

'How did you sleep, Professor Owolabi?'

Titus has asked that she call him by his first name but Zelda likes using the appellation, Mojisola can't work out why. They go together to Zelda's apartment to bring the trays. Once inside, she gestures, 'Have a puff.'

'Oh my goodness, on a day like today?' But Mojisola accepts the blunt and tokes deep. 'You've turned me into an addict.'

Zelda waves her hand in dismissal. 'Not with these quantities, my darling. When we reach addict proportions, trust me, you'll know.'

'How?' says Mojisola, taking a last pull and handing the blunt back, dusting her hands on her sweater as if removing evidence.

'How?' says Zelda. 'When you don't feel alive without it.'

Mojisola nods then turns her attention to the trays. 'Thanks for organising this.'

'Nothing at all. Lydia owed me a favour anyway. And don't look at me like that. No, it's not payment for dagga. Yassus, you really think I'm the Dagga Dealer of Vorna Valley.'

'Well…thank you, that's the thing I'm trying to say. Now… let's get these laid out before the…what do you call them? Mourners?'

'People. Let's just call them people for now. Mojisola, I wanted to say something.'

'Yes.'

'About Reginald.

'Was he your husband?'

Zelda shakes her head. 'My baby brother.'

'Oh, I'm so sorry, Zelda.'

Zelda shakes her head again. 'Back then I got...it's funny, it was so similar. Reggie and I hadn't spoken in a while. We'd argued about something, don't ask me to remember because I can't. We were always arguing about something. And then long silences. Then we make up. Except this time the fucking idiot goes and hangs himself before I had a chance to call and say: "Hey, jong, I'm sorry."'

Mojisola has her hand over her mouth.

'I got so stuck, Mojisola.' She wipes her nose with the back of her hand. 'I watch you and it's like watching myself. Trying to work it out...to decipher. And I can help you. Listen, I'm not a religious woman, not since I was nine and Father Buxley took me behind the toolshed to demonstrate reproduction. It's fine. As you can see, I turned out fine, but...there's no God. But I think you came here for a reason. There must be, everything must be happening for that same reason, there must be a pattern. You know? Some kind of logic. The scientists will explain it to us. Or I'll be dead maybe, by then but the young people will have it explained to them. There's no God but there's this...network. A lattice and they'll have calculations and mathematics, you know. It'll be science and it'll say that there is a reason.'

When they go back into Yinka's apartment, solemn after Zelda's sermon, arms laden with cakes and biscuits, Wicus is standing blocking out the sun and Titus has an expression on his face Mojisola cannot read. Yinka's artwork, transformed by the large wooden frames, has been spread along the edges of the room. Mojisola notices what may have turned Titus's face unrecognisable: he is holding the portrait of himself, the one in which he has no ears and an overweight mouth. The un-hearing fat-talking father. Mojisola looks for her portrait. The mother with eyes on only one side of her face. Seeing only half. Half seen. However grotesque, it is a natural thing Yinka has done, she thinks; we must account to our children, the same way we ask that our parents account to us. Mojisola clears her throat.

'Wicus this is my husband, Titus. Zelda, Wicus.'

The buzzer goes. The first person has arrived.

*

Mojisola had envisioned the memorial as a kind of trap, a snare for the culprit (guilty of what really? Argument is hardly murder) but instead it has exposed her. She feels to be the one caught versus the catcher.

The people who come are young. Except for Yinka's boss who looks to be in her late forties. *Even if she's 45,* thinks Mojisola, *I could still have given birth to her.* She looks all around the room and realises she could have given birth to everyone. Except Zelda and Wicus. And Titus, of course. But everyone else. Yinka's boss's name is Egizia. She is third-generation Italian. Her grandparents came with the goldrush. Born and raised on the Eastrand she explains, smiling, her teeth crooked.

'What sort of buildings do you do?' Mojisola asks. She's stayed right by the door, overwhelmed by all the youthfulness in the room. From the corner of her eye, she sees Titus standing by the drawing of Inanna, talking to a young man with a completely shorn head, save for a single braid that cuts his scalp in two, runs down his back.

'Uhm…we don't build,' Egizia says.

Mojisola's embarrassment lasts a few seconds. In that moment she gives it all up, relinquishes looking the part. She is a negligent mother and there is no hiding it.

'I thought Yinka was working for architects.'

'Oh.'

'She didn't tell us anything. When she left Cape Town. And…I don't know if you realise but we lost contact with her… in the last months.'

Egizia is looking markedly uncomfortable.

'I'm sorry, Mrs Owolabi. Yinka was an incredible artist. Great to work with. She—'

'You're an…artist company?' She knows that's not quite the right term.

'Graphic designers.' Perhaps out of habit, Egizia produces a rectangular card.

'Art-T,' says Mojisola, reading off the card.

'My partner and I started it about five years ago. We do a lot of online stuff but recently children's books. Yinka came on board with that.'

'Children's books.'

'She was incredibly gifted, Mrs Owolabi. Please. Take comfort in that.'

At some point Titus makes it across the room to where Mojisola is stationed, guarding the milk tarts.

'Who are these people?' he says half jokingly.

'Her friends.' Mojisola points. 'That one over there flew in from Durban. Those two drove from Polokwane.'

'Well,' Titus's face is drawn, 'the young man I was talking to …'

'With the…is that a plait, a braid — a real braid or fake? I can't tell the styles these days. And for a man to boot.'

'I think they call it dreadlocks, Moji.'

She scowls, not appreciating his tone. 'I know dreadlocks, Titus, but why does he have to keep it so long?'

'Moji, we're not here to critique the hairstyles of our daughter's friends.'

She bites her tongue.

'Now, let me tell you what I came here to say. The boy, his name is Porthos, he came in from Cape Town. He says he and Yinka were working on an exhibition.'

'Exhibition of what?' Maybe it's him, she's been studying everyone closely, as if an argument — even one from so long ago — leaves traces like gunpowder, microscopic argument-DNA.

'Are you listening? I said an art exhibition. They shared a studio in Cape Town. Says there must be more works other than what you found. That there was a man Yinka was communicating with online, a kind of art dealer.'

Mojisola begins to cough. Titus pours her a Styrofoam cup of mango juice.

'Maybe we can get hold of him somehow,' says Titus.

'I doubt that's possible,' she manages to squeeze out between gulps.

The rest of the day passes with Mojisola studying Porthos. *It's him,* she thinks. *They were working together, it's him.* As always her logic is wild, heady, but she garners conviction from the smallest bits of evidence. When she catches him staring at her for a second too long from across the room, Mojisola can almost hear her daughter pleading with him to...to what. Mojisola wants to test her theory on someone. She tries to catch Zelda's attention but she is in the centre of a gaggle of people, holding court, explaining the mating habits of goldfish. Titus is nowhere to be seen. Wicus, who'd stayed on after delivering the art, comes to say goodbye.

'Will you be going home?' he asks.

'I don't know, Wicus.'

He keeps his eyes with hers, tight, they stay locked.

'I don't feel as if I have anything really to go back to.'

Titus is sleeping so she stands alone and shakes everyone's hand at the end. She looks into their faces, into the atmosphere around their faces. She is not the kind of person to speak to auras but really that is what she is doing, staring down their auras for traces of her child's distress. She feels desperate. She holds each gaze with what she hopes is courage. If she can hold their gaze she can walk into the future, married or divorced, mother to a ghost. She can keep going until death strikes. Not tormented and half of anything, just bereft but still breathing.

'Thank you so much, ma'am.'

The faces are round. Some are pointy. To Mojisola these young people may as well be from a different planet, so strange are they in their bearing. There is one, she is uncertain of gender, whose hair is arranged into two antennae: they seem to be radiating out towards the world, sending signals of distress or hope — Mojisola cannot tell that either. There is a girl called Nandi, with a tattoo down the bridge of her nose, and when Mojisola shakes her hands, she feels the hardness of the metal on her fingers. Why walk around with such a weight? The young man with the braid — Porthos — hugs Mojisola and she can't help sniffing, trying to catch an odour. If he is puzzled by her behaviour he does not let on, simply pulls away and grabbing pen and paper from his bag writes down his number.

'Please, ma'am, call me when you get back into Cape Town.'

She reads Porthos Machiavelli and his number underneath. She sees it immediately.

'You're PM?'

Porthos looks shocked. 'Yinka used to call me that,' he says. Then his eyes narrow. 'Hey.'

'It was me, that day.'

He tears up with no warning. 'I'd been calling 'cause I'd been away...calling to say I was back. But she was already dead.' He wipes his eyes quickly and hugs Mojisola again. This time she doesn't smell him, lets herself be hugged by his young warm arms. He'd been away, they hadn't been in touch. Unless he is lying, it couldn't have been PM who argued with Yinka the morning she made a small firm decision, a decision of the darkest kind.

When they pull away, they watch each other. Mojisola is surprised to realise that as much as she has been sizing him up, he too has been appraising her. She feels that sting again — how did you let this happen?

'I have something to give you,' PM whispers.

'What do you mean?' asks Mojisola.

He starts crying again. The tears are wiped clean off his face almost as soon as they appear. 'I'm sorry. I was going to keep it.' He starts crying for real, unable to wipe fast enough. Mojisola leads him back to the couch. As she sits down with Porthos, she hears Zelda taking over the goodbyes at the door. Once he's calm, he looks at Mojisola and smiles.

'I'm sorry, ma'am.'

'What is it?'

He reaches into his bag and pulls out a notebook.

'She left it once. When she visited.' He places it in Mojisola's lap.

'What is it?' she asks again although it is clear what it is. In a way, she is asking something different. When Porthos doesn't answer she continues. 'And you weren't going to give it to me?' She tries not to sound hurt (not to pin that on him) but hurt is all that she is forever now, a mass of hurt, a big wound in the world, open and susceptible.

'I'm sorry, ma'am.' This brings new tears and when he dips his head towards his lap Mojisola rubs his back.

'It's okay,' she says.

'Please forgive me.'

'It's all right.' She thinks of herself, neurotically locking doors, trying to keep her daughter — whatever of her she'd ever possessed in the first place — trying to hoard it all. 'It's fine.'

When they are all gone (she can hear Titus snoring through the guest room door), Mojisola goes and sits on Yinka's bed. A small fury rises up, this time aimed at Titus. His snoring doesn't help, his conspicuous absence at the end of the gathering. Typical Titus, just disappear when things are hard. Is that what he did in their marriage? How about with Yinka? Mojisola recalls the phone call with him reminiscing about taking Yinka in to meet his students. She wonders about this, inspecting it, unwilling to be generous and simply see it as a father's affection and pride for his daughter. It must be linked to hubris, she thinks. Everything about Titus is about looking good. That must be it then, Yinka made him look good. It's a poisonous thought and it seeps into her dreams, bitter and self-righteous. Half-asleep, she promises herself not to give credence to his journal by reading it, not to be hoodwinked. Meanwhile, there is the notebook from PM sitting on the chest of drawers. Isn't this what she's been looking for; some words, a note, an explanation? A clear window into her daughter's mind. And yet she cannot go to it just yet. *Are they the same thing*, she wonders, *Titus's journal and Yinka's notebook.* For a few seconds she allows herself to notice that, by design or accident, she has in her possession the words of the two people closest to her — what she has known as family. A new bout of anger flares up inside her, this time loose and undirected. She curls onto the bed. In her dream there is a little yellow dog barking all day, all night. When she goes to inspect it, she realises that it is a talking dog, not barking at all but speaking a foreign language, human not animal but still indecipherable.

In the morning Titus has made breakfast.

'Did you ever love me?'

The question is so naked Mojisola is forced to avert her gaze, she studies the runny eggs instead.

'I—' she stammers, all her previous night's yellow-dog-resolve gone.

'Because I loved you. I love you, Moji. I know…I know I'm insufficient but…'

Insufficient. Even she finds it, in the face of his emotional nudity, a harsh assessment.

'I see you're not going to read the journal,' Titus signals towards the pages covered in waste.

He must have found it. She'd flung it into the bin at the end of the memorial, cleaning up, angered at his absence. Now she looks contrite.

'So let's talk then,' he says and it's like that time she was sick — an earnest Titus, a straightforward what-you're-seeing-you're-getting Titus.

Had she loved him? What was love any more anyhow? What had it ever been? Even without therapy Mojisola understands her early formative lessons in love were somehow warped. Titus was right that by the time she met him, whatever it was that might draw her in and have her cling to him could not be described in pure letters L O V E. Maybe love was too lofty a thing to reach for. Did she like him?

'Remember Aminata?' All that's missing is some weed but Mojisola feels protective over her and Zelda's ritual. She doesn't

wish to include Titus although she's certain if she offered, he
would accept.

'That's all I've been thinking about lately.'

'Oh Titus. We're not young anymore. We're not foolish.'

'But that's it Moji, that's precisely the problem — we've
never been foolish.'

*

Aminata Bar was the kind of place with little to no light inside.
You entered through a slanted doorway — the builders had
set the door askew either because they were drunk when
they made it or in a hurry or both, although drunk people are
seldom in a deliberate rush. They may hurry only by accident
because to go slow takes control and the drunk have none of
that. So that doorway was the introduction to Amin. Inside
you held onto the walls because, really, there was no decent
light to speak of. It was common to hear someone shouting
at the owner, 'Abeg fix the light now', 'Mommy, fix the light,
jòó.' But people didn't go to Amin for light. They went for
the first-rate palmwine, the peppered goat and the in-house
band of one. Many went for the darkness, for the pleasures
of remaining unseen and seeing nothing. Some went for the
smell; dank but not unpleasant, indecipherable. Addictive.

There was no stage at Amin. There were often candles
everywhere, which might be why the place eventually burnt
down. A man perched on a chair, like any normal patron,
except that at some point he'd begin to sing, making a stage
of wherever he had chosen to sit for the night. He had on
agbádá and a cap, abetí ajá style, the dog ears flopping about,
shining with golden threads. He cradled a şèkèrè shaking the
gourd every now and again to accompany his tunes. As was his
style, one second he sang Marvin Gaye or Chubby Checker,
then suddenly he'd start some serious Yoruba that made all
the patrons think of their grandmothers. The man was of an
indeterminate age although most put his voice at about 100.
The young men present at Aminata apparently didn't really

come for the voice. They came for the girls. And the girls came for the voice so in some circular way the young men came for the voice too.

'Do you take Guinness? What will you have?'

Mojisola shook her head.

'Star?'

'I don't drink.'

'Maltina? You drink nothing at all? How about water — H2O?'

'I'm okay. Thank you.'

Only when the young man turned to go back into the fold from which he'd emerged — a group from campus, no doubt, since few others were young and foolish enough to gather at Amin — did Mojisola realise to whom she'd just spoken. It was his walk that gave him away, even in the half-light of Aminata. She'd first noticed his walk on campus. Noticing walks was something she did initially without really thinking, and then it became a hobby, became something to look out for. She felt she could understand a whole person just from the walk and she reasoned with herself that this was not so far-fetched. There were cultures that read palms and others even further back that read faces, determined character from the posture of the face. Some cultures read cards and seeds, bones and sand. Well, she read walks. And this particular man, who had asked to buy her a drink, had a most peculiar walk. In fact, he had two walks. One walk happened when he was with his friends. They were a loud bunch. Some didn't comb their hair. Several walked around with books permanently clasped underneath their armpits as if the texts of their heroes — Cabral, Nyerere, Fanon — were an extension of their bodies. They occupied the cafeteria with their arguments and their loud display of brilliance, their certainty of a place for each in a bright future that was surely coming.

On first sighting Mojisola did not like them. Not because there was anything intrinsically unlikeable about them but rather because they were brash. If they came too close, she felt they would simply brush her out of existence. She knew the kind of women such men could go with and she was not that. But then one afternoon she saw one of them by himself. She was coming from a lecture, walking along the main drag back towards Queen's Hall. The sun made waves along the surface of the tar and she was sweating in places that embarrassed her. She was dreaming of filling her bucket with cold water, even finding five ice-cubes to put inside as she sometimes did, soaking her washcloth and wiping away the day's heat. Half-dreaming, she noticed this man coming towards her.

He wasn't tall. In fact, she could predict that, by the time they were side by side, she (not tall herself) would have a few inches on him. At first, she thought he was dancing, some odd slow dance. Then she thought maybe he was galloping, the way boys in secondary school had done. Those walks that she'd read as, on the surface, impressive. She'd come home from boarding school one weekend and walked that way in the yard. Her mother had pulled her ears. 'Are you a boy?' she'd asked, in such a way as to render the situation, the whole thing, absurd. Mojisola was absurd. Because of course she was not a boy: she was a girl. And yet she continued to study walks, particularly taken by the galloping boys of her brother school. Someone who walked like that, she thought, someone who walked with a gallop seemed to be in defiance of the human skeletal system. They gave a sense of bucking authority, of rebelling, which made them seem dangerous, even menacing. She saw that the girls liked it and the boys practised in their dorms.

The next time she was back in the yard at home she walked neat. By university days she had no particular longing to gallop around like a fool. As she'd grown older (become more practised at reading walks), Mojisola had read beneath the artifice of the male gallop. She'd seen that the boys were probably scared (just as scared as she was) and strategy had led them to employ a walk to protect themselves from the unpredictability of life, from scorn.

Maybe the man — now several paces away — was a galloper. He was walking asymmetrically; it wasn't a gallop, more an irregular shuffle of sorts. She recognised him as one of the cafeteria rabble-rousers. Alone, though, he looked quiet and injured. She'd liked him instantly then and smiled as he walked past. A smile he'd returned. Some regret now came up. On the basis of the shared smile he had found the courage to ask to buy her a drink. Might he now be confused by her stern refusal. Even for water. Simple H2O.

The singer was winding down his set. Mojisola knew because he began once more to sing the popular tunes as if he understood that he had entranced his audience with ancient notes and, for them to leave Amin and return to their grounded lives, he had to pull them out of the trance with high life, jiggle them back into the bustle of work and exams and alarm clocks and breakfast. 'Guitar Boy,' he shouted, and everyone shouted back, 'If you see mami wata o.' The morning light outside would soon threaten the shadows. To see Amin in full light was as scary as any juju curse. 'Better not let light catch you for there,' believers warned, but others were unbothered.

Patrons were clamouring for a last round, lovers were arguing, some were kissing. The singer slipped in a cassette and Professor Sir Victor Uwaifo took over. A crowd shook their limbs to *Joromi*, sliding on the grainy floors of Amin. The owner — a woman they called Moremi, famous for having only one breast — joined in, to the praise and excitement of her acolytes. Mojisola rose. Amin was just off campus grounds, not far, but still she dreaded the walk back to the dorm, more for the morose mood in which her nights out ended, rather than anything about the surroundings. She was thinking of some work she would need to complete once back in her room and so, her mind elsewhere, she bumped into her admirer.

'Sorry,' she said.

'No o, it's not your fault. The place is dark. Moremi, we need light now! People are bashing themselves!'

Mojisola smiled. Moremi was in the middle of the dance floor. Some young men seemed to be contemplating the wisdom of raising her (a hefty woman even with half a bosom) off her feet and carrying her above their heads.

'So,' he continued, 'you really don't drink water, eh? Either that or you don't like me at all at all at all.'

'I—'

'Titus.' He offered his hand.

She took it.

*

Titus falls asleep on Yinka's wingback, his mouth hung open but dry, face softened, disarmed. Mojisola finds herself staring. She's not quite sure what it is she is seeing but she finds something within her softens. Somehow bolstered, she goes not to his journal but to Yinka's diary. Initially Mojisola reads looking for an explanation. Over time she will learn to read it looking for nothing, fixing (absolving) nothing, but that skill takes her a really long time to master.

Her handwriting is as Mojisola remembers, except tighter, as if Yinka was worried she was about to run out of space. There are no dates. It even looks as if she doubled back to pages initially left empty, filling them. Mojisola eventually works this out when she realises lines end on one page and do not pick up on the next. Instead several pages along, often by accident, she sees the thread. Yinka writes as if she is stitching.

Mornings are the worst. The way the feeling comes upon me as if it can only approach in darkness. As if it's come through the night. I wake up with it on me. Like paint. It's heavy on my skin and it is chemical.

No dates, long expanses of blankness. Every few pages some scribbles. Mojisola treats each like a jewel. She would go on to keep the book for as long as she lives, reading until the pages threaten to crumble. Even so she doesn't panic, having, by then, committed all the words to memory.

I used to hide myself. I remember the feeling of being hidden.

Not easy to read. Initially she skips pages, sometimes she looks but blurs her vision. She wants to know. She wants not to know.

I want to feel beautiful. I want to stand inside my own body and a bright light to shine on my cheekbones and for the skin stretched over those bones to glisten. I'm gaining weight. I like it. I feel my thighs slide together. PM says I'm imagining. And he'll come up specially to check. Idiot!

Everyday I weigh myself. I feel more. Each day, half a kg. Like I'm spreading into the world more and more. It feels good.

I was remembering. I used to think Mummy was the one who was supposed to make me fat and beautiful. When I was young. Eight, I think. Auntie Modupe was always poking at me. Where are you, where are you? And then she'd shout at Mummy and say what are you feeding my child. And so I started waiting for her. To make me fat. But not with food. My body was wrong and she had to fix me with something much more substantial than just food. To take me out into the land and up a hill. At the top of the hill she would look for a rock. The size of the rock was important. Larger than a stone that could sit comfortably in the palm of a hand. Smaller than the hill. A rock of such a size that she would need both arms wrapped around to carry it, but small enough still to be carried. And at the top of the hill she would gather this towards us and say, 'Swallow.' The next several hours I was supposed to go to work. And even at eight, in my fantasy, I knew how hard it would be to swallow the rock. I knew it would be a special kind of agony. Swallowing the rock would involve first the mental audacity to think such a thing even possible. That I, with my eight-year-old body, can swallow the rock. And then I begin. I have to use my lips and tongue and teeth but it's too much and I have to use every other part of my body too. My whole body must do the work which makes sense since it's my whole body that will ultimately benefit. Swallowing the rock, when done well, does not tear the corners or rip the roof of my mouth, it doesn't file down my milk teeth or swell up my tongue. The wide rock is to work its way past my larynx and all its chapters, down the right hole as it were, into my stomach and settle. And then, like digestion, it must disperse of itself, work its way into my flesh. It's a kind of division. An apportioning. It is geometry and proportion. Rock becomes organised flesh becomes hips becomes bosom. It need only happen once and then my body is made, ready for use, for spectacle.

*

Two days after the memorial when Titus stands at the door like a schoolboy with his small luggage, when he hands Mojisola the now cleaned off journal and implores her to read it, she agrees. But then, as has been the case her entire life, the grounds shift. Titus returns to Cape Town and his earnest self — the self she admires — is back in the box. It's pompous Titus who phones and when he realises she still hasn't picked up the journal, he drops the phone on her. An email arrives soon after. He says his lawyers have advised him to cease all monetary transactions. She doesn't know whether to believe him. She's familiar with this side of him. He can bend you, knowing just where your breaking point is, knowing to go just right about there but no further. In the almost 40 years of their marriage Mojisola has never cursed her husband (not even in her head) but she feels, very strongly, like writing him a letter in response to his email and saying just two words: 'Fuck you.'

She doesn't reply for a few days and Titus writes again: 'If you come home you can have the house, think things through at your own pace and I will move out.'

'No,' she says. As per his threat Titus stops the automatic payments; when end of the month rolls around there is no familiar beep. She pays the rent on time, but her savings will last only so long. And so quite suddenly, after years of mastering that most undervalued of occupations (housework), Mojisola is looking for a new kind of job.

*

'What are you good in?'
    At Zelda's suggestion Mojisola makes a list.

    Organising documentation
    Cataloguing
    Drawing flowers, scientific
    Driving
    Au pair. Taking care of children

Everything she writes, Zelda feels compelled to add commentary.

    Drawing flowers, scientific: They have computers do that nowadays
    Driving: I've seen you reverse, not pretty
    Au pair. Taking care of children: Oh, Mojisola, is that really a good idea?
    Frail care: It's a lot of lifting. I know you're young at heart but, really, I wouldn't recommend it.

She has her degree. She wonders if she could teach primary school. She starts to send herself out, fill in job applications. A week passes, a week and a half.
    'We're old,' says Zelda one evening.
    Mojisola begins to think of what she can sell. Auntie Modupe had left her a small piece of land and a house in Akure. All these years, the cousins had occupied it. Could Mojisola now uproot them? It won't be easy, but it was good to know, if things got desperate, there was that.

*

D-Man sends Mojisola a text message.
Please reconsider and come

They banter back and forth.
I'll pay you
For what? How much?
She is not sure, of those two questions, which is the superior.
D-Man sends a smiley face.
What will you pay me for and how much?
R5000 2 hours of your time Similar to last time...with some additions.
What additions?
He doesn't reply immediately which is how Mojisola knows he knows he's got her. He's a cat now playing with its prey.
What additions?
We never got to use the equipment
Oh.
Yeah, those additions
I don't want to be on camera
You can wear a mask
You cannot touch me
I know
I'll be in control
Yes Mojisola that in fact is the point

*

I attended playgroup in a large double storey house within the grounds of the University of Ile-Ife campus. All the children, mostly the kids of lecturers, gathered together in an area at the back of the house, it had the feel of a veranda that had been closed-in. There was the alphabet on the wall in colour and 1-100 in black and white. Each day one of us was called to the front of the room, there was a deep ledge which I guess doubled as a stage. Each day one of us was called to the front of the room to recite 1-100 and read out the alphabet. Mrs Ositogun would give us a stick and we were to point to each letter or number and call it out. I was really afraid of the day when my turn would come. There was no escaping it, though. It was bound to happen, at some point every child had to do it, a playgroup rite of passage. When my day finally came the whole thing was simpler than I'd imagined. I stood on the small stage with the stick. I pointed to A and said, 'A for apple', and all the children staring back at me repeated, 'A for apple'. B for ball. C for cat. And we continued like that until Z for zebra. Then I did the same with the numbers and Mrs Ositogun asked me to sit back down. It was so easy. I'll never forget. Maybe I was six. Sitting back down and thinking that was so easy. I felt as if I could do anything. I felt superhuman, without limits. And later that same day, while the other children were drawing, I was just sitting. I can't remember why but I wasn't drawing. Mrs Ositogun was passing down the small rows between the chairs and desks, looking from left to right at the drawings of my friends. I remember looking up and seeing her. There was a boy sitting across the aisle from me, can't remember his name. She stopped to look at what he was drawing, to comment on it, I guess. She bent towards him and suddenly right in front of me were her buttocks. I didn't laugh or anything. Actually, I was mesmerised. The ìró she was wearing had this powdery blue colour, the fabric was taut against her body, hugging the flesh of her bum. Blue was one of my favourite colours back then. The fabric of the ìró and bùbá was lace. I couldn't stop staring at the holes, these beautiful intricate patterns. And through the holes I could see that Mrs Ositogun was wearing a silk petticoat. Black. Couldn't help it I just reached out my finger and began making little circles inside one of those holes, enjoying the shiny petticoat texture and the roughness of the threads holding the shape of the lace patterns. It was lovely. Her flesh underneath was warm. Soft.

*

Mojisola goes to D-Man. She goes to The Tower. She goes because she needs the money Jide has offered. There is rent. There is food to buy. And yet she is not that desperate. There are other ways, other means. Even Titus: she knows she can beg. He will extract penance but if she submitted, he would release funds. And yet she's tired of kowtowing. So she goes because she wants to. Because her daughter is dead and whatever ropes her life was previously strung by are unhooked, flying this way and that in a rough endless breeze. She goes because she has woken suddenly and remembered all her parts, swelling and aching. She has woken and she feels like playing, feels like being the very furthest thing from what society has called her already. What until now she has been boxed into. Shoe-boxed. She goes because her daughter wrote in her diary: *I want to be beautiful.* And when she was very young she asked: 'Are we beautiful?' She goes because she is angry and she thinks maybe this is the place to go. *Without limits,* wrote her daughter. Mojisola is tired of being afraid. She doesn't know precisely what lies ahead but she knows that what she and D-Man will do together is on the edge of what was written for her. She goes for no reason. She doesn't harass herself for reasons. She promises herself not to search for reasons.

Hebrew takes her up in the elevator and she wonders if he knows. He must know.

'I didn't think you'd come.'

D-Man is dressed in what she now regards as his familiar home garb. A silky black housecoat open down the front. The top of his body is bare, his nipples are glistening. *As if* thinks Mojisola, *he has applied Vaseline.* He wears silk pyjama bottoms and his feet are stuck in leather loafers that look more expensive than sexy. Mojisola takes him in, then moves past into his living room. She places her handbag on the sofa. She's not sure if it's an act or if really her joints are tight but she cracks her knuckles, glances once at D-Man and marches into the room where she knows everything is laid out, waiting. As before there is a camera, Mojisola can now tell that it is off. On the chaise longue is the mask he promised, with the golden whip and leather jodhpurs.

And there is an assortment of other things that she was either too flustered to notice last time or that he has since added to his collection. A pair of powder-blue diapers, man-size.

There is a collection of rope, varying in thickness from what looks like twine to the thick kind used for pulleys, hoisting grown men up the facades of ten-storey buildings. There is a pair of white gloves. Instantly, she remembers sitting in Aminata Bar with her left hand gloved and Titus trying to get her drunk. Why did Yinka pick D-Man? What was it about him that....There is a roll of what looks like cling wrap, not boxed as it might be in her kitchen but simply the roll, nude, and a small curl of plastic loose, easy to pull. There is a light grey feather duster that looks as if it's never feathered a speck of dust in its entire existence. There are gold-plated handcuffs. A wooden paddle that looks worn. There is something Mojisola would soon learn is a butt plug. There is a dildo made entirely of purple-tinted glass.

'We can't just jump right in, Moji. We need to talk first.'

She wants to ask him not to call her Moji. Not to shorten her name the way Titus had done their entire time together. Her throat is dry. She coughs.

'Moji?'

'Inanna.'

'Pardon?'

'Call me Inanna. Mistress Inanna.'

D-Man smiles. He puts both his hands up in front of him, willingly under arrest. 'Okay, Mistress Inanna. Let's talk first. In the living room.'

They sit beside each other on the couch. Mojisola packed the orange-handled knife (it is in her handbag, just an arm's reach away) but really there is no need. D-Man does not wish to hurt her. She can see it in the way he sits, the way he talks painstakingly about what is to happen.

'We could even do a switch.'

'Switch?' Why does she look at the light switch when she knows that what he is talking about has nothing to do with electricity?

'Ehn. Because my preference is to be sub but if at some point you want to do that too, we could switch.'

'Why did you offer me money?' Mojisola asks suddenly. She hadn't known she'd wanted to ask this until it was out of her mouth.

D-Man looks caught out. 'I didn't think you'd come otherwise. I have the money here.' He makes to rise but Mojisola holds him by the arm, keeping him seated.

'I don't want it.'

And somehow this gesture releases the evening. They finish scripting. Mojisola rejects any notion of golden showers or anything to do with defecation.

'I'm not particularly into that myself. The enema and the diapers I bought in case you—'

She shakes her head vigorously, uncertain whether to be thankful for his thoughtful nature or alarmed that he would have imagined she might want any of that. Does she really look like someone who would go for that? And then she recalls his comment that first night when she ran from The Tower as if from the Devil himself. *Do any of us look like anything?*

'No spitting,' she says towards the end of their interview. 'And no—'

'So, you're vanilla basically,' says D-Man.

Mojisola knows he's not talking about ice-cream. 'I...'

'You want normal stuff. Do you want sex? Penetration?'

'No!'

'Okay, good. I don't want that either.'

He wants her to restrain him. To hold him back the entire time. To tease him. He mentions that he would not be disappointed if she, at any point, got the urge to jerk him off, although he warns there will be no hard-on: he has a condition. 'It does not mean I will not like it... or you.'

Mojisola nods, overwhelmed by all the humanity.

'Just that my body betrays me sometimes.' He looks for two seconds like a little boy but it passes. Once more he is D-Man, the Money-Man who wants to be deprived and smothered. 'You mentioned you didn't want me to touch you.'

'Yes, that's right. And I'll keep my clothes on. No…fake penis.'

'Fine,' he says. 'No dildo. No strap-on. Will you wear the gloves when you spank me?'

Just in the short conversation, which D-Man refers to as 'the interview', something has moved in her. There is excitement in her chest, in the space between her breasts. She is five in the fields behind her home, running barefoot. She is 12. She is a young woman on campus; she is in her dorm bathing with ice-cubes on her nipples; she is lying naked beneath the whir of an electric fan, her skin changing texture under the cool breeze.

'Mistress Inanna?' D-Man says, when she doesn't reply.

'Maybe,' says Mojisola, and he smiles.

'I think we're ready, then.'

But just before they start, he says he forgot something really important. He races out of the room and returns almost ten minutes later full of apologies.

'What was it?'

'My daughter. She'd phoned earlier and asked me for something.'

'You have a child.'

'She's ten. Lives with her mother. We divorced two years ago now.'

'I'm sorry.'

'Me too. Love of my life really but…'

'But what?'

'I was…' he opens his gesture to take in the room and its contents. 'I was this and it wasn't going to work between us. We're best friends, though. And we're raising Sade.'

'What did she want from you?'

'The latest Harry Potter.'

At one point she asks him to lie down, forehead against the wooden boards, eyes bound. She knows he thinks, *Now come the ropes,* but she is intimidated by the strands of hemp: she has no idea how to tie, how to wind them around his torso.

'Mistress Inanna, I have displeased you.'

He speaks in a whine she had not expected, high and cloying.

'Mistress, will you tie me...because I have been naughty?'

She must learn the ties. She can study and learn them. She thinks this so quickly. The thought is there, just as someone else might think they must do a course on Excel or touch-typing. She must learn to tie rope, for God's sake. She thinks of adding that to her list, imagines Zelda's commentary and an involuntary laugh escapes her.

'Mistress?'

'Shhh!' she snaps. He has asked her to insult him, call him names. 'Keep quiet.' She looks on the bed for what else there is. She remembers the bookshelf in the lounge.

'Stay exactly where you are.'

'Yes, Mistress.'

'Do not address me unless I invite you to.'

'Ye—'

For that she gives him a slap on the ass then ducks into the living room. She can carry two in the bowl of her arms. She dumps them on the chair.

'Stretch your arms out, you...' this remains her shortcoming, she has no insults '...slave.'

'Ye—'

Another slap. D-Man writhes. It is hard for Mojisola to imagine that he enjoys it but he has told her so and there are words he can mention, coded words, to alert her that the pain is no longer pleasurable. She feels a surge of exhilaration through her. D-Man, flat on his stomach, naked as the day he was born, stretches out his arms. He looks like a fallen Christ nailed to the ground instead of the cross. She weighs his left hand down with one volume and his right with the other. His legs are still free; she decides to sit on him, using her weight to restrain the lower half of his body.

'Ah,' says D-Man.

Only now does she check which books she'd picked. A leather-bound Merriam-Webster dictionary and a hard-boxed special edition of the I-Ching.

'You're a rat.' She doesn't know her voice at this decibel. 'You're an animal. A very disgusting animal.' She needs to find a way to say 'motherfucker', 'bitch', 'asshole', 'cunt', 'dick', but her vocabulary resists.

'Yes,' whimpers D-Man and collects a slap that she delivers along his flank. She had not noticed initially but there are very small fine spikes along the face of the gloves. They will not break skin but already she can see the indentations her exertions have left on D-Man's body.

When it's over and she's walking in the streets, she thinks everyone must surely be able to tell. As when her girlfriends in university would tease each other that they could see when a woman had started having sex. They said she walked differently. Said her body took the light in a new way, and that her eyes were settled.

*

'You seem different.'

'Do I? How so?'

Zelda eyes Mojisola up and down then frowns. 'I don't know...just...'

Alarmed at how much weed she'd been smoking, Mojisola has invited Zelda over on the grounds that they drink simple tea and gossip.

'I don't understand why you're imposing this ban, Mojisola.'

'It's not a ban as such. I just feel...surely it's not good for us.'

'Look,' says Zelda, and takes a sip of tea. 'I've been smoking for the better half of my life and I'm perfectly fine, aren't I?

Tempted as she is to answer, Mojisola decides to treat the question as rhetorical. 'What's new?' she asks.

Zelda shrugs. 'Body corporate meeting last night. That nitwit thinks he should be paid more, thinks he deserves a raise.'

Mojisola frowns. She isn't confused so much as suddenly confronted with something she's never considered before. She can't find any insults for D-Man. Zelda saves all her insults for Percy the building manager. In fact Mojisola has grown accustomed to the special acid Zelda spits whenever Percy comes up in conversation.

'Do you like him?'

'Who?' She is so incredulous it fills up the whole house. 'Who, Percy?'

'It's just a question, Zelda.'

'Well it's a fucking stupid question, Mojisola. That's what it is.' With that she picks up and leaves, Mojisola too stunned to speak. Next time she sees Zelda, they barely exchange greetings.

'Zelda, I didn't mean to—'

''Scuse me, Moji — I need to attend to something.'

*

'What if your daughter said she was in love with a man who tied her up? What would you say to her?'

'I'd ask her if she liked it.'

Mojisola scoffs.

'It's true,' says D-Man. 'I'd ask her if he respected her.'

'How can he respect her if he's tying her up all the time?'

'With her permission?'

Mojisola shakes her head.

'Look, Moji, did your husband ever tie you up?'

She starts laughing. 'Of course not.'

D-Man nods. 'And, without a shadow of a doubt, can you look me in the eye and tell me he respected you 100 percent? Respected your body, mind, soul and spirit. Honoured you.'

Mojisola is unable to look at him. She cannot say yes but neither can she say no. The answer is somewhere in the middle. And perhaps that's his point.

'The world is full of lazy thinkers, Moji. It's true we have many, many problems on this planet. But I swear to you, BDSM is the least of them.'

'How so?'

'If you'd met Titus and, before the marriage he'd said: "Look, I'm going to love you but I'm also going to remain superior. I'll be interested in you but always with a touch of disdain. Throughout our marriage you must understand that my contribution will always be considerably more important than yours. And you must be prepared to constantly make sacrifices. Now, will you marry me?", how would you have replied?'

Mojisola cocks her eye at him.

'I'm serious. At least with BDSM it's all out there. In the community you know immediately what you are dealing with. My issue is never with people who call a spade a spade. Someone says: "I want to be a slave." Someone else says: "I want to own a slave." We vilify kinky folk but protect rapists and wife beaters. "She asked for it," we say, and the pastor coaches the wife to go back to her husband and do what? Surrender, try not to anger him. We demonise people who are interested in navigating the waters of trust and desire, but we raise our girls on Barbie dolls and our boys on toy pistols. Give girls one box to live in and boys another and say good luck.'

'So you're saying...'

'I'm saying some of my closest friends I've met on fetlife. Good people. I'll go into battle with them. Meanwhile, vanilla is full of cowards and hypocrites.'

Mojisola jerks back a bit, as if his words have hit her in the solar plexus.

'Oh, not to mention religion, which wants to own and decree anything to do with sex. Because what if, Moji? Enh? What if we just left people to plumb all the way down to the depths of their own desires? What then? Armageddon?'

'It's the pain element, the...inflicting of—'

'Please, abeg! We watch boxers beat each other up. Even better, we wage war. Oh...we go to the ballet.'

Mojisola looks doubtful.

'Listen to me, I'm serious. Ballet dancers. Have you ever gone after the show to look at the ballet dancer's feet?'

It's a rhetorical question and yet he waits. For dramatic purposes, figures Mojisola.

'Pain? You want to talk about pain. Bullshit. 'Scuse my French but it's not about the pain. It's that we want to pick and choose what to vilify and what to call art and entertainment. Pain ke!' He sucks his teeth.

It's hard not to like him just then. Just a little bit. Mojisola smiles.

'Why do I have to justify my desires? To whom?'

'But I'm sure there is a need. Because there are dangers in this kind of...this sort of...'

'Of course there are. And weirdos and creeps. But, look, there are creeps everywhere. Why do we pick and choose? It's just prejudice, that's what it is. Like people who see two men kissing and shiver.'

'You're not quite the typical Naija man.' And also she wonders, *Could we exist in Nigeria like this, you and I? Could anyone imagine us?*

'I'm not the typical anything.'

And just then, as if to underline his point, his phone rings and a man who, only half an hour before, had been begging her to lay a whip to his ass starts, in a soft enchanting voice, to tell a story to his daughter about to go to bed somewhere in the city.

'Once upon a time there was a little girl the size of a dragon...'

Mojisola lets herself out.

*

Zelda keeps up a cold distance and Mojisola is flabbergasted that an innocent question as to her love life could cause such a rift. It's as if by suggesting she has desire, Mojisola insulted Zelda. She recognises herself (her old self?) in the landlady's sudden stiffness. Mojisola goes to D-Man. 'You're not in charge here,' she tells him.

She learns how to insult him, learns that the abuse does not need to be vulgar. At least in D-Man's case what he desires is humiliation. Remembering how much he'd bragged about his job on their first date, keeping in mind the painstaking way his apartment is decorated for show, Mojisola learns to insult him where it hurts most. 'You're not worth much,' she says. 'You're a beggar, less than a beggar. You are rubbish. I don't see you. I can't see you. No one can.'

*

'Why do you think you need this?' She enjoys their chats afterwards almost as much as the sessions themselves.

'You mean?'

'I was wondering if you...'

'If I had a psycho childhood in which my father flogged me mercilessly?'

Mojisola looks sheepish. Sometimes when she asks questions, she sees the fatigue in Jide's eyes, just a flash before his good nature takes over.

'I guess I just wondered.'

'My father was the...God rest his soul, he was the gentlest man I ever knew. In all his life he never touched one hair on my head. The discipline was up to my mother and the worst she ever did was have me stand in a corner and look at the wall. I came after nine other boys, mehn. By the time I arrived my parents were tired.'

Mojisola laughs.

'I don't know why this is. I don't think about it much. When my marriage was dying, I did some therapy. My wife joined me in fact. My ex-wife. To be honest I wanted to be cured. I thought the therapist could say some things, give me pills and then I could go back to being with her instead of longing for things my poor wife could never give me.'

'But it's not a sickness.'

'Yes. And I know that now. I don't pathologise it any more. And you?'

'Me what?'

'Why do you think you need this?'

Her smile fades fast. She has the response ready — 'I don't'. And yet she knows that's a lie. And she knows that Jide knows it's a lie. So she says nothing lest she talk and he talk back, lest he say: 'That's a lie. Otherwise why do you keep coming?'

Because she does keep coming. Initially she has told herself she comes for Yinka, because of Yinka. She comes to know her daughter, know her dark secrets, the things she hid away. But there have been times when Mojisola has known that there is more to this. That for the most part she keeps returning not for her daughter but for herself. The weeks have blurred. Jide calls them play sessions, refers to her as a play partner. As from the first time he does not touch her. Despite his suggestion that, while not expected, it would be welcome, Mojisola has not touched his penis for any reason, least of all to bring him to orgasm. She can't pretend she doesn't enjoy it. That it isn't fun somehow. But what does that make her? What would Zelda say? What would her husband say? And Yinka? When she plays with D-Man she is cut loose from all that, from wife and mother, respectable friend. She is suspended in an enticing void of nothing, free even from the convention of feeling bad about inflicting pain on another; cut loose from civility and the constraints of politeness. D-Man continues to stare at her. He's waiting for an answer, but his face is kind, patient. Mojisola clears her throat.

'For no reason,' she says. And then, D-Man nodding, 'Because I like it.'

The conversation seems complete. They eat the sandwiches D-Man's chef has left prepared on the kitchen table. There is an ease between them. Mojisola has asked and knows that D-Man has other playmates. He's joked about making a set of shackles for Mojisola to use on him and that, if she wanted, he could use on her too. He has done this with other playmates. He knows a blacksmith deep in the city who makes them to specification. Despite the playmates, D-Man remains single. He's told Mojisola, though, that he would like to have a girlfriend; someone willing to switch. When he'd said it, he'd looked suggestive and she'd shaken her head vigorously. Yes, she enjoyed what they were doing but it felt like a course of medicine, to be taken and finished. When D-Man sees her to the door it takes Mojisola a few seconds to understand he is continuing the conversation she'd started an hour before.

'Sometimes when I'm in a meeting, there's a deal hanging and it's all on my head. My boss once told me, "Jide, don't sneeze. If you sneeze we lose a billion."' He's shaking his head. 'To be that kind of person...who can't sneeze.' He bends towards her and a small thrill climbs her skin. When their cheeks are almost touching, he hangs for a second. She's expecting a kiss then, after a beat, feels the sharp edge of his teeth as he takes her ear in his mouth.

*

Mojisola phones Yinka's ex boss at Art-T and asks if they need an illustrator. If Egizia is surprised she doesn't show it. She sounds kind on the phone and Mojisola worries that it will be charity: help the mother of the suicide girl.

'Send me your book,' says Egizia.

What book? Mojisola has no book but she goes downstairs and spends several hours in the garden drawing the cabbage roses, the bees that visit them and a butterfly consisting entirely of white. She remembers the project on Ife campus, her heart sore for only a second before she thinks, *Who would have thought that I would be here drawing again?* So many things have had to happen to find her here, drawing. She thinks she might finally cry but her sorrow remains bone dry.

She's never used colour — her previous work didn't call for it — but now she goes searching in Yinka's garage. At the bottom of one of the boxes there is a tin with rusty hinges and inside it ten squares of watercolour blocks. Something makes her keep rummaging, which is how she comes across a contraption that at first, despite using her eyes, she cannot see. In fact, she realises it has always been there, the first time she searched the garage there it had been and yet...she had not seen it. Perhaps she had not understood it. Dismissed it as bric-a-brac. Now after meeting D-Man, after their time together, her eyes are perhaps attuned such that she knows the thing she's looking at, picking up and hurrying off with it in the car, heavy and rusting and smelling like blood. When she gets to D-Man's Tower she hurtles past Hebrew.

'I'm not sure he's expecting you,' says Hebrew, but then he sees what she is carrying and is silenced.

She rides the elevator alone for the first time. When she enters D-Man's apartment he is in his underwear. Mojisola raises her fist and jangles the shackles.

*

'Are these yours?'

'Moji, I can see you're angry. I don't quite understand—'

'I found these in Yinka's garage. Among her things. Is this one of yours? Did you give my daughter this? Did you chain her up in this? Were you the one she argued with that morning?' Her voice is raised.

'What? No. Yinka and I never met. We never even spoke. And I have never seen those in my life.'

'Why should I believe you?'

'Moji, there is perhaps no reason you should believe me but…I swear I have never met Yinka in the flesh.'

He hesitates.

'What aren't you telling me?'

'Look, the site I met her on…'

'The dating site?'

'It wasn't a normal vanilla dating site. It was fetish, alternative.'

She'd missed that but she knows if she returns to it now, she'll see it. That is how life works, each time only seeing what your eyes can tolerate.

'What about it?'

'Yinka was…she…'

'Just tell me.'

'She wanted to be dominated.'

Mojisola has gone still as death.

'I recommended someone. I couldn't do what she...she wanted to be...paddled...hard. I knew someone good. Someone safe. All kinds come onto these sites. Novices claiming to be masters. People messing around.'

'You recommended someone?'

'Someone safe, Mojisola.'

'And you think this is his?' She rattles the shackles again.

'I think they...met up. Maybe a few times.'

She puts the shackles down and fishes in her bag.

'What are you doing?'

She'd joked once and told him she used to bring a knife to his place, when she'd still suspected he could be a serial killer. She wonders if he's worried she's about to stick him. Mojisola pulls out pen and paper.

'Write it down there. His address. What does he go by?'

'The Woodsman.'

*

She doesn't go immediately. She dreams he goes cloaked in navy blue velvet. That he walks with a staff. She dreams he speaks with a voice made from smoke, that his skin is sallow, his nails darkened by sheer wickedness. She imagines she will knock on his door and after she has threatened him sufficiently he will pull from his robes her daughter, small but intact, whole and alive.

Egizia rings. There is a job and the in-house illustrator sick with stomach flu. Mojisola draws flowers; her hand picking the lines as if it isn't almost two decades of time that separate her from that life in Ife, from drawing the flora, recording the biome. She finishes the job, the money is fair. She dreams that the Woodsman finds her hiding underneath a table. She is incredibly small or he is larger than giant or both. He fishes her out and goes around like that, with her hanging from his index finger like a puppet. 'Where's my daughter?' she keeps shouting, but he doesn't reply. Not because he's ignoring her. He doesn't reply because he cannot hear her: she is too insignificant to be heeded.

*

When Mojisola pulls up and walks into the warehouse she has a moment of realisation; that for the most part, life happens in circles, returning to the same place over and over again in big and little revolutions; if we're lucky life goes in spirals indicating some sense of progression, and if we're incredibly unlucky it's just one long interminable straight line.

'Mojisola, sjoe, didn't expect to see you again,' says Wicus.

'You're the Woodsman?' she asks, and it's as if she's ripped his clothes off, the flesh from his bones. His face bares itself. 'You're the Woodsman.'

Before Wicus can answer a young woman, perhaps she works at the shop, comes holding a cellphone to her chest. She addresses him as Meneer Kriel, rolls her eyes.

'Dis Lucinda. Should I maar just say the shipment isn't in yet?'

Wicus nods and signals Mojisola to follow him. He leads her to a room in the back. She assumes they will sit here — it looks like a storeroom. But there is a hidden door behind a stack of boxes. Wicus shifts these without much effort, opens the concealed door and, once more, Mojisola follows him through. Only now she is thinking, *He is going to kill me.* The thought is there but she also notices something else. It has always been there. All this time she hasn't recognised her own fear. She's noticed his kindness, always, but she was only ever looking because of something else she's never named, never known to name — he is menacing. Even his kindness produces anxiety, the sense that the kindness is there as mask, not material substance. They are walking along a narrow dark corridor. She remembers walking with Zelda through the belly of Cove Crescent to find a dead cat.

'Where are we going?' Her voice is shaking in a way she feels she needs to stifle. He mustn't sense her fear. He will eat her.

'Not far.'

She can now hear the menace in his voice. He can no longer hide it from her. She hasn't packed her orange knife, all this time taking it to the wrong criminal. Here's the real monster and she comes unarmed. Just when she's about to shout, 'Stop!' and turn around, Wicus slows. He opens a door and they are in a small room, concrete walls and floors. The walls are of particular interest. A dado rail runs along at eye-level and dangling from ornate hooks, equally spaced, is an assortment of what Mojisola can only think of as instruments. Long. Some thin. Most are made from wood. She recognises an array of wooden spoons varying in size. There are three sjamboks hanging together like cousins. There are paddles — she knows these, recognises them from D-Man's small collection. She wants to say something but finds herself struck dumb. Wicus seems to be in no hurry, now that they have stopped walking and have come to this small closed off place. He simply stands, occasionally looking at Mojisola, occasionally surveying the room as if it's not his, as if he's never seen the things it contains.

'I...' She is slowly finding her words again. But then she turns and catches sight of something. 'That's a...'

'It's a spanking bench.'

'Is that for...for...'

'Mojisola, please allow me to explain.'

*

'My name is Lodewicus Helmut Kriel. I supply paddles. I make them myself, usually from bamboo. Some know me as the Hangman, for my ropework. But mostly in the community I'm known as the Woodsman.'

They are sitting — he'd produced two folding chairs.

'I've been in the lifestyle for some time now. I first realised I was into kink when I was about nine, maybe ten. We were playing cops and robbers. Me and my cousin. He was the robber. When I caught him I decided to tie him up. That was it, I guess. I was hooked, please excuse the pun.'

Mojisola is not in the mood to excuse anything.

Wicus continues. 'Later I convinced the same cousin, we were…11 or so, I asked him to let me punish him. We were the same age, in fact he was bigger than me, if you can believe that, but for whatever reason he let me punish him. Maybe he liked it.' Wicus shrugs.

'What did you do with my daughter?' She is no longer scared now.

Wicus puts his hands out as if he's under arrest. 'I only met with her once. I know you must have many questions, Mojisola. I can explain.'

He takes her back to the first time Mojisola appeared at his shop. At the mention of Yinka he'd remembered the young girl who had come to him. They'd only met once but it had been memorable, 'I don't get a lot of black partners, even fewer black women.' Mojisola winces as he speaks.

'She was curious. Mostly we just talked but—'

It's Mojisola's turn to raise her hand. She wants to know. She doesn't want to know. Wicus nods.

'So you do this?' she asks, looking around. 'This is what you do?'

'I run "We Do Boards" and then in my other life, my non-vanilla life, I have play partners. I'm a sadist and I'm heterosexual but I punish women and men. It's a mutual pleasure. Consensual and safe.'

He could be explaining how best to invest her pension, or something technical about the hard drive of her desktop computer. He could be talking to her about the political state of the country. Matter-of-fact and with no sense of irony.

'At first the idea of having my fet life right next to my vanilla seemed tricky…but I had the space for it. I'd bought this place way back when it was still bush all around. Built the warehouse. And now there's an entrance for the dungeon — that's what I call it — on one side and the entrance to "We Do Boards" on the other. Like two sides of one coin.' He looks amused but Mojisola does not smile. 'Sometimes I rent this side out for fet parties or events. The money isn't bad. As I got more into it, I started learning to make the paddles. I sell them through an online shop. I'm good at paddles — I ship to customers in Bahrain.'

'When you found out who I was, why did you lie to me? Why didn't you just come out and tell me that you and Yinka...'

'I didn't mean to be deceitful. After that first meeting, we would chat occasionally. Then she mentioned that she wanted to frame some of her works; from there it was pure business for a while, then silence. Until you told me Yinka had passed on, that day in the kitchen, I did not know. In this world, in the community people do just drop off. They fall away. They disappear. When Yinka didn't respond to my calls and emails I just assumed she'd had enough. It wouldn't be the first time someone moved on with their life. I thought of her but...' He shrugs.

'Then I showed up.'

'Then you showed up at the warehouse. Initially I thought maybe Yinka had sent you. Maybe she was embarrassed, sent you instead of coming herself. So I thought that was what it was. I had no way of checking. I certainly wasn't going to tell you I knew your daughter. You must understand that so many people — I include myself — live this in secret. Not from shame, although maybe that is there too, but...there is so much judgement.'

Mojisola thinks of her and D-Man's long conversations. Wicus continues speaking.

'Sometimes I see people on the outside. I once saw a man — a regular playmate — in a bookshop. He was with his daughters and his wife. We just walked right past each other. That's how it works. That's how it has to work.'

'And when I told you she'd died? What then?'

'I liked you. Very much. What a crazy situation it was. A young girl had come to me. And then mysteriously she'd taken her life. And then her mother shows up. And there was... something about you, Mojisola.'

'Are you married?'

'No.'

'Divorced?'

'I've never been married, Mojisola. I'm single.'

She nods.

'Have you ever,' says Wicus, 'found yourself somewhere, in a situation and waiting for the moment to extract yourself, explain yourself, waiting for the right time? That's what it was like. Suddenly I was thinking about you. Thinking about kissing you. Can you see that I didn't know what to do, what move to make? I thought my task was to do the job — the framing — and then disappear from your life. My desire was to know you deeper but that could never be possible. Not without either living a lie or disclosing something so delicate I didn't have the words for it. When you came that day and said you were married, that we couldn't continue, I thought, *Ah, well, there it is.* I thought that was all. That we were done.'

All these weeks Mojisola has been visiting The Tower thinking it silly, trivial. A distraction from grief perhaps. But really, looking back, she sees she has only been doing what she came to Jo'burg to do. Tracing her daughter's footsteps, tracking her.

'What did you do with her? Show me.'

Wicus is shaking his head before she's finished speaking. 'I can't do that, Mojisola.'

'Yes, you can. Now.' She gets up and moves towards the closest dado rail, picks at random one of the paddles. The one she has chosen looks like a cross between a slender cheese board and a meat tenderiser. 'This one? Did you use this on her?'

'Mojisola, please.'

'No, Wicus! You need to show it to me. You must. How about these?' She goes to the cousinly sjamboks. They are identical. She picks one and tests its tail in the air, cutting the room. 'How does it go? Does she undress? She's naked, my daughter, my Yinka, isn't she? And then she leans over, like this? Here, Wicus, take this cane — show me. Pick one of your whips and show me, Wicus!'

She has leaned over and, the pressure of the padding on the spanking bench pressing against her solar plexus, her voice is deep and raw. She waits ten beats, breathing deep from the work of shouting. She cannot see Wicus. The bench is positioned in a corner and their seats are behind her now.

'Come, Wicus,' she's dropped to a whisper. 'Show me. I command you. I'm her mother. Show me how you killed her.'

'I didn't kill Yinka.'

'She was powerless here, not so? Isn't that the point? She was powerless with you…and powerless with life. One may have been a game, Wicus, but the other was real, not play.'

'I have a fetish.' She can hear he is defending himself from a position of defeat — she is familiar with this, she does it too. 'She had a fetish…her death has nothing to do with any of that.'

'How do you know?' His denials enrage her. She lunges, like a cat, from the bench and is instantly in his face. 'How can you be so sure? What was she doing here? What brought her here?'

'I—'

'No!' She cannot bear to hear another word of protest. 'Bend there.'

'Mojisola, I don't—'

'I said bend there. Bend!'

Perhaps on account of her rage, which she realises only later must surely have been terrifying, or the strength of her accusation, Wicus slides (it can hardly be called a walk) and slumps over the spanking bench. Quickly Mojisola straps his arms in place. He doesn't protest, as if she has conquered him with her fury. When he is strapped in, she starts to work his pants down his waist. It takes effort and at times he seems to oblige, lifting first one hip and then the other. They are both breathing deeply, her upper lip is damp. Once she's worked past the waist, the khaki shorts fall to the floor, a pile around his thick ankles.

'How hard did she like it?' Her own voice surprises her, steady, anticipating. His bottom — backside, ass, Auntie

Modupe would say nyash — is there, flat pale buttocks awaiting impact. 'Answer me!'

But the man cannot talk. Mojisola picks up the tenderiser cheese board, which she had set aside. When she turns to strike Wicus's bottom the tears, Zelda's tears, are right there. Easily they come down her cheeks and drip off her chin. Her hand goes limp.

'What's wrong with you people?' she whispers. Wicus does not hear her. 'Why didn't you send her home? She's a child.' She thinks of her little girl, ferociously slender. 'You should have sent her home to me. What's wrong with you?'

'I'm sorry,' Wicus shouts, as if those two words are to be his last and he wants to be sure they are heard, heeded.

Mojisola puts the paddle down. She releases Wicus's wrists from the straps and stands aside, wiping her face. For some reason they both sit down, Wicus after pulling up his shorts. They sit on their respective chairs for what seems like hours.

When she gets home, she climbs into bed and she must have fallen asleep for a long time because when she jerks awake it is dark outside. Before her final departure from "We Do Boards" she'd turned and asked Wicus, 'What did you argue about, Yinka and you — that morning. What was it she was begging you for?'

Wicus had looked confused. She'd had to repeat the question two more times before she realised he really did not know what she was talking about.

*

Despite the diary, the drawings and whatever Zelda has been able to tell her, Mojisola is as ignorant of the reasons Yinka took a knife to her wrists as she was when she first walked into Cove Crescent. It seems an ugly thing not to have an answer and still to need one. Something, maybe it is the episode with Wicus, sends her back to the diary, flips through, past the many blank pages at the back. On the very last page there are random notes, reminders. A few phone numbers, an account number Mojisola recognises vaguely as Zelda Petersen's. Written boldly is: call Daddy, followed by a Cape Town phone number Mojisola does not know. But when she studies it a bit longer, she realises she's seen it before. The number Yinka had dialled the day of her death. Mojisola remembers seeing it on the call log of her daughter's phone. She'd dialled it and there'd been no answer.

Mojisola reaches for her phone, sighing, thinking she's operating more like a butcher than a detective or coroner. She's hacked through Yinka's life, hacked her computers, hacked through her friends and diaries and secrets. Call Daddy.

'Moji?'

'Yinka called you?'

He doesn't answer immediately and for the second time in only a few days Mojisola begins to cry.

'Moji?'

'Why didn't you tell me? What was it?'

'Moji, I'm so sorry.'

Everyone has been sorry.

'Moji...'

'Tell me.'

'I'm telling you. She — she called me...I couldn't take the—'

'What number is this? I don't recognise it.'

'My new office number. I didn't tell you, I moved offices.'

'I'm not understanding, Titus. Why did she call you? That morning.'

'Please, Moji.'

'Why was she calling you that day? Titus, why did Yinka call you on that day?'

'I don't know...Moji, are you there? I...Can't you see I couldn't have known? I couldn't have known, Moji. Can't you see that? I couldn't have known.'

*

It arrives in the post. Now she has the whole thing.

Professor Titus Owolabi: Journal

The morning of her death Yinka phoned me.

Mojisola puts it down and goes to bed. When she comes back to it, she moves many pages forward. And she reads on in this way, skipping parts too raw to digest. She handles the thing like a landmine. Any page, any day now an explosion.

3

Professor Titus Owolabi: Journal

i

She's asked me to write a journal. The therapist. Thembi
Minyuku. Contact of John's. Didn't really intend on going
but then the appointment was made. Then decided I'd go but
not return, but now I've been 3 times. I feel a bit ambushed.
No one's forcing me though. John suggested it, I couldn't say
no, the way he framed it. John does that. The way he said
'work things through' and then mentioned Gita's Cancer so
I couldn't say anything in response. If he's referencing his
wife's Cancer well — it's all over. So I went thinking I knew
what to expect. Some stuffy personality telling me rubbish
(what exactly is psychotherapy after all?...made up stuff...
fiction?) Anyway point is Thembi was not what I'd imagined.
She's a small woman, the smudge on her left cheek which
when we shook hands looked like dirt turns out to be some
sort of birthmark. I keep forgetting though, each time I see
her my first thought is — the woman's face is dirty. Then I
remember she has a birthmark. Her hair, at least for the few
appointments so far, is always in a wrap. Her eyes are hard,
made even harder perhaps behind wire-framed spectacles.
I'd really imagined someone large-boned, easily flustered,
wearing comfortable Green Cross shoes, firmly past middle
age. Married. I'd certainly imagined her much older. She's
somewhere in her mid-to-late thirties I'd say. Too young I

thought, what qualifications could she possibly have to listen and cure me?

We did niceties first. Her accent is American — hadn't expected that. She explained that her family was from South Africa, but her parents divorced when she was young. She and her sisters grew up with her father in exile. They'd left in the seventies when she was still a baby. Before the riots she said making me think, where was I in the seventies. When children were being shot at in the streets. I would have been in Ibadan, a young academic trying to read Cabral and singing Sonny Okosun. Fire in Soweto. A burning all the people. I asked her what brought her back to the country, out of exile. Love she said. Which made me feel a little sick in my stomach. She asked what brought me there, to her upholstered wingback. Love, I said, not just clever but honest. She said a few things, I wasn't paying 100% attention at this point. But I heard her mention a journal. So here I am.

ii

Somehow despite my misgivings Thembi has won me over. Sometimes I think she's tricked me, that it cannot be the case that I'm going of my own free will. As if she has juju or something. If I believed in juju. Which I don't.

I haven't been writing here so regularly but I've certainly been going for the sessions. 50 minutes. Medicine I suppose. Talk-medicine. Who knew? I'm as surprised as the next. Me Titus Owolabi discussing my personal things with a perfect stranger. Some young woman barely off the breast. When I was walking into the session yesterday, I was actually looking forward to the conversation. Caught myself. My first reaction was to feel embarrassed, to check that she hadn't noticed how happy I was to be there. She was too busy settling her dog Roxy (Alsatian and superior, attends all our sessions) to notice me. I was relieved. Then I thought why do I enjoy the sessions so much. Would that mean that I was sick. That something was wrong with me. A weakness somewhere.

Driving home afterwards I think I got it — all my adult life I've applied as keen an intelligence as possible to certain kinds of data. The life of an academic. In my case the data involves wars, conquering, loss, pillage. It involves conflict and the impossibility of resolution, truces and false truces. In my career I have engaged with scholars from far afield, attended conferences and delivered papers in six of the seven continents, sat on panels with more than ten languages jostling for currency. But when I sit for 50 minutes with Thembi Minyuku, I'm struck by this simple fact: it is the first conversation I have ever had that involves turning the sharpness of my intellect inwards. It's the only time in my day, the only engagement in which I'm not trying (in fact there's nothing) to win.

iii

Interminably long faculty meeting. I'm here now pretending to take notes. I am taking notes. Just not to do with the meeting. John's sitting next to me so I've angled my notepad and besides my writing is fabulously illegible.

Moji not responding to my messages. Not picking up my calls.

The other day in session Thembi asked me to describe myself. What a bizarre thing to ask was my first response but she just nodded. She does that a lot, very disarming. I say something and she nods. And so I find myself saying more. It's deceptive of her really but perhaps for a good cause. She nods whether she agrees with me or not. She nods. And when I see her nodding more words want to come out of my mouth. They just come pouring out. Witchcraft.

Short. Handsome.

Not physically she said, can I describe myself in terms other than physical.

Intelligent.

Your temperament, she said.

Calm. Straightforward. Affable.

Perhaps I should ask the question differently, she said. How would your wife describe you? How would Yinka describe you?

Didn't really like her in that moment. Or myself. Which was maybe the point.

iv

Earliest memory, Thembi asked.

When I was about eight, I asked Sister Immaculata whether I'd been sick. I remembered a cast on my foot. I asked her about this. She said, many times, you were sick many times — repeating it like that.

When I meet people for the first time I try and tell if they've noticed my limp. Of course they've noticed my limp. My limp is noticeable and yet so much of my time is spent concealing it. I learnt to walk in a particular way that I believed disguised the limp. Walk properly, Sister Immaculata would say. Walk well, repeating it like that. She always said things twice. Twinning her admonitions as if discipline only works if it comes in twos.

I didn't need a brace. I never wore caliper shoes.

You were sick many times, Sister Immaculata said and I told her I remembered and she said no you would have been too young. Too young.

Nothing bothered me till primary school. Not my legs. Not Sister Immaculata, austere and white. Nothing struck as off-kilter. Not until primary school. The Sister had taught me at the kitchen table. Her idea of an education was numbers in French, Latin and English. Although when she became my guardian she'd been living in Nigeria for ten years already, her grasp of Yoruba, spoken in the regions she'd missioned, was poor. The little Yoruba I went to school with Kemi taught me. Kemi was the Sister's helper, hoeing yams at noon, blowing soil off the harvest when the time arrived. She cooked and cleaned and when Sister Immaculata got old, she tended to her, nursing, brushing, sponging. Burying.

It was Kemi who gave me passable Yoruba. And a few stories about Obatala which the Sister eventually forbade. From the Sister I learnt Greek history, which she regarded simply as an introduction to the birth of Jesus Christ. I learnt to recite the entire first book of the Old Testament, with particular emphasis on Adam and the transgressions of Eve.

I entered primary school.

Everything was fine until the children laughed.

I've studied war but there seems to me nothing quite as vicious as the mocking laughter of children.

v

I now have a de facto useful way to spend my time during faculty meetings.

Except then at the end of yesterday's meeting (I'd written my fourth entry and was reading back, admiring my writing and so on) John asks to have a copy of my notes. He says he was distracted during the meeting and missed a few key points but he noticed how diligently I'd been scribbling. All I could think was fuck.

vi

If someone looks a bit too long I think it's the scars even though that was so long ago. A few have a small keloid to them but mostly there's nothing to see. It's funny that although I know there's nothing to see still if someone looks—

I told her, Thembi, that the other children would chase me home, throwing rocks. They wanted to see how funny I looked when I ran.

vii

I remember being in agony. Physical agony. There had been a succession of operations, over several years, to fix my leg. I remember doctors, Auntie Kemi's prayers. And Sister Immaculata trying to distract me. Who's a boy? she'd ask. It was what she said whenever I started to cry: Are you a boy or a baby? And if this did not succeed in getting me to stop, if the crying continued, she'd scrunch her nose, which was how she showed displeasure and say, Look who's a baby. On the rare occasions when I (at four or eight or even ten) mastered my emotions then Sister Immaculata would smile, proud, and say, Look who's a boy. I remember once not being able to speak for a week because I had bitten my tongue raw trying not to cry out in pain.

viii

Sometimes I wonder if in Mojisola I didn't find something familiar. I said this during a session and Thembi asked me to explain. I loved her on sight. Instant. And yet I'm not sure I'm romantic enough to believe in love at first sight. I think instead she was deeply and profoundly familiar. Thembi didn't get it, she thought I meant our backgrounds were the same. I meant our emotional — not that I knew to call it that before I started therapy but that's what it is — our emotional…there's a word Thembi uses…code. Emotional code (can you imagine, kai!). Anyway, emotional code. What we live by I suppose. And then the word floated up, the way words seem to do when I'm sitting on the wingback barely a metre away from Thembi Minyuku. Suppression. It's as if I knew, on sight, that we would not be messy together. We would be emotionally neat. Neat emotions. We would have a clean marriage.

ix

Look who's a boy.

x

Dinner at John and Gita's. Initially didn't want to go but I thought maybe it's good. Besides didn't want another night of cornflakes. Ursula, that damn tarot card reader, was there. Luckily we sat apart. But she couldn't help herself and leaned, shouted over three others to ask about Moji. I could hear Gita clearing her throat, umming and aheming, trying to get Ursula's attention. Obviously no one had told her about Yinka. It's so unmentionable no one had even dared whisper it.

On the way out she comes at me again asking if I want another reading. The first time we'd met she'd made us pick cards, Moji and I. She was sat between us. She'd done the whole thing — bringing the deck to the dining table is apparently a thing of hers and you invite her to your dinner party for entertainment and intrigue. In the middle of dinner she pulls out two decks, says pick one to Moji. Does the same to me. What am I supposed to do, the woman is being a nuisance but decorum beckons. I pick. Moji picks. And we both picked the same card so Ursula screeches. Even worse once she realised we were married. She made this big thing about it. Texted a few times after that first meeting suggesting we do a proper reading, that she could help us. I still remember the cards we picked. A naked man and woman standing beneath an angel, the succulent hanging apple, the serpent. But the worst of it, the title of the cards, burnt a hole in my ear, so many years later I still hear Ursula calling it out — oh my, my my she'd shouted — Lovers Upside Down.

xi

I tell Moji I'm writing a journal and I can hear from her tone she thinks I'm ridiculous. Or stupid. Or both. She seems to think I'm lying somehow. That even in my journal I'm pretending. Which means she thinks I'm a fake, through and through.

xii

Got Moji on the phone and she was very sarcastic about this
whole thing. This journal thing. With her being snide I read
over it. The journal or whatever I'm supposed to call it. What
is it? Why is it? What am I doing here really? So I decided to
stop but obviously I haven't stopped because here I am writing
this now. I can't seem to stop. Who knew there was a journal
waiting inside me all this time, waiting to be written. That I'm
a journal sort. I mean I'm not a journal-sort. So what then.

I've written many things. Papers, my publications. My lectures
obviously. The other day when I was reading back over the
journal (can I say enjoying or does that make me an asshole
— enjoying my own journal) I was imagining delivering it at a
podium. I suppose that's wrong then.

I suppose Moji is right then.

The way Thembi said artifice. I almost didn't hear anything
else. Except I did hear when she reminded me about my
descriptions of myself. She wanted to know if the description
might change a little, how would you describe yourself now,
she asked. True, I couldn't think of any adjectives. I won't, I
said. Okay, she said. Not bad.

Been thinking a lot about how we met. Maybe looking for
where we went wrong — I don't know. Are the seeds of fate
sown right at the beginning, the way we shake a person's hand,
the way we stare.

      After bumping into her that first time at Amin I tracked
Moji to the library. She was reading a textbook. Geography.
I had come to flirt and I turned it on full-charge. I asked her
if her subject was difficult, was that why she was sweating so
much. She smiled — the thing filled her face. I tried to convince
her to take a break but she said no. So I said later and invited

her to a film — that was our first date. We went to Moola, watched an Indian film, the details of which were forgettable. At the end I asked to see her again — why not? She agreed. We said we'd go to Aminata.

Before Moji there had been others. I'm not saying many, I'm not saying few. Look, I wasn't the greatest of lovers. I fumbled. How was I supposed to know what to do with a woman's body, I barely knew what to do with my own. Nothing in Sister Immaculata's tutelage had taken copulation into consideration. In fact I don't think she'd ever so much as mentioned 'sex' to me. The word 'girls' was as far as she went to describe an entire world of pleasure and sin. Don't go out at night in the dark. Don't go with girls. Don't go with girls at night in the dark. And yet that's precisely what was required.

Initially the little I knew, believe it or not, I picked up from the good book itself. Bible passages such as: 'May her breasts satisfy you always'. I remember that one in particular. Soon after I came across it, I started having wet dreams. I was about 14. Confused. Sticky and damp in the dawn.

Second year I put away the Bible Sister Immaculata had given me and bought my own. With my new ideas I thought I needed a new book.

In the beginning, once I started being intimate with women, I thought God would send lightning down on me. Hard to fathom but it is true. Eventually those fears fell away. Before that though I thought the best way to protect myself was to consult only the Bible in preparation. Surely if I took sex-advice from the good book it couldn't be a sin? 'Let us go to the vineyards to see if the vines have budded, if their blossoms have opened and if their pomegranates are in bloom...' Song of Solomon. This piece of advice would prove eternally helpful: never have I sought to enter a woman's vineyard before it was clear that her pomegranates were in bloom.

xiii

Sex was finally somewhere to put everything.

xiv

Sometimes I do wonder what a life in the seminary would
have been like. Not wistfully but I wonder to myself if Father
Titus would have had an easier life, more peaceful. No real
discussion but I guess once I hit high school the Sister saw
there was no use in continuing with her ambitions. What did
she see? I can't recall this, I can't recall a specific day when she
stopped pushing me towards that end. But surely there would
have been a moment for her where she saw I was not that.
I was bright enough so it must have been something lacking
in my character. By UI days I'd lost that church-boy Sister
Immaculata had worked so hard to raise. Not lost really, like
a set of housekeys. Rather I set him aside, like a key that no
longer worked, was rusted, or opened a room I no longer
needed to enter. I simply wanted to go elsewhere. I wanted
to taste things that were neither just sweet nor sour; I wanted
to feel the dampness of the most hidden skin, those bits of the
flesh that seldom see daylight; I wanted that dawn feeling, wet
and heavy, again. And again. I learnt quickly, watching the
older boys, I learnt how to want and, mostly importantly, how
to get. When I met Moji I was ready to put into motion what
had been gathering for years. And yet all that preparation to
nought — things between us stalled.

    We had been seeing each other regularly — the cinema or
at Amin — but something about her prohibited intimacy. We
didn't return to Moola but I took her to Obisesan, tried plain
old English-language films, not that that made a difference. I
suggested we go for a walk, determined to take her hand once
we were on the path only to find my hands empty, hers too.
We would spend a night dancing in Amin and, while walking
her back, I would be certain as to the task at hand — take her
in my arms and kiss her — only to find myself waving as she

walked off past the porter's lodge into the dorms, unkissed. I had many pictures of the thing. To touch her neck. To put my hand on the side of her face, caress her ear. After some weeks, when none of this transpired, I thought perhaps I was setting my sights higher than was possible for the time. I resorted to giving compliments, imagining that I could start casual-like (your hair is nice like that) and skilfully edge into more intimate terrain (your eyes are beautiful, I like your lips, your hands are soft, can I hold you?).

In between our times together I felt a sharp sense of rejection. I was failing at something fundamental. Despite having become popular my time as a young boy and teenager returned, a time of misfit and social agony. I often couldn't hold Moji's gaze for fear she could see my undesirability, my scars, my hideous walk. I felt self-conscious about my height. Perhaps she found me gross. But, no, she seemed to like me. She must do. She kept agreeing to meet again. Then I thought maybe she was cruel and laughing at me behind my back with her girlfriends. But that didn't seem right either. Eventually I worked out that we were simply stuck, suspended in a cordial interaction that was doomed to stay so if I didn't act. I couldn't discuss it with my friends. They would laugh. It was then I did something I hadn't done in a while. I obeyed Sister Immaculata and opened the good book. There's a lot of kissing in the Bible, mostly between men. Very little of it instructional. Then again mostly people came to the Bible for help with their soul, not their inability to get laid. Except at that time in my life the two seemed caught up, one and the same thing. I was simultaneously miserable and enraptured. Mojisola wasn't like anyone I'd previously encountered, male or female. Her body, the way she moved and spoke, seemed to be imbued with the certainty of life's dangers, ruled by caution, governed in hesitations. She was filled with a concrete silence, which isn't to say that we didn't engage in conversation during our meetings, even robust ones, but rather that, whether speaking or not, there remained a sense of quiet about her, as if her very centre was dead. Not as in old and rotten. Dead as in the condition before life, not after. And then right on cue her smile would spring forth from that deathly core: this remarkable joy would fill her face and scatter my mind.

xv

Moji not answering again. I texted. But nothing still.

The night we first kissed we'd been to Amin. On previous nights I'd been trying to get her — not drunk, I'm not that person. But loose. Open her a bit. She always declined my offer of beer. This night she asked about my parents, that kind of thing. She'd wanted to know if I remembered them. I'd said my first memory was of waking up in hospital. Born in crutches, I'd said which became something between us when gentle soft things still grew in the space two people can cultivate. But that night I felt determined. Not in my usual gra-gra way. A very light certainty, maybe some kind of wisdom that the reason nothing was working was because I'd been trying too hard. And maybe what I needed to do was not try. I gave up on the beer and asked her to dance. Many lovers have danced in Amin. Some famously dance sitting down, enveloped in each other's arms, necking, vibrating. But Mojisola and I were not lovers. Boyfriends have been known to come upon their beloved with another and vice versa but we had no others. We danced shy, exposed as if naked to Fate, to the ways in which life will consume and ruin us, for what is it to have really lived but to be ruined, to die spoilt and finished?

xvi

Moji not picking up. I should just fly there.

We've been discussing human frailty, Thembi and I. I brought it up. I didn't call it human frailty though. I asked Thembi what she thought of all this, my recollections, my childhood. She didn't give a straight answer but instead said there seems to be something recurring about "weakness" and "frailty".

xvii

Some people call it cheating. For me I had simply found, on arriving in SA to the Chair, all the fuss, the prestige — I found that I needed somewhere to explode into, a place to drip-dry, somewhere to put everything that was building up all the time. And so there were women. Not students, I'm happy to say, since it was often on offer. I took my erections and emptied them into women who were not my students. There was a lot of sex: now in my maturity I can concede that it was mostly bad. But the flurry of it, the fact that it occurred in small spaces (once on Beach Road in the back of a car), all the drama that surrounded the actual lovemaking gave the immediate impression of hotness, of something bursting, urgent and magnificent. Often, I bruised an elbow. The women complained, a sore neck from straining too hard, an embedded ache in the rib cage. Sometimes they complained I'd gone too hard and that their insides were bruised. We were always rushing, with the sea just there, standing witness. I was married. Often the women were married. They were white and married to poets. They were black and poets themselves, starving. Or satiated and married to bankers, bankers themselves. They were everything, every kind of body, so large was my appetite. Some were older than me, one by a decade. 'You're not very good at this,' she'd said, and we never repeated the event. Younger girls were preferable. They never said: 'You're not very good at this.' There was Lakshmi and Nobantu and Ursula. There was Mary-Ann. There was Teresa, Agnes and Nolayi. Some were the wives of people I'd met, people I knew, some were strangers. Some were just the one time and never see them again; others made appointments. I made time, I found the time. As if the reason I lived, the batteries for my heart, were to be found in all those vulvas, the mouths, the bushes of hair.

At the time I'd decided that Moji did not know. I took risks, perhaps deliberately (the thief that wishes to be caught) but always she presented me with a face of stone.

xviii

Moji was attacked at Yinka's place. Attacked.

Can't write anything. She was attacked

xix

The thought of Moji dying. My daughter is already dead and then my wife dies. The thought of that.

xx

Human frailty. There was a period of time in Nigeria when Moji was ill. The doctor said terminal, she was on a ventilator, often under sedation for days. Every night she was in hospital I dreamt that I was lying in bed with my wife. The dream started with an awareness of her presence in the bed with me, the feeling of being accompanied. And then a slow achy swelling, not only in the Y of my underpants but a full unfamiliar experience of my entire body being weighed down by desire. As if someone had taken a smooth flat piece of cool slate and laid it on top of me, gently so it balanced and pressed down, inflicting no pain, just a pleasant encumbrance. I wanted so much, in the dream, to reach for her but the desire was a hand pressing me down into the mattress making me shiver. In another dream I managed to reach her. Soon we are fitted together, in rhythm when, as I move inside her, I remember that she is dying, and I wait for my erection to fall but instead I grow bigger. In yet another dream she is dying and far away and I phone and ask her to come home and she says no, she's buying things and I should send money but please leave her alone. In all the dreams she is dying. In the most devastating, the one from which I would wake up as if from a fever, she is something I cannot remember. All through the dream I know there's something I've forgotten. Then finally when I see her I ask, 'What are you? Please remind me what you are.' And then she says, 'I am dying.'

After her illness nothing was the same, as if she went to hospital and never came home. When we got married we'd made such reckless love. But after Mojisola's brush with death the sex slowed, still sensual but laggard, followed by the earnest nervous kind, then careful love and, after mechanical, none at all.

xxi

The thought of Moji dying. I've decided I need to tell her. What's the point of not telling. How did that help Yinka. Will she hate me, possibly. But I'm tired. Describe yourself says Thembi. Tired, I say. Alright, she says. Okay.

Moji calls. She is having a memorial for Yinka, trying to catch someone out. She's acting as if we're a detective story. I suppose we are a detective story.

I need to tell her.

I've decided to surprise her. To arrive unexpected.

xxii

I hate airports. There I've said it. I hate especially, Arrivals, that section. People waiting, expectant. The theatre of reunions. I hate the smell of other people's expectations. I hate the young adults smelling of sex that is to say smelling of youth. I see Yinka in all their faces, male and female.

Yinka.

I cannot think about her. I must not. I cannot write about her.

xxiii

Moji remains beautiful. Hers is sensed rather than seen. A beauty that emanates from within her skin rather than sitting on her face. Her limbs. The heavy way in which she walks as if she's three times her weight. The way her eyes are cool. She doesn't mention the affair (or does she know there were many? Plural.) and without much fuss puts me in the guest room. Fine.

xxiv

I gave her a few of the journal pages. The beginning bits. I'll post the rest. I guess this isn't really a journal after all then. I guess it's a letter? When I imagine reading it I'm no longer at a podium. I'm on my knees. I'm reading to Moji.

I hate Joburg.

Found journal in bin. That's what she thinks of me. The damn bin.

During those early years in South Africa, all the spirited fucking around, I'd felt myself grow big. Not in a metaphysical sense but actually. I would be approaching a doorway and have the intuition to duck. As I neared it, I would slow my pace and worry the door jambs might brush my sides.

After Yinka's death and Moji's departure I'd looked in the mirror again and seen someone puny.

These days when I arrive home especially after a session of therapy I look in the mirror, notice with surprise that I look like myself, just my size, neither bigger nor smaller than I'd ever imagined.

xxv

divorce

xxvi

Out of the blue Thembi asks — how long have you been depressed? Just like that. I told her I'm not. Sad? she said and the simpler word somehow made it easier. As long as I can remember I said.

After the funeral, and after Mojisola left I asked my psychiatrist to up the dosage. Instead the doctor suggested I see someone, that more medication was not going to help. John had given a name, the same one he'd offered Moji. That was Thembi Minyuku.

Sadness.

I never took notice. I thought that was just how things were. Or that something was wrong with me but I simply had to bear it. I didn't think it had a name. Depressed. Not till it got bad. When we came here, to South Africa. When I really wasn't coping. Then Dr Naidoo prescribed pills and we managed it. Why the secrecy? Thembi asks, her belly slightly swollen although she hasn't told me anything yet.

Why the secrecy.

xxvii

Where do you put sadness.

It doesn't fold.

A few months into Yinka's life Moji started crying at night. The first few times it happened I tried holding her but that didn't work. One night she asked me to call Auntie Modupe who was one door down in the guest room. Auntie Modupe, as far as I could make out, was always awake when I opened the door to the guest room. What else would explain the way she sprang out of bed on hearing the words, like a Jack-in-the-Box. An Auntie-Modupe-in-the-Box. Definitely if someone was to be in the box, someone reliable, you'd want Auntie Modupe. She was always ready, it seemed, perhaps even waiting. Either she never slept at all, I thought, or slept little and lightly. Then she'd come to my wife, her niece, and hold her. Cradle her. And I'd leave, go to the guest bed and sleep till dawn. The next day, home from work and frightened of the approaching night I suggested to Auntie Modupe, avoiding looking into her eyes as I did so, that she sleep in our room for a while, that I take the guest bed. She didn't object. Yinka was three months old; we would keep that arrangement for the next six months.

Did I give in too easily? I sometimes wondered, afterwards, if Moji resented my absence, my emotional incapacity. But it was self-preservation. The depths of her grief which I witnessed for a few nights and never again, scared me to my core. The Moji I had married, with that tacit unspoken agreement to exclude the mess, had disappeared. In her place was a woman wrought with feeling, overcome, too much feeling to give coherent expression. Raw. I left her in the capable hands of Auntie Modupe. In place of being an emotional support I took on more housework. We could easily have afforded a house-help, we could have afforded three, but Mojisola vetoed it: she didn't want anyone, even a helper, to see her in such a condition. She could barely withstand my own gaze, which, even when innocent, even when admiring (she was, despite everything, still beautiful to me), was met with challenge.

I found myself scrubbing toilets; the bleach made the skin around my cuticles grey and wrinkly; I found that I cared; I discovered shea butter. I made one meal and Auntie Modupe forbade me from ever attempting it again, saying 'you'll just kill everybody'. She really did consider my cooking bad enough to do harm.

Although we spent many hours of the day in each other's company (Mojisola often retired to bed earlier than us), Auntie Modupe and I never spoke about what was happening. I didn't know what she was thinking but from my side I felt to mention it would be to create it for real. And to create it would be to present myself with a problem. The problem of having a sad wife, a sad mother. During the day I went about my work: I taught, I supervised, I was collegial, I wrote and marked, sat in meetings and panels. No one must know, I thought. Look who's a boy.

After several weeks I began to wonder. Having moved out of my bedroom (to make way for Auntie Modupe's ministrations) I had no way of knowing whether my wife still cried at night. I couldn't ask Auntie Modupe at breakfast because we had no language for what was going on. When I greeted Mojisola and the baby before going to work I could not tell, just from looking, what the night had brought with it. I began to hope that Auntie Modupe, Empress of All Things Big and Small, would volunteer, would update me somehow as to Mojisola's condition but she never did. The closest I came to raising it was when I came home from the university one day and asked, 'Shouldn't we get a diagnosis or something?' but she shook her head, she didn't seem to think that there was anything going on that required diagnosis. I left it.

When the whole thing finally ended it seemed as if it was always going to end and any anxiety on my part had been foolish. But that came only with the clarity of hindsight. While Moji was afflicted, the condition — night after night — had seemed interminable. I always came back to the actual truth of the matter: Mojisola was remarkably sad and Auntie Modupe was somehow the person required to care for her.

I see it now. That's what we are. People with nowhere to put the sadness. We try, everyone, we try stuff it away. And sadness doesn't really fold.

xxviii

I sometimes think we are soldiers, Moji and I. We are some kind of love-soldiers (Lovers Upside Down) battling it out on a large invisible field whose coordinates stretch to lives before us and will continue into lives that haven't yet been lived. What are we fighting. Not only each other but love itself, wrestling, attempting to shape the shapeless, to dominate water or air. Fighting what does not fight back, fighting ourselves.

I wanted love so badly. I remember seeing Moji, most definitely the minute I saw her, and thinking, that's it, that's what it needs to look like. If I could just get her in place — like a chess piece finally on the right square — then the picture is complete. That's it, I thought. And we've been wrestling ever since.

xxix

I once got a long rope. I was going to kill myself. Young me. Sister Immaculata found me. She took the rope and beat me with it. I still remember she wouldn't stop beating me. She wanted to see me cry. Twelve or so. After years of teaching me not to cry, to be brave, be a boy not a baby, she just kept on beating me, trying to get me to cry.

xxx

When Yinka left and cut off communication something hardened inside me. Congealed. Moji occasionally got her on the phone but Yinka refused to speak with me. I felt dirty and furious.

I remember getting the call from the police at Seapoint. We have your wife. When I saw her face I didn't need any further explanation. It was there, plain on her face — Yinka was dead. I don't know how else to say it, her child was dead — there it was all over my wife's face.

I asked Thembi if Yinka was dead because of me. She didn't answer. I suppose she wouldn't be a good therapist if she had an answer for that. Did my secret kill her? Worse was it hereditary? Did Yinka inherit my sadness?

I told Thembi I would live with that (that question-answer) on me, like a mass. When she asked me to explain further I told her about Hornbill.

Hornbill lived in the village with all the other animals, but he would not conform. He refused to follow the rituals of the village — particularly the death rituals. When a member of the community died Hornbill refused to join a funeral procession and, to the great annoyance of his fellow animals, he would not acknowledge the separate place for the dead, apart from the living. Some villagers ignored Hornbill, spat at him, others pleaded but no matter the treatment, Hornbill refused to comply. One day his own child died. No one came to partake in any rituals with Hornbill, to prepare the body, to carry it in procession to the place for the dead. At the death of his own child, Hornbill was unable to observe the customs of his kind, simply put, he did not know them. Desperate, Hornbill wrapped the body of his child in the best way he knew how and, carrying the weight on his head, went wandering in search of the burial site. But he could not find the place and anyone he asked said, 'I do not know.' Hornbill walked and walked and walked. Days passed and no one would tell him. 'I do not know,' they said. 'I do not know.' Eventually the corpse of his child began to decompose. So that's the hornbill. With its dead. Buried on its head.

The morning of her death Yinka phoned me at the office. H took the call and came to tell me who it was. Yinka had been the only person brave enough, once she found out about my affairs, to condemn my behaviour. Even Moji, it turns out, looked the other way. But Yinka looked me right in the eye and said you're a wrong-doer, a fake. She didn't use those words, typical Yinka, respectful even as she cut me down to size. She condemned me then disappeared to Jo'burg, disowning us both. I had stewed in that time. I resented my own child, I resented her integrity. By the time her call came in that morning I was ripe for some kind of pay-back. I told H to tell her I was in a meeting and that I would call her back. Apparently when H delivered the message an argument erupted. Yinka, realising the woman was my lover, shouted at her and also she begged her to put me on the phone. Like a fool. Like a fool I said no. I said no.

4

Lovers Upside-Down

One evening at Aminata, to steel herself, Mojisola declined the soft drink and requested a beer.

'Is the Queen visiting?' Titus asked, indicating her gloved left hand.

Amin attracted enough eccentrics that Mojisola had hoped her glove-wearing would go unremarked but, she supposed, while in the company of eccentrics she did not quite pass as one herself. The gloves on her were conspicuous.

'It's nothing,' she said, and before she could repeat her request for alcohol, Titus reached to touch the gloved hand.

'Style?' He was curious in a way she couldn't brush off.

In the week a rash — the same from her childhood — had flared up. This was not unusual, it happened on and off.

'I'm really a lefty,' Mojisola said, looking Titus in the eye.

Despite all the darkness Amin was not really a place for confessions. Both shifted in their seats.

'I was a lefty,' Mojisola dropped a voice. 'But my mother showed me how to write with my right hand so...I'm no longer a lefty.'

Titus cleared his throat into the silence. She could see she had made him uncomfortable.

'Lace àbí?' he asked.

'Yes.'

'It suits you.' He smiled, then drummed the table. 'Óyá come, let me buy you your beer.'

Mojisola brought the open beer bottle up to her chin, picking up the scent. She held it like that for a beat.

'Cold enough?'

She nodded, putting the bottle back on the table without having taken a sip. The evening carried on; she was distracted, remembering a week ago when, after a stroll, Titus had walked her back to her dorm. Already she'd been thinking that something was wrong between them: she knew something more ought to be happening. But she was a young 21, had entertained no suitors before Titus and was too shy to ask for guidance from any of her girlfriends. That night, after the walk, he'd shaken her hand as usual. She'd said what a lovely time she'd had. He too. She'd turned and was walking through the gate by the porter's lodge when she had an alarming thought. She realised that he'd applied a special pressure to his handshake. Almost imperceptible, a quietly urgent pulse that hadn't been there before. It put her on guard for something, she wasn't sure what. The next time they went out, there it was. And walking away she couldn't hide from the fact that she was the problem. She was somehow disallowing things. Not in words but in action, ruffling when the conversation died, troubling the kind of silence a kiss could grow up in; coughing and mumbling — disturbing the delicate fibres intimacy needs for weaving. She'd driven the poor guy to start sending smoke signals in the form of pressured handshakes. Well, tonight was the night.

'You haven't touched your beer,' Titus said, as the man began to sing.

Mojisola scooped up the bottle and plugged her lips to the mouth. Beer is sour, she thought. Outside Queen's Hall, Titus leaned in and she held still, waited. She didn't think to part her lips. And she felt it was beautiful enough (soft, wet even) without the addition of their tongues.

*

Once she is finished with the two journals she puts them away. She has a picture of something, her and Titus fumbling as parents, confusing their daughter somehow, trapping her. And yet there are pieces in Yinka's journal that seem triumphant. She knew more than they did, didn't she? She understood what perhaps they are only just learning. That if you attempt to clean the messiness of life you end up scrubbing the life away from living. We can't excise joy from pain. We can't draw, Mojisola, without fainting occasionally, without slipping and falling to the floor; because we don't stop looking in an attempt to avoid going blind.

And so Mojisola Owolabi cries for real. She cries until her ears pop and the muscles in her face ache. She cries, and the snot that comes out from her nose gets in her eyes when she wipes them, makes them sting. She cries and beats her chest because she is the criminal in this crime story and it seems so unfair to the dead girl that she, the criminal, is also the investigator. How incompetent a world that chooses her. How can such unfairness roam unchecked? How is the world designed this way? She cries and wishes she never set eyes on Titus, never conceded to his ardent attentions. All the better to have lived a barren life, free of complication and struggle and agony. And yet Mojisola cannot bear to cut out Yinka. Cannot bear to pray for a world where such a being had never existed, even if to spare herself from a pain so deeply embedded in her body she would need to be minced — put in a grinder — to be relieved of it. She cries until her eyes swell up. She punches a wall and the skin on her knuckles break.

Later Mojisola goes to the kitchen cupboard and takes the orange-handled knife. She starts stabbing the air and jamming the knife into the cupboard doors. She finds a hammer and bangs away on the knife for almost a minute. When she realises her rage is not useful, she calms down. She finds a star screwdriver. Carefully, meticulously, she takes the knife apart. She kills the knife. The blade once removed from the handle looks pure evil. She gets the blowtorch. Slowly, on the granite counter, she melts the blade to a molten mass of metal. She then applies the torch to the plastic orange handle. She has to stop and open a window. In the end, she wraps the carcass in some newspaper.

She carries the parcel around in her bag. On the day she leaves Johannesburg, without the means to send it into outer space, she will dump the whole mess into a bin at the airport.

Mojisola lies back in bed and closes her eyes. Quite suddenly a flood of pictures comes through like a videotape with no sound. Pictures from the last few months, snapshots, little puzzle pieces. She falls asleep, her clothes on, her teeth unbrushed. She dreams she is a giant and Yinka the size of a ladybird. 'Pick me up,' Yinka keeps saying. 'Mummy, pick me up.' But the child is so small and Mojisola so big, she tries to pick her up but her fingers are too fat and really it seems she might crush her.

In that way that you can only know what something is after you have lived it, when Mojisola wakes she thinks she understands what she came to do at Cove Crescent. To collect her child, to root her out of her hiding place. In the process, she has collected herself. It is a strange feeling to know Yinka in death so much closer than she knew her in life. Stranger still to know she had to lose her daughter in order to find herself.

'I've seen my parents,' writes Yinka in her journal. 'I've seen Moji and Titus.' She doesn't write any more on this, yet Mojisola can read, just as clearly, all the things that are unwritten. She thinks of the drawings from D-Man. Titus with no ears and a mouth larger than science could explain. And her with her two eyes but restricted to one side of her face. Yes, Yinka had seen them. And yet in so many ways, she had not. In the same way, up until her death Mojisola's mother, the woman who'd raised her, had remained inscrutable, profoundly unavailable.

*

Mojisola knocks on Zelda's door. She's packed. This is now the last thing to be done. When Zelda cracks open the door, her face hard and closed, it is difficult for Mojisola to imagine her any different. And yet they'd smoked weed together, they'd sipped Rooibos tea in the kitchen and laughed, Zelda had masterminded her daughter's memorial and they'd buried a cat.

'Mojisola, I'm just busy do—'

'Let me in, Zelda. For God's sake, let me in. I cried!'

'What do you mean you cried?'

'You told me I had to cry? Well, I've finally cried. And now I'm going home. Stop being so pig-headed and let me in so I can say goodbye properly.'

Mojisola's fury has come as if from nowhere. She hadn't realised how upset she's been by Zelda's behaviour. The truth is she is more sad than angry. Zelda is the closest thing she has had to a best friend since varsity days.

'You're an idiot, Zelda! Cooped up in this house, wearing black. Visiting funerals. You're supposed to tend the living, not the dead! Open the damn door.'

Zelda seems at a loss in the face of Mojisola's torrent. She steps back and Mojisola, instantly calm after her outburst, walks past into the living room.

'When's your birthday? I'm going to buy you a couch.'

'You have no money.'

'With the first cheque from my divorce settlement I am going to buy you a couch, Zelda. And they'll deliver it. And you'll need to ask Percy to help you set it up.'

At the mention of the name, something flashes in Zelda's face.

'Why do you hate him so much?' asks Mojisola, flummoxed.

'I don't hate him,' says Zelda. 'I don't hate him at all.'

Mojisola does not pry. They sit and talk, and the weeks of distance fall away. She doesn't quite confess her darkest secrets to Zelda but hints at the world she has, ever so briefly, glimpsed. They have a hearty goodbye, both women dabbing the corners of their eyes, pleading eye infection and pollen allergies when the truth is simpler. They wonder when they will see each other again. In fact, the friendship will continue even though they are cities apart. For years to come they will write to each other in longhand, defiantly eschewing email and other technological advances in a world dispassionately overtaking them.

Somehow the conversation turns a corner and Mojisola is talking slowly and deliberately.

'Titus and I took a while but then we got used to each other's bodies. He claimed to be this great Casanova. Well, I've never been with any other man so I cannot really know what I might have been missing but...in the early days he seemed as much at a loss as I was — a virgin. Still, we worked at it. Not with books or anything as avant-garde as that. But we...I suppose we loved each other and wanted this to be something fun so...we put effort into it and...we got good. I learnt to...to orgasm. What I mean is I experienced immense pleasure, deep within and all around me. As if my pleasure could somehow change the molecules of air around my physical body. And we enjoyed that for a time. When Yinka was born we took a while to love again. I had a lot of pain and I struggled with depression. But we came back together eventually. My aunt...well my...let's call her my aunt, helped me and Titus and I came back. The first time we made love, after the birth, I knew immediately. Of course it's not the child's fault. It's just we'd lost something. Something slippery that you can lose in the dark. You can lose it very quickly in the dark and you wouldn't even know it. You'll carry on thinking you're managing. And you know, Zelda, you think, *I'll pick up that thread in a moment. In a moment when there's some light again, when I have time, when I remember. I'll pick up that thread and we'll be fine again, we'll love again.* You think all that but it never happens. At least not until it's just about too late. Then maybe, if you're lucky, it happens then...but...you can just lose things, is what I'm saying. You can just lose an entire thread and be gone...you can forget what it is you ought to hold onto, what you ought to let go. Watching you is like watching myself Zelda. Listen to me — I can help.'

They hug at the door. After almost a minute Zelda tries to pull away but Mojisola holds on tighter. She thinks of Titus's description of them as love-soldiers, wrestling, even their lovemaking a form of wrestle. She thinks of Zelda and D-Man. Even Yinka. We're all love-soldiers — life's unwavering assignment.

*

When Titus invites Mojisola for a session with his psychologist, she is not surprised. It has been some weeks now since he gave her the news about what he calls his sickness; he'd mentioned the pills he'd been taking for such a large portion of their marriage and Mojisola had been filled with a now familiar sense of shame and failure.

'So...will you? I...I...'

'Yes, yes, I'll come.'

Once settled in the straight-backed chair (Titus takes the couch), Mojisola perceives a bulge in the woman's waistband and can think of little else but the pregnancy during the entire session. She feels overcome; unaccustomed to outpourings, Mojisola holds back, giving one-word answers wherever possible and stiff responses where more words are necessary. Eventually Titus is doing most of the talking. She listens to bits, distracted by thoughts and the companionable pulsing of her feelings. It is true there's a different tone to his voice. Halting. Maybe softer. She sees there is something improved in him. She worries for several minutes (Titus's lips are moving but she isn't paying attention) that perhaps she is jealous. Is she jealous?

Minyuku asks if she has anything to say in response. She has nothing to say: she was not listening sufficiently to be able to respond with any intelligence, and although this is meant to be a room for truth, Mojisola is unable to confess that she hasn't been paying attention. Titus and the Minyuku woman look at her (can they tell?) and she feels for a moment that they are a team and she is on the other side of the net: who exactly has won this match? As the session closes Mojisola declines to join the group therapy and is happy to leave when the 50 minutes are over. She shakes Thembi Minyuku's hand, thinking she'd be too young to smoke weed in Zelda Petersen's universe. Titus follows her out, sees her busy with her phone calling a taxi.

'Let me give you a lift.'

Mojisola is hesitant. Really, she doesn't wish to be in a car with him, such a small space, contained for a period, alone.

'Come on, Moji. Come, I'll give you a lift.'

A fury is suddenly in her throat but it is gone as quickly as it emerged. Titus, none the wiser, smiles. He jerks his head to indicate where he has parked.

'Please, Moji,' he says, and because she has no recollection of him asking her anything with such tenderness, she goes to the car.

They drive towards Table Mountain, distant and straight.

'Why have we lived such a life, Titus? Why have we been so useless at the truth?' So confused, so back to front.

She hears him breathe in sharply, but doesn't hear him exhale. They do not say anything else for the duration of the journey. When they enter Rondebosch, Mojisola gives him directions. She doesn't care that he will now know her address. He parks outside the block and releases his seatbelt. She cracks open the car door.

'You're right,' says Titus.

'What?'

Suddenly he is quick on his feet and around to her side of the car before she has swung out her legs.

'You're right,' he says, holding the car door open. 'We have been useless at the truth.'

Mojisola closes her eyes, when she opens them she sees that Titus is half a person and she decides, only there, to restore him. They walk together into the block and up the interminably long flight of steps. Mojisola opens the door and they enter her flat. The floor is parquet, the sun fits through a window. Mouse comes to greet Titus by swirling around his left leg.

'Hey,' says Titus.

Yinka's drawings are spread along a wall, small, framed and blazing. Titus spends several minutes staring at them. He doesn't say a word.

Mojisola leads him to the couch and they sit beside each other with their hips pressing. As if understanding the need for no witnesses, Mouse promptly disappears. Titus puts his arm around Mojisola and she senses the shape of a person and what she has missed. She feels his shape grow heavier, his hand come deeper around, move up and down in a caress. She dips her head, angles it, nestles beneath his chin, takes in his smell. He rubs her shoulder. And, perhaps because the lights are low, neither of them startles when they begin to kiss. They reach for each other. He kisses the back of her left hand — the latest bout of rash has healed, the mottled skin only a little tender. She too looks for him. She looks for the bump of nipples, skin both rough and soft. There is more of him than she remembers. She looks for the strawness of damp hair, each separate strand. She wants certain sounds as from a memory box with a wind-up screw.

Afterwards, they spend several minutes catching their breath. She thinks she hears him wheezing but doesn't want to draw attention to it. She is shy for a few seconds, but it passes like a breeze, a carefree thing moving about regardless of bad news and hopelessness and failure.

'What's it like?' Mojisola asks, allowing him the few seconds to fully understand what she's asking. When Titus had mentioned his depression, she'd heard it clearly in her head, Yinka's voice: sad all the time.

'It's...long.'

She nods, encouraging.

'We eventually found; my psychiatrist and I, a combination that worked but while we were still trying to get it right...or when, let's say, I don't take the medicines...everything just becomes...very very long.'

'What do you mean?' But she's thinking; sleeping, not dreaming.

'Endless and with no reprieve. Final. Unbearable.'

She's quiet for a while, contemplating being possessed by this sort of monster. Titus is staring at her. She can feel his eyes on her skin, but she isn't interested, just then, in meeting his gaze. Maybe she is enjoying the pressure. It does feel lovely. He has not looked at her this way, if ever, in a really long time.

'I wish I'd met your mother,' he says. It surprises her. 'I'm sorry about the way I've scattered our lives.'

'Shhh,' she says, because she can hear that he might cry. And then, 'You did meet her.'

'I don't understand.'

'You met my mother.' She wonders if she'll have to tell him clearly, spell it out word for word. She watches, in the small light, his face change shape, and only when she's certain he's fully understood does she continue. 'We only spoke about it once, just before she died, she told me. But it's funny, just now I suddenly understood something else she'd told me way before, that time soon after Yinka was born? When...when I wasn't well. Those months were so hot, so heavy with my grief. One night when she came to lie with me, I begged her to explain why the pain was so sharp. What was this thing? And she said, "You're crying because you miss me." I said, "But you're right here, Auntie." And she said, "No, you're crying because you miss me from before."'

'My God.'

'I hadn't really understood, and I guess was just too distracted by my own sorrow to ask my crazy Aunt to explain herself. But it all made sense later.'

Titus nods.

After a while she whispers, 'Let's lie down.' And, because he lags, she realises he might not understand this as, 'Come into my bed.' To clarify things she stands up and tugs at his arm.

A bigger canvas. With more room, she enjoys the second time better. She wonders if he'd needed the first round to remember her, to rediscover, and now there is room for playfulness, the desire to go in search of those little soup bowls of pleasure. She even thinks she is young. Thinks they are making a person, this time consciously and in earnest. As if they both know (secretly) that sex is not only for pleasure and sowing seed but can make a grown child reappear, whole and happy. They make love to each other's portraits. Those delicate lines, those places on a face that make life a mystery. They are not foolish. At one point, Mojisola gets up to draw the curtains. They know morning will bring light, and light will bring vision, and vision will bring something they can't quite tell, so they want to do this first and fully before uncertainty takes hold and cautions them. It feels good, like a sip of something ice-cold on a scorching day, the caress of something soft and giving when life has always negotiated.

In the dark morning before the sun comes to accuse, Titus lets himself out. Mojisola stays lying flat on her back. She imagines her daughter dialling a number she had probably memorised even though she'd also written it out clearly on the back page of one of her journals. That seems like Yinka. Her memory had always been sharp, yet simply to remember the number must have felt insufficient. She'd written it out, clearly. Unaware — how could she have been? — that there would be a day when her grieving mother would come across it, dial and unravel the mysteries. She would have memorised the number when she still hoped, believed things could be repaired, believed no one needed to be sad all the time. Even as she packed for Jo'burg. She'd memorised the number, but what for? Did she mean to appeal to Titus to stop the affair? That didn't seem right. After all, on discovering the affair, Yinka had called her, held her to account for tolerating something she found intolerable. No the act, memorising the number, filing it away, had nothing to do with Titus's affair. Rather it seemed to Mojisola that it was an act of preservation. Yinka was, by her own admission, sad all the time. The number in her head, her father's office number, must have simply formed one of many lines she may one day need to use to tie herself down, firm and safe. And although she'd rebuffed her father's calls over the months, in a final moment Yinka had dialled that number. In that same moment, informed of his daughter on the line, Titus had chosen not to answer. Pride. Hurt. *Same thing, really,* thinks Mojisola. She knows that now. Pride is all the flesh you've grown, by necessity, around the bones of your pain.

And then what? thinks Mojisola, still lying in the dark. Determined for the first time to go all the way, to complete every piece of the puzzle. Mouse climbs onto the bed and she strokes him for a few seconds but then, as if her caresses are only pleasurable for a short time, he moves off again, searching for the next thing.

Yinka had lived a mostly quiet life. Lived what would be her last months, last days at Cove Crescent. She went into work at Art-T, under what appeared to be the kind gaze of her boss Egizia Giannone. Mojisola has continued to work for the company, grateful for the money, modest but adequate, grateful for this late break into a career as illustrator, something she could never have imagined for herself. Something she sometimes feels her daughter handed to her, something she took from her daughter's hands — all the stories bunch up and she is afraid to look too closely to see which is true, which is the truest.

When Mojisola was still in Midrand she'd occasionally drive through to Art-T for meetings with Egizia, to discuss a brief, to show her a concept. A few times she'd sit at an empty desk. No one was brave (or foolish) enough to tell her it had been Yinka's, and neither was she foolish (or brave) enough to ask. She assumed it was, though, and she'd sat and worked, looking up occasionally, searching for a clue to confirm her suspicions, opening drawers, hoping to find more pieces of her daughter left behind. Yinka had sat in that chair, sketching, answering emails. And then she'd driven home in the car Mojisola had become familiar with. The Ford Ikon, clean-clean. She'd rescued a cat, as she'd done with Mouse. Rescued Inanna and attracted the disapproval of Zelda Petersen. By Zelda's description the animosity was understated, passive-aggressive mostly. Yinka paid her rent, they stayed out of each other's way.

Before she'd left Cove Crescent Mojisola had made friends, once more, with the guards. Three of them, Moses, Phillip and Buntu. She asked if they remembered the very thin girl with the cat and they did. But there were no revealing anecdotes. She was nice, they said. She was a good person. Sometimes, on request, she bought them a cold two-litre bottle of Coca-Cola. Did loneliness lead her to the website where she encountered D-Man? Or had she always had an inkling for such things but never dared do so while living under her parents' roof?

The pieces of a life, even when put together, assembled, never amount to the life itself. Mojisola knows the pieces. D-Man. The jokes, the invitations parried, the relentless flirting. Was she writing in her journals throughout, and writing to D-Man and deleting sometimes and writing? Deleting, hiding what from whom? Shocked, perhaps, by her own audacity, by the terrifying darkness of her deep desires. Mojisola remembers perfuming her thighs on that first visit to D-Man's Tower and even now, after everything, her cheeks are hot with the memory. And throughout it all, was Yinka sad? All the time? Was she thinking of the calls to her father that she hadn't taken? Was she thinking of the lies, of the family she'd run from?

Occasionally Yinka would take Mojisola's calls but those conversations were always weighed down by duty, stifled by guilt. At 23, was Yinka trying to work out how to fix things, how to be okay, how to get from day to day? Mojisola sees what until now she hasn't wanted to see. That whatever Yinka was doing with the Woodsman, it wasn't the sickness itself but rather, the search for a cure. She'd wanted it, no one forced her, she did it for relief, for rescue.

It is painful that Yinka did not call her mother that morning. Why Titus? Maybe because she wished to apologise for ignoring him all those months, maybe she'd felt bad, longed for redemption? Had she thought it might rescue her, *he* might rescue her? That if she could just start something with him they could pull a thread, start the unravelling, if she could just start it everything would follow? At the end they'll have a ball of wool again, the thread worn (used) but loose, set free of the things they had gotten bound up in; loose again, ready for a second go, a second chance. *But I'm on my way*, Mojisola had wanted to tell the policeman who'd called her with the news. The same sentiment. *I'm coming, to start again, to try once more, to do better.*

She'd called Yinka just a week before. As usual the call had lasted only a few minutes, Yinka straining to get off, Mojisola finding more excuses to keep on talking. But she could never come up with anything truly compelling so she asked mundane question after mundane question, knowing how much such triviality must annoy her daughter. Yes, I've eaten. Yes, I've done my grocery shopping. Yes, I'm keeping warm. Work is fine. I'm fine. Yes, I have enough money. The call remains distinct in Mojisola's memory for only one reason. It was the first time she ventured to suggest that she ought to come and visit.

Yinka, of course, had shot down the idea. 'No, Mummy, there's no need…I'm hardly here…I'm really busy at work… you'll be bored.' Yinka's blocking of the idea may have seemed like a failure to anyone else but at the time Mojisola had felt a small sense of triumph. She had managed to convey to her child that she wanted to see her.

The next time they spoke Mojisola intended to build on her initial request to visit. Eventually she wanted to work her way through to imposing herself, imposing her authority as mother, and her every right to see her own child. She intended to invoke the powers of Auntie Modupe from all those years back when she used to descend on them from Akure, inspect baby Yinka and cook 'proper food' for the family. In fact, Mojisola had spent the week before the final day fantasising about her visit. Maybe alone, without Titus in the house, they could find a way to reach each other. When the police officer called to say her baby was gone, Mojisola had been day-dreaming about her trip to Jo'burg. 'But I'm coming, I'm literally on my way, she cannot be dead, I'm just around the corner.' As if humanity knows Death to be mindful of the proximity of mothers. As if Death is reasonable. As if Death says: 'Oh, since your mother is on the way, in that case, pardon me — I had not realised.'

Titus hadn't taken Yinka's call. 'Why not?' Mojisola had asked. She knew it was a cruel question but a necessary cruelty. At this stage there was no avoiding cruelty.

He'd just shaken his head, tears down his face. And she'd nodded. Because she too had been scared many times but most of all, on the day that Yinka had looked her straight in the eye: 'I'm sad all the time.' Nothing had prepared her for that, and nothing had prepared her for the fact that in life some things present themselves only once. So much is taught about second chances. Gurus write books about not giving up, keep at it, failure is normal, recover. But also Mojisola knows, in the way she knows water will quench thirst only for a period and then to quench more thirst more water is required; some things are never recovered. Her daughter told her something and she'd had only one moment to answer. They should teach you that too, thinks Mojisola. They should teach you that sometimes you have only one chance.

She sees clearly now, even as the sun is coming up, bringing the light she has so feared. She sees that it all got too much for Yinka. After that call, after her father's secretary saying whatever she may have said: 'Your father is busy, he'll call you back.' Or 'Your father can't come to the phone right now, let me take a message.' Or 'He's in a meeting. I'll tell him you called.' Or whatever other stupid insignificance the woman may have uttered, she would have had no idea that she was sealing Yinka, her lover's child, into a box with no more gaps for air to pass through. It was final now.

Mojisola knows that that day Yinka did not go into the office. Egizia had expected her but had been distracted with a looming deadline. Employees of Art-T were known to work from home, it was not unusual so no one had thought to check. *Did Yinka go out that day at all?* Mojisola wonders. She'd asked Buntu, who would have been the guard on duty, but he'd looked apologetic and said he couldn't remember. Anyway, where could she have gone? Her habits were particular but few. She was a regular at Blessed and Bounty but the appointment she'd made — the one Mojisola stumbled upon — was not for that day. She saw the Woodsman but by the day of her death they hadn't seen each other for almost two weeks. Correspondence with D-Man was harder to track because of the deletions but Jide had sworn on his life that when Mojisola wrote to him on the website — posing as Yinka — he had not heard from her in months.

It's painful to think of it in this way but Mojisola cannot avoid the sense that Yinka was winding her life down, exhausted somehow, at the end of her options for reprieve from an all-the-time kind of sadness. After the call to her father, did she grab her keys and go for a drive? Or did she huddle in the shadows of that small apartment and finally, as night began to fall, did she fill the bathtub? Did she fill it knowing — or at that point, the steam rising, causing her skin to moisten, was she still full of strong intentions? Was she trying to be brave? And the knife? Had it been in the kitchen all that time before, helpfully slicing open tomatoes and chopping onions? When did she first recognise it as a possible weapon against the tyranny of sadness? Did she have it with her or did she have to get out of the tub, dripping, fetch it from the kitchen drawer and then re-submerge? Was Inanna about? If the damn cat could actually talk, could she have said, 'Yinka, please don't. Please. Nothing is irretrievable, dear. Not even your happiness. We can go in, I promise, we can go in and pull it from the very depths of your darkness. Your parents are useless but come to me, Yinka — come here to me.'

The knife was sharp (blade-like) but even so she would have had to apply a fair amount of pressure to break the skin. Mojisola has searched online, desperately looking, trying to imagine. There are many posts about how hard it is to kill oneself by slits to the wrists, how painful it can be if you get the wrong spot, how difficult it is to locate the artery. The articles make her cry because somehow, regardless of emphatic article after emphatic article as to how near impossible this method is, Yinka cut whatever it was she had to cut, she bled, passed out, drowned.

She sees it right through, Mojisola does, all the pieces of the gross puzzle. She eventually sees Zelda opening the door with her spare key, calling in the police, cleaning up the mess. She sees it all, this horror movie, and then she closes her eyes and sleeps for a very long time. She doesn't get out of bed even when she hears Titus ringing. On the seventh day she rises, weak, headachy, and takes a shower. She eats an apple, then holds her head — heavy — in the palms of both hands.

*

One day, far into the future, a parcel arrives. Despite her name on the box — Zelda Petersen — the address is written in a hand Mojisola does not recognise. Her skin tingles. A small note says, 'Zelda wished for you to have these.' Grief comes like an old friend. Mojisola has had opportunities to practice, she knows it now. The sense of panic is first to arrive, atavistic, instinctual, the horror of death however ubiquitous, the shock of its ordinariness, that casual way death arrives in all lives at all times reminding how small we are. 'I'm just here, I'm always here," says Death and "No," says Mojisola, "Please no, not today'. But Death keeps taking. In the box are several balls of yarn of varying thicknesses, orange, olive green and teal. Yellow. Did Zelda knit? Mojisola has no recollection of ever seeing her friend working knitting needles. And yet there are a pair of steel needles. When Mojisola does some research, she realises they are special needles, expensive and sophisticated. At the bottom of the box are several items Mojisola can only guess Zelda actually knitted. Socks for someone very little. A child? Zelda had none. A baby that never arrived? There is an adult-size sweater knitted in purple cashmere. Mojisola puts on the sweater — it holds Zelda's scent. There is a photograph of a girl and boy, the girl a little taller, straight-backed with Zelda's unmistakable green stare. Tied with sewing thread — fine and white — are a bundle of letters, the ones Mojisola wrote to Zelda. Mojisola takes and puts them beside a similar bundle — the letters Zelda wrote back. There is no talk of a funeral or memorial and no phone number to call. Zelda is leaving Mojisola's life with as much mystery as when she entered it.

Zelda the closet-knitter, weed-smoker, cat-lover. A sad smile
comes on Mojisola's face and stays there for many days. She
promises to learn to knit.

And as if ghosts visit in pairs, in that same week Mojisola
walks into a coffee shop in Observatory and inexplicably hones
in on a table off to the side. A man sits there. It is Jide Lawal,
the Money Man, D-Man. Initially, after she'd left Jo'burg,
Jide had kept texting. He apologised for not telling her about
the Woodsman, explaining his fears and concerns. After a
while he started asking her to visit him in Jo'burg; he offered
to organise a ticket. Sometimes he asked to visit her in Cape
Town. She hadn't responded to any of his messages and over
the months they'd dwindled, although, every now and again
one popped up. 'No one does it like you do,' he'd say, and 'I miss
you.' Eventually though the messages had stopped. Mojisola
still thought of him, memories accompanied by sensations she
no longer feared or questioned.

Sitting with Jide in the coffee shop, Mojisola has no doubt,
is Sade, his daughter. She looks to be a teenager with the
commensurate affectations of her age group: an awareness
of body in the strange way she sits, a sense of becoming into
womanhood in the playful way she tips her head. The waiter
is approaching to ask if she will be sitting alone. Mojisola
turns before he gets to her, before Jide looks up. Out on the
pavement, she takes deep big breaths.

*

There is no end to this. Such a fallacy that grieving can be
mapped, that it begins and also bottoms out. Day after day
Mojisola remains locked up in thoughts, tracking through
her life to find the actual moment of her crime as a mother;
the actual second it was that she let her daughter fall. She is
thinking as she does her grocery shopping, as she manages her
online banking, as she browses for nail polish. Regularly she
feels unable to eat, allows the now familiar malaise (the fever

of her failures) to come upon her, take hold and stay. She has looked in Midrand, she has snooped around, she has smacked the naked bums of strange men, her hands gloved, her rashes protected, healing. She has done all this and yet here it comes again, the sickness, the empty pit.

Titus says they'll never know. The problem is, she knows. She knows she failed. The question is, where exactly? And perhaps one answer eludes her because there is no single place. Instead, unhelpfully, there are many. But sometimes she thinks it's South Africa. It was during that decade in South Africa that she really lost hold. She was overcome by strangeness. The foreignness of the land, the foreignness of herself to herself, the foreignness of the child — all the distances seemed to gang up against her and, in their monstrous strength, make jest of any attempts, any short strides she could have made to cover the gaps. It was in South Africa where her motherness was finally defeated. Where she really didn't know her child, where she really couldn't help her. She couldn't plait her hair. She couldn't comment on her daughter's confession of sadness — the moment had passed. She couldn't advise on boys (what did she know) — Yinka mentioned none. She couldn't fraternise with the other mothers — she found them too unfamiliar, unwavering in the authority of their knowledge.

Snatches of her days right after Yinka's birth creep in; how she had felt on the outskirts of humanity, how everyone else in the world knew things and she knew nothing. The mothers had occurred as versions of her mother and Auntie Modupe — in full possession of themselves and their daughters. She cowered away. She hid.

It has taken Mojisola decades to learn the fault lines in her own thinking. She was not at all on the outskirts of humanity. In her loneliness, lack of confidence, fears and terrors, she was right in the centre, along with everyone else. She had seen wrongly; or it had been a trick of light. Her mother's fragility and devotion to a God she hoped would save her, save them both; Auntie Modupe's regrets and earnest but clumsy attempts to repair. Even the mothers at Yinka's school, impeccably made-up. Mojisola now imagines the make-up, the heels, as part of a suit of armour. Ferociously slender. And even as we lose (such is the design of war), we fight. That's what she'd been seeing all along, seeing and not knowing what it was she'd been looking at. Not perfection, not people who never faltered, but rather the opposite. And so now, finally, she can include herself. Now she walks in the streets as if she built them with her own hands. Now she stares into faces as if mirrors; she sees herself, her fragility, her ugliness and wonder. She sees her shame and her courage, her capacity for failure but also for magic.

*

Friday, late afternoon, Mojisola finds herself walking in the city bowl. They'd had an agreement but, at the last minute, Titus had phoned to apologise profusely, said he couldn't make this week. She ducks into a bookshop and stays for a while. It is almost 4pm and there are people slowly spilling in. Mojisola likes the quiet, the comfort of wall-high books. She feels young, just then, a youth she almost can't remember ever feeling and sometimes believes never existed. Suddenly too agitated to stay indoors, she leaves the bookshop.

It is busy outside. She walks down Harrington, the buzz of the coming weekend taking hold of East City as people leave their jobs and go back into their lives: as they walk away from Parliament, as they walk with purpose towards Cape Town station, towards the taxi rank, as they think about having a drink, having sex. Mojisola walks along with the crowd and, when she gets to Darling, cuts left and then over the street onto the Parade. In some weeks it will be a year. She's been wondering how to spend the day, no fixed idea has emerged but she brushes that aside for now, enjoying a breeze on her cheek. A host of pigeons have settled on Edward VII. They are amusing, shitting all over the stone waistcoat of the playboy king. She stands to watch the birds for a moment and a sweet sound suddenly comes up. It's a woman's voice, seemingly from close by, but Mojisola can't see where. She thinks she's inventing it, she must be, but then, looking around, she realises that other people are hearing it too. She notices a few people staring at something on the ground. They are looking down a manhole. 'There's somebody inside,' a young boy shouts. Someone disagrees with him and another person tells them both to shut up.

The first sounds Mojisola catches make her think she is listening to Yoruba. She remembers Aminata Bar again, but quickly realises it is a lullaby sung in a language unencumbered by words, universal. The melody mushrooms up from the old canals of the Cape, mushrooms from those violet tunnels into the late-afternoon light of the Grand Parade. Some of the people rushing home slow their stride, stop. A woman standing some metres away from the hole puts her hand to her mouth. A young woman puts her bag down and lies on her back upon the asphalt. Not far from the hole, an old man is sitting on a wooden crate; Mojisola asks if she can join him and he shifts. There is someone down there, someone singing a lullaby at 4pm, her voice, from the depths, a reminder of the chambers below and invisible histories. Mojisola thinks she might cry but then there's nothing. The woman's voice wavers for just a second, Mojisola wonders if, standing underneath there in the blackened canals — is she scared? And it seems as if this is why she'd come out this afternoon. Not to meet Titus who cancelled at the last minute but to walk in the city and stroll into the Parade and hear this woman singing. To hear this woman singing something ancient but new; an invitation to stop for a moment. Mojisola can hear, in the treble notes, that the woman is explaining to her, giving her the world as it is in its resplendent chaos and horror and not as she longs it to be, safe and known.

She thinks of her mother, Auntie Modupe, herself and Yinka. There has never been such a time, but she imagines them standing, all four, together in a line, talking fast, back and forth to each other — finally saying all the things that count. The woman is still singing, and it is good to hear the music, hear it all told. After enough generations, Mojisola wonders, would someone look back and see the lives lived, laid out side by side? See a pattern? It would have to be someone from outside looking in or up (maybe a woman in a hole) or, at the very least, Mojisola understands that it cannot be her; you cannot read the story when you are the book.

Mojisola closes her eyes. She feels buoyant but also tightly bundled. Swaddled. When it is all over a stranger taps her gently on the shoulder.

Acknowledgments

Rahma Mire, you opened your home to me when I needed a place to stay and write — thank you.

Over the time it took to write this book, several organisations provided the luxury of quiet space, guidance and unforgettable artistic camaraderie for which I am deeply grateful. Thank you to the University of East Anglia Etisalat Fellowship and NoViolet Bulawayo for making the fellowship possible in the first place. Johannesburg Institute for Advanced Study, Miles Morland Foundation, Africa Centre Artist in Residency Programme, Bundanon Trust and OMI Artist's Residency: these are places peopled by the kindest and most committed, the difference you make for artists is tremendous — thank you.

In the final scene of the novel, the artwork (including its description) situated in the Cape Town Grand Parade is inspired by and borrowed from the joint artwork by Kim Gurney and Pauline Theart called *Cape Town Under: The Third Voice.* Thank you, Kim and Pauline, for giving Mojisola a space to sit in.

So many people, friends and strangers alike, responded to my emails and phone calls, requests for interviews, information and support: Jane Alexander, Lien Botha, Fritha Langerman, Gabrielle Le Roux, Stefan Hubert Krynauw, Anya Mendel, Woody Oliphant, and Rebecca Townsend for invaluable insight into art and art-making. Simidele Dosekun for your support and Dr Abosede George for helping with my research. Thanks to Dr Sairita Maistry, Dr Wale Adeosun, Dr Reinders and the dedicated staff at St Luke's Hospice. Mandy Russel and Mary Anne Botha — one day I will write about Prince Albert! Prof Ladipo Adamolekun, Prof Niyi Akinnaso and Prof Kole

Omotoso for sharing your experiences at the University of Ibadan. Dr Eve, Mistress Baton, Mark and Mark — for trusting me as I explored a new world.

Which comes first, the writing or the idea; as I wrote to find the story, thank you to those who waited, guided, encouraged: Elise Dillsworth for your steady unrelenting passion, incredible commitment, and belief; Hazel Orme for your close reading. Mahreen Sohail, Jacqui L'Ange, Zukiswa Wanner, Jumoke Verissimo, Katarina Hedren, Britta Rothman, Rachel Zadok, Colleen Lindesay and Karen Terera: thank you for having my back and reading and commenting on the story in its many previous incarnations.

Bibi Bakare-Yusuf, thank you for giving this book not just a physical home but an intellectual one. Layla Mohamed for your insightful editorial work and patient collaboration.

Through chance encounters I've been fortunate to know the special long-distance but enduring friendship writers can offer one another: Mahreen Sohail, Anakana Schofield, Tsering Lama and Mireille Juchau — thank you.

To my family and friends, you are the dearest of beings and I am made better for knowing you. Uriel thank you for all the laughter, the union. Taiye and Kehinde thank you for choosing me.

Support *An Unusual Grief*

We hope you enjoyed reading this book. It was brought to you by Cassava Republic Press, an award-winning independent publisher based in Abuja and London. If you think more people should read this book, here's how you can support:

Recommend it. Don't keep the enjoyment of this book to yourself; tell everyone you know. Spread the word to your friends and family.

Review, review, review. Your opinion is powerful and a positive review from you can generate new sales. Spare a minute to leave a short review on Amazon, GoodReads, Wordery, our website and other book buying sites.

Join the conversation. Hearing somebody you trust talk about a book with passion and excitement is one of the most powerful ways to get people to engage with it. If you like this book, talk about it, Facebook it, Tweet it, Blog it, Instagram it. Take pictures of the book and quote or highlight from your favourite passage. You could even add a link so others know where to purchase the book from.

Buy the book as gifts for others. Buying a gift is a regular activity for most of us — birthdays, anniversaries, holidays, special days or just a nice present for a loved one for no reason... If you love this book and you think it might resonate with others, then please buy extra copies!

Get your local bookshop or library to stock it. Sometimes bookshops and libraries only order books that they have heard about. If you loved this book, why not ask your librarian or bookshop to order it in. If enough people request a title, the bookshop or library will take note and will order a few copies for their shelves.

Recommend a book to your book club. Persuade your book club to read this book and discuss what you enjoy about the book in the company of others. This is a wonderful way to share what you like and help to boost the sales and popularity of this book. You can also join our online book club on Facebook at Afri-Lit Club to discuss books by other African writers.

Attend a book reading. There are lots of opportunities to hear writers talk about their work. Support them by attending their book events. Get your friends, colleagues and families to a reading and show an author your support.

Transforming a manuscript into the book you are now reading is a team effort. Cassava Republic Press would like to thank everyone who helped in the production of *An Unusual Grief:*

Editorial

Layla Mohamed

Uthman Adejumo

Design & Production

Deepak Sharma (Prepress Plus)

Leah Jacobs-Gordon

Marketing & Publicity

Niki Igbaroola

Kofo Okunola

Fiona Brownlee

MORE TITLES TO ENJOY

Men Don't Cry
Faiza Guene

Pub. Date: 27th July 2021
ISBN: 9781911115694
Genre: Literary fiction

Is it possible to make your own path in the world while upholding your family legacy? That's the question at the heart of this tender and poignant coming-of-age story from the widely-acclaimed author of *Kiffe Kiffe Tomorrow.*

Born in Nice to Algerian parents, Mourad is fuelled by the desire to forge his own destiny. His retired father spends his days fixing up things in the backyard; his mother, bemoaning the loss of her natal village in North Africa. Mourad lives in fear of becoming an overweight bachelor with salt and pepper hair, living off his mother's cooking. When Mourad's father has a stroke, he makes his son promise to reconcile things with his estranged sister Dounia, a staunch feminist and aspiring politician, who had always felt constrained living at home. Now living in the Paris suburbs himself, Mourad tracks down Dounia and battles to span the gulf separating her and the rest of the family.

Unbury Our Dead with Song
Mūkoma Wa Ngūgī

Pub. Date: 29th June 2021
ISBN: 9781911115984
Genre: Literary Fiction

"Part mystery, part road novel, part philosophical enquiry, [this] is a dazzling journey to discover the meaning of music and it's immense power over the human soul." — **Aminatta Forna**

In the heart of Nairobi, four musicians – The Diva, The Taliban Man, The Corporal and 70-year-old bartender Miriam – gather for a once in a lifetime competition, to see who can perform the best Tizita. In the audience is tabloid journalist John Thandi Manfredi, who is enthralled by their renditions of the Ethiopian blues.

Hoping to uncover the secret to the music that haunts him, he follows the musicians back to Ethiopia. Manfredi's search takes him from the idyllic Ethiopian countryside to vibrant juke joints and raucous parties in Addis Ababa, set to a soundtrack of stirring Tizita performances.

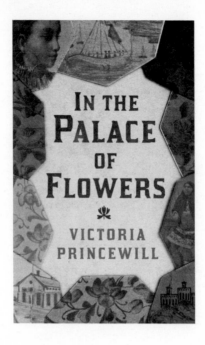

In the Palace of Flowers
Victoria Princewill

Pub. Date: 25th February 2021
ISBN: 9781911115755
Genre: Historical fiction

"...historical fiction at its finest... a book in which unpalatable humanistic truths and disquieting historical details undergird a truly enrapturing story." **– Yorkshire Times**

Set in the opulent Persian royal court of the Qajars at the end of the 19th century, *In the Palace of Flowers* is an atmospheric historical novel following the lives of two enslaved Abyssinians, Jamila, a concubine, and Abimelech, a eunuch. Torn away from their families, they now serve at the whims of the royal family, only too aware of their own insignificance in the eyes of their masters. Abimelech and Jamila's quest to take control over their lives and find meaning leads to them navigating the dangerous, and deadly politics of the royal court, both in the government and the harem, and to the radicals that lie beyond its walls.

Love, friendship and political intrigue will set the fate of these two slaves. Highly accomplished, richly textured and elegantly written, *In the Palace of Flowers* is a magnificent novel about the fear of being forgotten.

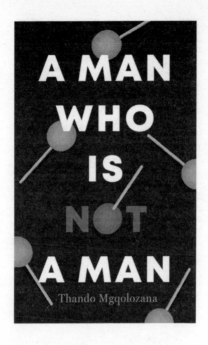

A Man Who Is Not a Man
Thando Mgqolozana

Pub. Date: 12th January 2021
ISBN: 9781913175023
Genre: Literary fiction

A Man Who Is Not a Man recounts the personal trauma of a young Xhosa initiate after a rite-of-passage circumcision goes wrong.

This powerful story follows Lumkile's journey into manhood, from crime and violence in Cape Town, to education and first love in the village, and finally to the harrowing isolation of a mountain hut where the protagonist faces the unthinkable and unspeakable.

A Man Who Is Not a Man challenges the code of silent suffering expected of men, and provides a subversive depiction of masculinity, in all its varied forms. Set within South Africa's Xhosa community, this is a local novel with big and universal themes: the confusion of boyhood, trauma, truancy, love, male tenderness and the making of men through violence.

"Highly original." – **Nadine Gordimer**

"His straightforward no-frills prose tells an effective story of a botched circumcision and its consequences." – **Zakes Mda, Sunday Independent**